LOVE HARD

BLACK ROSE KISSES #4

EVA ASHWOOD

No.

Not Rory.

Please, fuck, no.

The rest of the world stops mattering in a split second. My vision narrows down to a single point as a rush of pure terror floods my body.

I run to Rory and drop to my knees, hovering over him. He's bleeding heavily from a spot on his arm where he got shot, and I press my hands over it, trying to put pressure on it to stop the flow of blood.

But I don't know if it's helping.

There's just so much blood.

So much *red*, shining darkly in the crackling light of the flames that devour Jen's house like hungry monsters.

The hot, sticky blood coats my palms and spills out

between my fingers, and the ground beneath his body is wet and saturated with it.

It's not like the shot went in at his chest or his side, where it would hit his vitals and fuck things up, so it doesn't seem like it should be this bad, but my fingers are slick with the proof that it's much worse than it looks.

Fuck. How much blood does the human body have to lose before it stops working?

I don't know the answer to that. I can barely even think.

I can't focus on anything else but Rory. His handsome face is too pale, too slack. I've never seen him like this before. He's always smiling, always laughing. There's always a light in his eyes, and that wicked spark of teasing mischief lurking somewhere. But now it's like he's just... a body. Like the Rory I know and care for isn't even here anymore.

I want to plead with him to open his eyes, to smile at me, to say something. Anything. My heart feels like it's breaking, and at the same time, my pulse is hammering through me, anxiety and panic rushing through my system.

It's an odd mixture of being keyed up and numb at the same time, and it turns my stomach and makes me want to vomit on the grass of Jen's lawn.

I can hear the sounds of voices around me, of the rest of Jen's house burning, the wood cracking and splintering with the heat. But it's like there's a barrier around me, a wall of glass that keeps everything out. Nothing really seems to penetrate my mind while I keep my eyes on Rory.

I can't lose him.

Not now.

Not like this.

Not *ever*, ideally, but him bleeding out and dying in the middle of the lawn after getting shot by a Jackal is not the end that Rory deserves. This can't be it.

The muted scream of a siren splits the night air, and the dim light of the street lamp is overlaid with the flashing blue and red lights. But I don't look up. I just keep my gaze on Rory.

I feel hands on me, trying to grab me and pull me away, and for the first time since I saw his body on the ground, I find my voice.

"No! No, let go of me!"

It's only been a couple of minutes, but I sound raspy and devastated, and I don't want to leave him. The fear that if I take my eyes off him he's going to disappear and die grips my heart like a vise, and someone has to keep trying to stem the tide of blood pouring from his arm. I can't leave him now. I can't leave him alone.

The hands get more insistent, dragging me up to my feet and away, and I thrash in their hold, trying to fight to get back to him.

"No," I gasp again. "Let me go. I have to—I need to—"

"Mercy."

It's Levi's voice in my ear, and the familiarity of it washes over me, filling me with relief. He's alive, at least. He's okay. In the moments of chaos following Rory's shooting, I almost forgot that Levi and Sloan are here too. Thank fuck neither of them got shot.

"The EMTs are here," he says, rubbing his hands up and down my arms. "They'll take care of Rory, okay? We have to let them do their jobs."

The logic of that cuts through the panic enough that I stop fighting. He's right. In the end, there's nothing I can really do to help Rory. I can't put him back together at all. I'm not a fucking doctor.

When the fight leaves me, I give in to how tired I am and slump back into Levi's hold. I can feel his heart beating against my back, strong and steady, and it gives me comfort that he's fine at least.

And Sloan's somewhere nearby, probably angry and ready to fight, so that's something I can hold on to as well.

Levi and I watch as the EMTs move into the space I vacated, surrounding Rory and carefully getting him onto a stretcher. He still looks so pale, so lifeless, and watching them strap him down and then haul him into the ambulance spikes panic inside me again. Like if they shut the doors and drive off, I'll never see him again.

"I'm going with him," I hear myself say. Before anyone can try to stop me, I pull away from Levi and climb into the ambulance after the EMTs. They glance at me and nod, and when no one protests or tries to throw me out, I relax just a little. They're not trying to take him from me.

Through the open doors, I can see Sloan approach Levi and say something. Levi nods, and Sloan puts a hand on his shoulder and then climbs into the ambulance with me.

"Levi's going to take Jen and Piper and meet us at the hospital," he says, his voice deep and flat.

I nod. Levi's the best choice for that anyway. He's so level-headed and sweet. Even if he's just as upset as Sloan and I are, he won't let it show enough to send Jen and Piper into a panic.

The doors bang closed, and the ambulance starts up, pulling away from the driveway and onto the road. Part of me wants to look and see if I can catch the blazing inferno of Jen's house, but I can't take my gaze off Rory.

Two EMTs are in the back with us, working on him. They put pressure on the bullet wound and take his vitals, murmuring to each other as they work in tandem. I know enough to know they have to get him stable before we get to the hospital, and I feel like my heart is in my throat just watching this.

Sloan has settled next to me on the long bench seat off to the side, and he grips my hand hard as we stare at Rory. I squeeze back just as hard. It's clear we're both in the same headspace—devastated at Rory's condition, too rough to even talk to each other while we watch and wait.

Sloan's hand is large and warm and solid in mine, and when I look down at our hands joined together, I can see that his are also covered in drying blood. It's all Rory's, I know, and it makes me feel sick to my stomach all over again.

He lost so much blood. It's all over my hands and the front of my shirt, and there's still a puddle of it in the grass outside Jen's house. It's way too much, more than he can possibly afford to lose, and I have no idea what's going to happen to him.

That, more than anything else that's happened tonight, terrifies me to my core.

I don't know what's going to happen, and whatever it is, there's nothing I can do to stop it now.

I've never felt so goddamn helpless.

Still not speaking, Sloan and I sit together, holding on to each other, because there's nothing else we can do. We watch the EMTs work, and they never stop moving, never stop and give us those regretful eyes that say they did all they could and they're sorry, but he's gone. That's something, at least, but the ride to the hospital feels like it takes hours instead of minutes. It crawls by, and every second we spend on the road is a second Rory probably can't afford to wait.

Eventually, the hospital comes into view, and the EMTs leap into action as we near it. The ambulance pulls up into place outside the large building, and the ambulance doors bang open a split second later. Two people move around from outside to grab the stretcher, and the two inside with us help ease it out.

They hurry to wheel it into the hospital, and Sloan and I follow wordlessly.

We make it inside, and the EMTs say something to a woman in scrubs who's waiting when we get in.

She gives us a sympathetic look but holds a hand up to stop us as the EMTs take Rory back past where visitors are allowed to go. Tears burn the backs of my eyes as I watch him get wheeled away where I can't follow.

What if this is the last time I get to see him? Is this how I'll always remember him? Not full of life and vigor, teasing me about everything under the sun, but pale as death and just as silent?

I hate the idea of that. It makes my soul ache.

"Follow me. I'll take you to the waiting room."

The woman shows us to the waiting area, and at least it's blessedly quiet. A few minutes later, Levi arrives with Jen and Piper, and the woman goes over to talk to them too.

I just stare off into the distance, not sure if I should sit down or stand up or what. I don't feel like myself. I don't really feel anything but numb fear.

I blink slowly, and my eyes feel gritty and sticky. The world seems to flash by in disjointed images, like I'm watching a poorly made stop-action movie. One minute, I'm looking at a carefully neutral picture of a seashore on the wall, and the next, there's a nurse in front of me. She's an older woman with graying hair and a kind smile, a few inches shorter than me.

"Let me have a look at you, honey," she says softly, and it takes me a second to realize what she means. I'm sure I look a hot fucking mess, covered in soot and ash and someone else's blood.

I just nod at her and follow her back to a little room off to the side. She nods me over to the sink, and I wash all the blood off of my hands, watching the water run red, red, red as it swirls down the drain. It's even under my fingernails, and I take the time to scrub it out, not wanting to wear the visceral reminder of how much blood Rory lost.

The nurse looks me over and takes care of the few minor scrapes I got in the fight, disinfecting them with a spray and then covering them with bandages.

"There we go," she says, smiling at me when she finishes. "You have some bruises, but they'll heal fine on their own. Do you feel any pain anywhere else? Anything hurt when you breathe?"

I take an experimental deep breath, just to make sure, and then shake my head. I still feel so numb and out of it, as if this is happening to someone else and not to me. Like I'm watching it on TV instead of living it.

The nurse keeps smiling, as if she can make everything okay just by pretending it is. "Then you're good to go. I'll check on the rest of your friends."

I follow her back out and watch her move from person to person, helping them clean up and taking care of their injuries. Sloan and Levi have the same scrapes and cuts as I do, and Jen comes back with some kind of ointment on her arm that might be for a burn or something.

Once everyone is patched up, the nurse gathers her things and addresses all of us. "Your friend is in surgery," she says. "I'm sure someone will come out to update you once that's done."

"Thank you," Jen says. At least she can still make words come out of her mouth. It's more than I seem to be capable of at the moment.

The waiting room is small, decked out in the way hospital waiting rooms always are. Uncomfortable chairs in muted colors, and paintings of landscapes and bowls of fruit on the walls—things that won't make the people looking at them feel any kind of way about them. It's all supposed to be calming, or at the very least not *more* upsetting, but I don't think there's anything that could calm me down in this state.

Levi sits with Jen and Piper, murmuring softly to the little girl who seems so out of it. Like her dad, every time I've seen her, she's always been bright and happy. Full of life. Now she seems quiet and afraid, clinging to her mother with both arms while she looks at Levi.

Jen's eyes are unfocused, and I know she's probably thinking about how much worse it all could have been. Her daughter was in danger tonight. They both were. Anything could have happened.

Aside from Levi's soft murmur, we're all just quiet. There's nothing really to say. Everyone seems to be in the same state of shocked numbness that I feel, and I don't blame them.

Of course, then there's Sloan.

Where everyone else is sitting down and staring off into the distance or down at the floor, Sloan is pacing.

I can feel the waves of anger rolling off him. He walks from one end of the little waiting room to another, his footsteps padding on the ugly patterned carpet. Every time he passes me, it feels like he's gotten more and more worked up, his shock and sadness turning into rage. The way it always seems to with Sloan.

He's pissed off as fuck, hands balled into fists, jaw tight as he grinds his teeth.

He passes me one more time and then turns like he's going to pace the length of the room again. But instead, he stalks off down a random hallway.

My stomach clenches with worry. Levi pointed out once that Sloan and I are a lot alike. We love hard, and we fight hard—and we're not good at controlling our emotions when people we love are threatened. Given how I feel right now, I can only imagine the turmoil that must be raging in Sloan's soul.

I get up and follow him, heart in my throat again.

He walks down the hall, and I can tell he's a second away from doing something stupid. Even through his shirt, I can see the muscles of his back are tense and bunched up, like he wants to haul off and hit something or someone. This is so not the place for that, and if he tries to leave and take on the Jackals himself or something right now, he could get himself killed.

I can't let that happen. I can't let anyone else I care about get hurt tonight.

There's nothing we can do now but wait, and I need to make sure he knows that.

Coming up behind Sloan, I reach out to touch him, hoping I can get him to see reason. But before I can get any words out, he whirls around in a fluid motion and grabs my wrist in a bruising grip. His fingers are tight around my wrist, squeezing my bones, and even if I wanted to, I wouldn't be able to break away. He hauls me toward him roughly, and I stumble a little as our chests, collide. I crane my neck, staring up at him to try and get a handle on what he's feeling.

He just looks right back, staring down at me with steel gray eyes that burn with so many emotions I can't even catch them all. His dark blond hair is still streaked with bits of ash from the fire, and his full lips are pressed into a hard line.

I always thought Sloan looked too damn much like a male model to be a down and dirty gang member, but now, he looks like something else entirely. He looks like the personification of pain, like whatever's inside of him right now is too *much*, too big and too violent for his body to contain.

He looks broken, and I wish I knew what to say to patch him back together.

I have to say *something*.

But before I can do anything at all, he releases his hold on my wrist and grabs my shoulders, pivoting our bodies and shoving me against the beige hallway wall.

Then he drops his head and crushes his lips to mine.

2

I CAN TASTE the anger in Sloan's kiss.

The desperation.

The heartbreak.

The helplessness.

This man has never been the *sit and wait* type in all the time I've known him. He's always been ready for action, ready to fight, and now that there's nothing here to fight, it must be tearing him up inside. He can't storm into the operating room, grab the tools, and perform the surgery himself—as much as I know he'd probably like to.

He can't do anything to save his friend.

And I can *feel* how much that fucks him up.

My body responds to the pressure of his lips immediately. I gasp softly into the kiss and arch against him. All the shock and anger and pain and grief I've been feeling crystalize into this single moment. Into the pure, desperate connection between me and Sloan.

It's always been like this with us. We put our feelings into physical acts, and more often than not, we end up fighting or fucking when shit overwhelms us. But at least this time, we aren't raging against each other. This time, we're clinging to each other.

The kiss escalates quickly, like a brushfire started by a bolt of lightning, getting hotter and more desperate with every passing second. Our mouths crash together again and again, and when I part my lips to make a needy little noise into Sloan's mouth, he plunges his tongue into my mouth, kissing me like he wants to devour me.

I cling to him, giving back as good as I get, chasing his tongue with my own.

When he pulls back a little, it's just to bite down on my lower lip, and I shiver against him, hands roaming over the broad planes of his chest.

I can feel my heart racing and my pussy throbbing, but I'm also vaguely aware of the distant beeping of a machine. It reminds me that we're still in the hallway of the hospital where anyone could walk by and see us going at it right there.

I grope behind me, hoping for a door that doesn't lead to an exam room or something. When my fingers find the cold metal of a door handle, I grab it and turn.

Luckily, it's a supply closet. A quick glance around

shows that it's packed with cleaning materials and has a mop leaning up against a back corner, but I barely register more than that. It's a room with a door, and that's good enough for me. I grab the front of Sloan's shirt and haul him inside, and he kicks the door closed behind us.

As soon as the door shuts and it's just the two of us in here, it's like the last thread of Sloan's self-control disappears.

He grabs me again, hands on my hips with almost bruising force. He shoves me back against the shelves and drops his mouth to mine once more.

I can feel how hungry and desperate he is, how he's holding nothing back now.

His touch is like a force of nature, and I might as well be standing in the path of a tornado.

It's all I can do to hold on. To kiss him back and try to keep my footing as the intensity of our emotions rises to a peak that feels like it could devastate us both. But he needs this. *I* need it. I want him to make us both feel something other than the panic and worry that seems to be eating us up from the inside.

His hands leave my hips to roam all over me. Up my sides, across my chest, over my shoulders and neck. My hands follow and do the same, mirroring the movement on his body.

It's almost like that time at the warehouse after I fought Baldy, when Sloan was so angry and so intense. But this time, it's not just chemistry and lust between us—it's a whole ocean of emotions.

It's so much more powerful than it was before, and it nearly overwhelms me, threatening to drown me like a heavy black ocean. All I can do is cling to him and kiss him back like I never want to let go.

Because I don't.

I *don't* want to let go.

Everything outside this closet is chaos and worry and anger, and in here, we're building a little haven of safety and hope with each fevered kiss. It feels somehow like clinging to each other and giving in to the way we both feel is the only thing that can save us. The only thing that can preserve the little family the four of us have built between us.

As if the two of us can somehow save Rory by feeding the connection between us.

Sloan shoves his hand down the front of my pants, and I echo the action, sliding my fingertips past the waistband of his boxers. I can feel him hot and hard against my palm, his cock tenting the front of his boxers, and it almost seems to leap into my hand when I touch it.

I know that he's going to find me just as hot and soaking wet between my thighs, and the second his fingers touch that spot, I moan softly and spread my legs a bit wider.

I need to feel this. I need the heat and the desire that's

consuming me. I need to feel something other than the heartache that's eating at my chest, and I know Sloan probably feels the same. I've never seen him look so wrecked, and I don't think I'll ever forget the haunted look in his eyes for as long as I live.

Trying to drive that image from my mind, I wrap my hand around his cock and stroke him with the limited movement I have. When he manages to bury his fingers inside me, I thrust my hips forward.

"Fuck, Sloan," I moan, my breath ragged.

He doesn't reply, but I can see the heat simmering in his eyes, burning out some of the anger that was there before. It's pleasure and pain all at once, and I chase the feeling.

"I wanna feel you come for me," Sloan rasps. "Do it, Mercy. Now."

It's the first thing he's said since we got to the hospital. His voice is husky and low, and I can hear the pain that he's still holding back. I can see it in the way he holds himself, the way he thrusts his fingers in me so deeply that it feels like he might split me open.

And it's not like I don't want to come for him, or like I have a choice in the first place. My hand stills on his cock, and I focus on the way he's working his fingers inside me, unable to think about anything else.

His fingers are thick and calloused, and they know how to stroke me by now. Sloan knows how I like it, hard and fast and unrelenting, and he works his wrist with as much movement as he can get. Considering I'm pinned between the shelves and his body, there's nothing for me to do other than feel it and give myself over to the maelstrom of desire and pain that swirls between us.

Maybe my body is responding to Sloan's command, or maybe it's just desperate to feel anything other than pain for once tonight, but every nerve ending inside me responds to his touch, tipping me over into an orgasm that steals my breath for a second.

I moan his name softly, hips bucking as I grind against his fingers, riding out the pleasure until I can breathe again.

Sloan barely gives me time to catch my breath. The second the last shudder washes through my body, he yanks his hand free of my pants and then goes for the button and zipper, shoving my jeans down until they're around my knees. His eyes burn with desire when he looks at me, and the air in the small closet is already thick with the smell of sex and arousal.

His hands go to my hips and he turns me around in a single sharp motion.

"I'd brace myself if I were you," he growls, and if it was Rory who said those words, they would be teasing, but I can tell Sloan means it. He's going to ruin me, and that's exactly what I need right now.

I brace my hands on the shelf and stick my ass out, openly begging for everything he can give me.

The pain.

The destruction.

The *release*.

"Fuck, Mercy..."

Sloan grabs my hips again, and when he presses in behind me, I can tell that he's gotten rid of his pants as well, leaving his cock free to push against my bare ass.

He's rock hard, and I can feel the smear of precum against my skin as his fingers dig into the flesh of my hips. I'm expecting him to plunge right into me, giving in to the storm I can tell is raging inside him, but instead, he rubs his cock between my thighs for a few strokes, *almost* giving me what we both need.

I can feel the smooth, velvety skin of his cock against my pussy, and it makes my legs shake like leaves. I want him in me so badly that my body is screaming for it, but he's holding out, holding back for one last second, as if he's afraid of what he might do if he lets himself go entirely.

I can feel it building inside of both of us, the intense need for release, for some kind of reassurance that we're both still here.

That we're still breathing.

Still alive.

And that Rory will live too.

I'm more desperate than I can ever remember being

before, and I hear the whimper spill from my lips before I've even registered that I'm making the sound.

"Sloan," I gasp out, hips working so I'm slowly grinding against his cock, trying to get him to push into me. "Please. Fuck, I need this. I need you so much. Please, Sloan." I can hear the plea in my voice. It cracks on the last word, the need pushing through, and Sloan lets out a heavy breath behind me.

"Fuck," he groans. "Fuck."

Yeah. That about sums it up.

He pulls back, leaving me even more alone and empty than I was before, and I whine, near tears by now. "Sloan."

"Hold on, baby," he manages. "I'm here."

And then he drives into me.

It's hard and fast, and he doesn't take the time to let me adjust or anything. He seats himself in me with one smooth, fluid motion, bottoming out until he's balls deep.

He's never been gentle before, but this is something different than I'm used to. He pulls out until just the tip is left inside me and then drives in again, hitting that spot in me that makes my mouth drop open and stars swim in front of my eyes.

I can barely catch my breath, can barely hold on to the shelves in front of me. Each deep, brutal thrust sends me forward, and we're just seconds away from knocking boxes of paper towels and gloves onto the floor.

But neither of us care about that. At least, I sure as hell

don't. I'm only focused on the feeling of our bodies together. The way we meet in the middle again and again with the sound of skin slapping skin that echoes in the small space.

Sloan's fingers dig into my skin so hard I know I'm going to have bruises later, and yet somehow, it's barely enough. I want *more*. I want him to break me, just so I can reform into something stronger. He fucks me like he's trying to chase the demons out of both of us, like he's trying to purge our goddamn souls.

It's the most fierce and wild sex we've ever had, a strange alchemy that turns pleasure into pain.

Every thrust is punishing and deep, and I can feel my body cresting closer and closer to the edge. It's not going to take much more for me to come. The deep ache of a soul-stealing orgasm is already building up in my core.

I have no idea how loud I'm being or if people outside the closet can hear. It would be beyond fucked up if someone came barging in to see me bent over and taking it from behind, with Sloan fucking me like he wants to drive me through the shelves.

But when I'm this close to the edge, this lost in breathless delirium, I can't really bring myself to care about that at all. All I want is to come for him. To clench around his cock and feel him empty himself inside me.

It's a desperate need at this point, beyond anything rational or logical.

"Mercy," Sloan pants, his voice a low growl in my ear. "Fuck, you feel so good. I'm—close."

"Yeah," I manage to get out. It's hard to say if that's me acknowledging what he said or me saying I'm close myself, but when he plunges into me one more time, roughly and without mercy, I fall apart completely.

My pussy squeezes around his cock as waves of pleasure course through me, like it wants to milk him of his release while I'm having my own. I manage to slap one hand over my mouth in time to keep from crying out and making too much noise, and I stifle it down to a whimper instead of a loud-ass moan. My knees buckle a little, and without Sloan's hands on my hips and the shelves in front of me, I'd probably be in a heap on the floor, overwhelmed by how intense it feels.

Sloan isn't far behind. He slams in a few more times, his cock pulsing and swelling, then fills me in a hot wave, groaning and cursing in my ear as he comes undone himself. Even once he finishes, he keeps grinding his hips against my ass, pushing his cock in as deep as it will go as his fingers hold my hips in a bruising grip.

I feel sore and a little battered, but not as terribly numb as I did before. My brain is fuzzy, but it's from the remnants of my orgasm instead of despair.

Sloan is still behind me, breathing hard, and instead of pulling out or moving away, he tucks himself in closer, curving his body over mine from behind. He wraps his arms around me, and I can feel the hammer of his heart and hear him panting for breath in time with my own gasps.

For a little while, we're both quiet, coming down from the violent sex and the rush of feelings.

"Mercy?" Sloan murmurs quietly.

"Yeah?"

"I need Rory to live."

His voice is broken and hoarse, and each word hits me right in the chest.

"Me too." I swallow, blinking back tears. "I just... I need him."

Imagining the man with the bright green eyes and lopsided smile not being here, not pulling through this, is unthinkable.

I thought my desperate fuck with Sloan chased away the worst of the pain, but maybe all it really did was distill it, because tears slide down my cheeks as I let myself rest in Sloan's embrace. I can feel his own tears falling on my shoulder, and something about that makes me accept my own grief and fear more easily.

It's a moment between us that we haven't really had before.

In the beginning of all this, Sloan was the one who was most reluctant about sharing me. The most averse to letting me be a part of the tight knit group he and his two friends had formed. He tried to keep me at arm's length until finally, neither of us could fight it anymore.

But right now, it feels like we both understand how much we need this little family that we've built.

The four of us are a unit, and we need each other—more than I know how to say.

Rory's such a huge part of what we all have together. He's the heart and the soul and the laughter. He keeps us all from taking things to seriously, and without him, I don't even know who we would be.

I rest my forehead on the shelf in front of me and let out a shaky sigh. There's a moment of shuffling, and Sloan pulls out of me, leaving me a sticky mess. He turns me around and wraps his arms around me, not worrying about the cum dripping down my thigh or the fact that my pants are around my ankles and his are shoved down as well. He just clings to me, holding me tight, and I let him.

I wrap my arms around his waist, holding on to him with everything I have. It's comforting, maybe even better than the sex, a way to ground myself and not get lost in the tide of dread and uncertainty that I can already feel pressing in at the edges of my mind all over again.

Sloan's arms are like warm, solid bands around me, and as we breathe together, I'm not sure who is holding who up at this point.

Maybe we're both supporting each other.

3

I'M NOT sure how long we stay in the supply closet, holding on to each other, but eventually our breathing evens out a little bit. My heart still feels like it's beating too fast, but I know that's more about the worry than the sex.

It's still eating at me, that worry for Rory. This moment of connection with Sloan helped, reminding me that I'm not alone in this. We all care about Rory, and we all want him to pull through, so he's not alone either. He'll never have to be alone with so many people here, gathered to wait for news and hope he comes out of this in one piece.

I care so much about him.

No. More than that. I love him.

I hid from my emotions when it comes to these men for a long time, but I can't do that anymore. I love him, and there's not a single doubt in my mind about that.

But everyone who came here with us tonight can say the same thing. Sloan and Levi consider him a part of their team, practically a brother. Jen and Piper are his family, and they need him just as much as we do. Everyone in the waiting room out there loves him, and we're all pulling for him, throwing our energy out into the universe.

And with that much love in Rory's camp, death should know better than to try to take him from us.

"He's not alone," I murmur to Sloan, because I think he needs to hear it too. "He has all of us. We all love him so much, and he knows that. He's going to be fine. He has to be."

I lift a hand to stroke it up and down his back a bit, trying to be comforting. I can remember my dad doing that when I was younger and had nightmares or a bad day at school.

"He knows we're here for him," I add, hoping like hell that my words are true. "Somehow, he knows we're here and that we've all got his back."

Sloan shudders against me, and I can tell he's listening, taking my words to heart. I let my had trail up his back and into his hair, stroking through the fine locks for a second.

He draws back and looks down into my eyes, holding my gaze with his haunted gray stare.

"I'm so fucking glad you came into our lives," he whispers, and I can hear the emotion behind every word.

Before I can think of anything to say back to that, he's

drawing me closer and leaning down to kiss me again. It's not heated like how we were kissing and groping at each other before. This kiss is just sweet and deep and meaningful, the two of us reminding each other that we're here and we have each other and it's all going to be okay.

It all *has* to be okay.

Eventually, we draw apart. We can't hide out in the damn supply closet forever, and if a nurse or doctor comes back with news about Rory, I know we both want to be there to hear it.

We're both a mess though, so we take a minute to straighten up. I clean up the cum sliding down my thigh, then pull my pants up and run my fingers through my hair, trying to make it look less like I just got fucked in a closet, since Jen and Piper are still out there in the waiting room.

Sloan smooths his clothes and hair down as well, and we listen at the door to make sure there's no one coming before slipping out of the closet and heading back down the hall to the waiting room.

The way the seats are arranged, Levi is the first one to see us coming. I meet his gaze as I'm walking, and he gives me and Sloan both a slow once over with his perceptive chocolate-brown eyes.

I can tell just from the look on his face that he knows what happened, and I brace myself for whatever I'm going to see of his reaction. This is all still so new, and even though Rory and Levi have been the ones with the least amount of jealousy in all this, things can change. Especially in times of crisis. Maybe he'll see it as some kind of betrayal of Rory, or of himself, that Sloan and I just had sex.

But Levi doesn't look jealous or angry as Sloan and I enter the waiting room. There's actually a flicker of something that looks like relief on his face. Maybe he saw the same manic energy in Sloan that I did earlier and can tell that some of it has drained away, and that Sloan is less likely to do something reckless that could get him killed or arrested tonight. Levi nods at me a little, and I give a small smile back.

When I pass his chair, he loops an arm around my waist, snagging me and pulling me down to sit in his lap. He wraps both arms around me, holding me close, and I relax into his grip, letting out a soft sigh.

"How are you holding up?" he murmurs.

I shake my head. There's a lot I could say to that question. I could tell him that sex with Sloan was a very good outlet for my raging emotions and that it calmed me down, but the anxiety is still there, gnawing at me relentlessly. I could tell him I don't know how to picture my life without Rory in it, without all of them in it, and just thinking about it makes me want to cry. I don't say any of that, though because the truth is, I feel like my heart might break if I speak at all. I've never been great with words, and I don't have the right ones to convey everything churning inside me right now.

Levi seems to understand. He usually does. He strokes a hand over my side gently, looking up at me with those steady dark eyes.

"It'll be okay," he murmurs. "I promise. He's going to be okay."

His voice is even and steady, as if he's willing his words to be true just by saying them. He's so sweet and strong, holding me close like he can protect me from all the bad things out there, and for a moment, I almost believe him.

Sloan hasn't sat down, and it's clear that even after what we did, he's too agitated to let himself rest even a little. At least he's stopped pacing, instead standing against the wall with his arms folded while we wait to hear something.

Jen's sitting a little ways away now with Piper in her lap. Piper is curled against her, her head on her mother's shoulder, face tucked against her neck, and it's hard to tell if she's asleep or just hiding from everything. Jen's eyes are haunted, and she's staring into the middle distance, almost unblinking.

God. Just watching them makes my heart break all over again, and I have to look away from them both. I can't even imagine what they must be feeling.

Somehow, I feel like it's my fault that we're all in this mess. That *they're* in this mess especially.

I shouldn't have gotten involved in their lives. Rory invited me in, let me spend time with his family and get to know them, and because he did, I blurred the line between his work and his personal life. Between the gang and his family. Between them being safe and... this awfulness.

He was always so good about keeping them safe and keeping things separate, but then I came along, and now their house has been burned down and Piper has to live in a world where she knows there are people out there who would hurt her dad. It's horrible.

I swallow hard past that lump of guilt and look up in time to see a doctor coming down the hall.

"Are you the ones here for Mr. O'Shea?" he asks, glancing around at all of us.

We all leap up, eager to hear what he has to say. If he thinks we're an odd bunch to be sitting here waiting for Rory, he doesn't say so. Instead, he consults the chart in his hands, then looks back at us with a solemn nod.

"The surgery was successful. Mr. O'Shea came through it well, and his vitals look good."

Just hearing that is like a weight off of my shoulders. I can finally draw in a full breath again, and my knees go a little weak and wobbly as if they want to give up and dump me back in my chair. I manage to stay upright though, and I even manage to tune back into what the doctor is saying before I make an idiot of myself.

"His injuries aren't too bad, but because of where the

bullet entered his body, there was some very serious blood loss." He demonstrates, gesturing to his own arm in the area where Rory was hit. "He's had a transfusion, and we were able to stop him from bleeding out. The prognosis is good."

For a second, I feel such a strong wave of relief that it makes me dizzy. That feeling of almost wanting to faint comes back, but I muscle through it. Rory needs me in one piece. Everyone else does too.

"He'll need rest once he's discharged," the doctor continues, glancing around the group of us like he's not sure who he should be directing this information to. He glances at me and Jen in particular, probably assuming that one of us has to be Rory's wife or something. When his eyes settle on Piper in Jen's arms, he seems to make the decision that they're his family. And that's fair. They are. "We'll send him home with a sling," he says. "And he needs to use it. He'll be sore for a while, and he'll need to avoid aggravating the injury more."

We all nod at that, and the doctor gives a small smile. "He's in recovery for the time being," he says. "He should wake up in a little while, and then you can go see him."

"Thank you," Levi says, since he seems to be the only one who has the words to speak right now. "For letting us know and for... for saving him."

The doctor nods and withdraws, leaving us alone

again. One by one, we drop back into our seats, settling in to wait longer.

The atmosphere is different now than it was before, though. It's like some of the tension and despair that was filling the little waiting room up until a few minutes ago has been sucked out of the air, leaving it lighter and easier to breathe. Sloan's jaw isn't clenched hard enough that I'm worried about the integrity of his teeth anymore, and Jen's gaze has cleared from that horrible haunted expression to something lighter and more hopeful. She strokes her hand down Piper's back and whispers into her ear, probably translating the doctor's words into something a small child can understand.

The waiting is terrible because I want to see Rory now, but I manage, jiggling my leg a little as I sit in one of the uncomfortable chairs, trying not to glance up at the clock on the wall every few seconds. Rory's fine now. There's no need to worry. He's just resting, but there's a part of me that won't believe it until I see it with my own eyes.

Finally, a nurse comes around the corner, smiling warmly. "Mr. O'Shea is awake," she tells us. "You can go see him now. He's still a little groggy from the surgery, but he's asking for you."

Somehow I know she means all of us.

We are all on our feet in a second, and we follow her down the hall and around a couple of corners to the room Rory's been given. The door is propped open, and I can see

Rory, still horizontal in bed and paler than he should be, but alive and whole and smiling.

My heart finally knits itself back together, and I can feel my eyes itching with tears. But I hold them back for now. Jen and Piper walk in first, and Piper, who has been a trooper through all of this, squirms in her mother's arms and reaches for Rory insistently.

Jen smiles and sets her down on the bed, and the little girl scrambles up to crawl into her father's embrace. Rory wastes no time in wrapping his good arm around her, holding her close.

"Be careful, baby," Jen murmurs to Piper. "Daddy's hurt, and you need to take care of him, okay?"

The blonde-haired little girl nods, not even looking at Jen as she gives Rory the gentlest hug I've ever seen. She reaches up and pats his hair, smoothing down the mess it's become, and he laughs softly. His green eyes, almost a perfect match to hers, shine with love as he looks up at her. He seems like he's still a little out of it from the meds, but I can tell how happy he is to have her there.

Eventually, Jen lifts a reluctant Piper off Rory, and the two of them share a look. Jen's side of it is full of relief and care, and I can tell that she's so grateful he's alive. There may not have been anything romantic between the two of them, but it's so clear how much they care about each other. They're good friends, and even now that Rory and I are together, I could never be jealous of the relationship they have.

Rory smiles at her and clasps her hand tightly for a moment before letting go and looking around the room. His gaze lands on me, and I give him a shy little smile, not sure why I feel so tentative all of a sudden.

He gestures me over with a crooked finger, and that, plus the look in his eyes, is enough to have me crossing to him immediately as the tears I've been holding back finally begin to fall.

They pour down my cheeks and drip off my chin, soaking into the collar of my shirt, but I don't even care. I only have eyes for Rory and the way he's grinning at me. Even with the drugs and the pain he must be in, he still looks like his old self, that light in his eyes bright and ever-present.

"I knew it," he murmurs teasingly. "I knew you cared."

I laugh, and it's a helpless sound. As I stand at the side of his bed, I can't help but lean down and kiss him, clasping his face between both of my hands. It's a long, slow kiss, reassuring myself that he's here—warm and solid and alive. I pour all of my affection and love into it, just in case he ever had a reason to doubt my feelings.

"You know," I whisper when I pull back, my gaze tracing over his face. "If you really wanted a confirmation of that, there are other ways to find out how I feel besides getting shot."

He chuckles, and it's that incredible, warm sound I've gotten so used to these days. He leans up and kisses me again, nuzzling my cheek a little before he draws back.

I can feel Levi and Sloan at my back, and I move out of the way so they can have their moment with Rory too. Levi's been the most calm through all of this, but his relief is clear to see on his face. He leans down and hugs Rory for a few seconds and then pulls back, letting Sloan move in to grip one of Rory's hands in his.

I can see the same look in Sloan's eyes from before. That desperate need for Rory to be okay and the relief now that he knows he is. Sloan cares about him so much, and it hits me that now that I've seen this side of him and I know the lengths he's willing to go to for the people he considers worth it, it's hard to believe I ever thought he was cold or uncaring.

"Don't do that again," Levi says warningly. "You asshole. We've been out there worried sick about you."

His words are light and teasing, and Rory gives a vaguely sheepish grin in response.

"I know, I'm terrible. So damn inconsiderate, getting shot like that. What was I thinking?"

"You weren't," Levi and Sloan say at the same time, and all of us laugh at that. It's not even particularly funny —*none* of this is—but I think we all need the release, something to break the tension that's been hanging over us.

"It's good that you can make jokes about it," Jen puts in

35

dryly. "At least we know you're not suffering badly enough that it affects your sense of humor."

Rory flips her off, and she rolls her eyes, but the fondness between them is clear to see.

This moment of lightheartedness is so welcome after the last few hours of adrenaline and fear. Seeing Rory and how many people care about him, how many of us want him to pull through, makes the painful lump in my stomach ease a bit. He's alive and he'll be fine. Getting him to get the rest he needs will be a challenge, I'm sure, but other than that, everything's okay for the moment.

Although Rory is still a bit groggy, he doesn't seem like he's in any hurry for us to leave, and none of us want to go anywhere, so we settle in around the room and hang out for a while.

We don't talk about the Jackals or revenge or anything serious like that. Partly because Piper is still here, struggling to stay awake in the middle of all of this, even though it's well past her bedtime probably, and partly because I think we all need a break from it. Celebrating Rory pulling through from his injury is much better without the ever-present shadow of the looming gang war hanging over our heads.

A little while later, a nurse pokes her head into the room and clears her throat. We all look up, expecting to be thrown out or called out for being too rowdy or something, even though we've been trying to keep it down.

"Um, the police are here," she says gently.

Rory nods and Levi and Sloan tug me out of the room. We pass two cops on their way in, and I don't meet their eyes. It makes sense for Jen and Piper to stay in there with him, to help complete the picture of Rory as a family man whose house was broken into.

That's the story we'll all be sticking to. It's not like we can tell the police what really happened, and our cover story isn't even strictly a lie. Jen's house *was* broken into, and Rory's family was threatened.

We stand in the hall while we wait for them to question Rory, and I can't help but glance at the door every now and then.

"Is it going to be okay?" I ask in a low voice, not addressing either of the men in particular. "Rory's in a gang, after all. That's not going to come back and bite him in the ass with this, is it?"

Levi shakes his head. "Nah. He doesn't have a criminal record yet, so he's in the clear. And in a way, it's lucky that none of the Jackals who attacked Jen's house were killed in all that mess. They'd deserve it, those fuckers. But at least there were no dead bodies to account for at the scene. So the story holds up."

I let out a relieved breath I wasn't even aware I was holding. That's good. One less thing to worry about.

Sloan, Levi, and I camp out in the hall the whole time the cops question Rory and Jen, trying to stick close by while also staying out of the way of the harried looking nurses and doctors who hurry up and down the hall.

I've never liked hospitals. They're too clinical, too clean. Someone's probably dying at any given time, and it's just not pleasant to think about. At least Rory's alright. No matter what else is going on, I can keep telling myself that. Rory's alright, and he'll be able to come home soon.

The police stay in with him for a while, and we're still standing near the door when they file out. I watch them go, following them with my gaze.

They seem like normal cops, talking to each other as they head out, one of them flipping through a note pad in his hands. I feel like I'm holding my breath all over again, waiting for them to turn the corner and be out of sight already. Like I can't wait for them to go.

It hits me in a sudden rush how much my life has changed lately. There was definitely a time, a while ago now, when I might have been glad to see the cops come. Happy to turn this whole mess over to them and let them handle it from here. They're the authorities, and it's supposedly their job to handle shit like this, but now I know the truth of the matter.

In this situation, there's nothing they can do to help, so it's better that they stay out of it.

Because my men and I are going to have to help ourselves.

Getting cops involved in the crossfire just means more lives in danger, more people who might get hurt or worse.

What's looming on the horizon is going to get messy and bloody. It already *has* gotten bloody, so there's no use pretending there's any other way to get through this. No one is going to swoop in and save us. It's on us to protect each other and deal with this ourselves.

It's war, plain and simple.

And it's up to us to end it.

4

THE DOCTORS INSIST on holding Rory at the hospital for another few days, just to make sure that there are no complications from the transfusion or the surgery. It would be nice to have him back at home, but it makes sense for them to keep him under observation. There wouldn't be anything the three of us could do to help him if there was an issue, other than take him right back to the hospital anyway.

I don't go to school during those days. I can't even imagine myself sitting in class and pretending to listen to what the professors say. It was hard enough to focus on school when we weren't poised on the edge of an all-out war with the Jackals, but now it just feels impossible.

So I let it go. Right now, my priorities are different. They have to be. I have to focus on what's coming.

At least Rory is healing well. The doctors come in from

time to time to check on him, monitoring the injury and checking for infection and whatnot. The biggest thing was the blood loss, and not any broken bones or internal injuries, so really, Rory was much luckier than he could have been.

It's clear that he's anxious to get out of the hospital bed and go home. Once his head clears from the drugs and his gratitude at having survived wears off a bit, he's furious about what the Jackals did, ranting for a solid five minutes about the nerve of them coming into Jen's house and burning it down.

They hit him in a sensitive place, coming for his family like that, and the steel in his eyes when he talks about it proves that he doesn't intend to let them get away with it. Levi and Sloan are just as angry, just as riled up, and all of us are eager for vengeance.

Underneath all of that is Rory's natural restlessness. He's always up and about, usually with more energy than he knows what to do with, so being bed-bound, even for his own good, is definitely taking a toll on his nerves.

"Rory," I say for the third time in one visit, watching him try to get up so he can start pacing. I don't even have to finish the thought before he makes a face and settles back among the pillows, running his good hand through his messy brown hair.

It's weird to see him in a hospital gown, and even having the bed adjusted so he can sit up with a pile of pillows at his back and his tattooed arm in a sling doesn't make the sight any better. Or make it easier for Rory to bear, clearly.

"Maybe I'd be more likely to stay in bed if you got in with me," he fires back, winking at me.

"I don't think that would help you heal at all," I tell him, raising an eyebrow.

"Maybe not physically, but emotional well-being is important too, you know. And having a gorgeous woman in bed with me is good for the soul."

I roll my eyes at him and shake my head. "I'll go see if I can find one for you then. Any preferences?"

He tries to make a disapproving face, but his eyes are bright with the laughter he manages to smother. "Hm, lemme think. Dark hair, green eyes, about your height with a mean right hook. Oh, and an ass that won't quit. That part's important too."

We both give up on being serious and laugh at that, and I shake my head again.

I don't mind the teasing or the flirtatious comments at all, even if it *is* hard to make Rory be a good patient. Seeing him be his usual self, flirty and irreverent, reminds me that he's really okay.

It's impossible to forget what happened, and sometimes when I look at him in that hospital bed, there's like an overlay of him from the night it happened, broken and bleeding out on the grass. It sits heavy in my chest, like a weight on my heart, and I can tell it's going to be a while before I'm able to let it go.

On the day he's discharged, Levi, Sloan, and I all go to pick him up from the hospital. Jen and Piper aren't with us, although we've promised to give them updates as soon as we can.

Rory had them moved to a safehouse as soon as possible, with people he trusts guarding them and watching them all the time. When I asked him about it, he admitted that he wasn't willing to take a risk again, not with their safety. And as much as Jen didn't want to be sent away like that, she understood that it was for her daughter's safety.

As shitty as it might be, it's necessary, because tensions are at an all-time high with the Jackals.

Every time we leave the house, we're constantly aware of it, looking over our shoulders and trying to make sure we're not being followed. On the drive back from the hospital, Sloan and Levi both keep an eye out for any sign of a tail or other hints of trouble, and I do the same. The Jackals haven't made any moves since the night of the attack, but now that we know what they're capable of, none of us want to underestimate them again.

We make it back to the house without incident, and Rory looks thrilled to be home, smiling and giving a content little sigh when we get through the front door. His arm is still in the sling, and he flops right onto the couch in the living room, wincing a bit when he jostles the arm.

"Damn. I never want to spend that much time in the hospital again," he declares.

"Then stay out of trouble," Sloan replies shortly. He frowns and looks down at the phone in his hand when it starts to buzz. That can only mean it's Gavin, calling about something probably not great.

Sloan steps into the kitchen to answer the call, and I can hear his low voice as he talks to his dad.

I know that there were other locations hit the night of the attack on Jen and Piper. Other members of the Black Roses have people they're close to and places that matter to them, and the Jackals didn't hesitate to strike those too.

I've been so distracted by taking care of Rory and worrying about him that I haven't been very involved with the rest of the aftermath of the attack. But Sloan, as the leader's son, has been dealing with the fallout from it all on top of everything else.

From what I know, there were a few losses, and even though the Black Roses were able to hold off the Jackals in most cases, it just makes everyone pissed as fuck at them and hungry for revenge.

Things were already tense enough before these attacks, and now it's even worse. I don't know what's going to happen next. It's impossible to predict. Even with Hugh making more aggressive moves as their new leader since Samuel died, I never would have guessed that the Jackals would go after Jen and Piper, of all people.

For a long time it seemed like it would be best to avoid an all-out gang war, but now it seems like that might not be possible anymore. And even if we *could* avoid it, I don't know how much I want to.

I've never thought of myself as bloodthirsty, but seeing Rory almost bleed out in the street has changed all of that.

Sloan seems like he's in deep conversation with Gavin, and Levi and Rory both head upstairs. Levi to shower and Rory to, supposedly, get some rest. Even though he's been released from the hospital, he's still supposed to be taking it easy and not putting too much stress on himself.

I head upstairs myself and peek into his room to see him sitting up in bed, scrolling through his phone one-handed.

"Hey," he says, looking up to grin at me. "What's up?"

"Nothing. I just wanted to come check on you. Make sure you're actually resting and not up here lifting weights or something."

He laughs and motions me into the room, so I step inside and sit on the bed next to him.

"I'm fine," he says. "I promise. I'm sitting in bed like a good boy, not stressing myself out or anything. Are you proud of me?"

Rory flutters his eyelashes dramatically, and I can't help but laugh.

"So proud," I reply with a teasing grin.

"Come here." He leans over and wraps his good arm

45

around me, pulling me into an embrace that I settle into gratefully. We lie side by side, with my head tucked into the crook of his shoulder.

"You're sure you're alright?" I ask him, tipping my head to the side so I can see his face better.

"I'm sure," he promises. "I've still gotta recover more or whatever, but I'm going to be fine. You guys worry too much."

"Well, we can't help it. You just matter to us."

"I know," he says, smiling. "I heard even Sloan got choked up while I was in surgery. Takes a lot to get that guy to get emotional. I'm really flattered. It feels like I won an award or something."

He's teasing, but I can hear the deeper truth behind his words. We all rallied around him when he needed us, and I know that means something to him.

It shouldn't have gotten that far in the first place, and thinking about it makes me feel the familiar wave of guilt again. Jen and Piper shouldn't have to be in a safe house, locked away because someone wants to hurt them for simply mattering to Rory.

It's easy to go down the path of worrying about that and letting the guilt get to me, and I've definitely done it more than a couple times while Rory was first brought to the hospital. I try to keep my thoughts off my face so that he won't be able to tell how fucked up I am about it all, but he can read me better than that.

He gazes down at me with bright green eyes that seem to penetrate my soul, and I know if I look away, then it'll just confirm his suspicion that something is wrong. I try to keep my face neutral, to hide it better, but it's a lost cause with Rory.

"What's the matter?" he asks, stroking my side with one hand.

"Nothing."

He lifts an eyebrow at me. "Now I know that's not true. Come on. Talk to me, Hurricane."

That last word tugs at my soul. It's just a nickname, something he's been calling me practically since we met, but it feels so much more like a term of endearment these days. It makes it hard to hide from him.

I sigh softly, trying let out some of the tension that's building in my chest.

"I just..." I shake my head. It's hard to get the words out. How do you say *sorry I got involved in your life and almost got your family killed?*

But Rory keeps looking at me, and his green eyes are patient and kind and concerned, so I know I have to say something.

"I'm just sorry," I finally get out.

"About what? You didn't do anything."

"I feel like I did. I feel like... like this is my fault. Like if I hadn't gotten involved with your family, they would have been safer. I'm a member of the Black Roses now, and you always tried to keep distance between them and Jen and Piper, but then I went and blurred the lines, and..." I trail off, clenching my jaw to try to keep my emotions in check. "And then they were in danger. They could have died."

Rory's quiet for a moment, and there's a little spark of fear in my chest that makes me worry he's going to agree with me. That he'll tell me my guilt isn't irrational, and that it really is my fault. But instead, he pulls me closer, and I sink gratefully into his warmth, lifting my head toward his.

He kisses me gently but with purpose, using his good hand to smooth my hair back from my face. His eyes are intent on mine when we separate, and I don't look away.

"It's not your fault, Mercy," he tells me gently. "I don't blame you for any of this. If anything, it's on me."

"What do you mean?"

He sighs. "I was wrong to think I could separate things like this. I thought if I pushed Piper and Jen into a little box and kept them separate from everything else in my life, it would keep them safe. But it didn't, and it was only a matter of time before something like this happened. The honest truth is that I shouldn't push the people I care about away, no matter what. Instead of trying to keep up barriers between the two parts of my life, I need to hold what I love even closer."

I'm quiet for a bit, taking that in. I've never thought of it that way.

It does make me feel better to know Rory doesn't

blame me, although it's hard for me to let go of the feelings that grip my heart like cold fingers.

As if he can sense me trying to fall into guilt again, Rory kisses me firmly, holding me as tight against him as he can with one arm. I wrap my arms around him, draping myself partway over his solid frame as we kiss.

"That goes for you too, you know," he murmurs against my lips. "I love you, Hurricane. And I'm going to hold you close and protect you and take care of you for as long as I can."

I love you.

My heart races to hear those words, and I have to swallow hard past the emotions welling inside me.

"I love you too," I tell him softly.

At the hospital, I had a moment of pure clarity where I admitted to myself that I love this man—that I've fallen in love with all three of them. But this is the first time Rory and I have said those words to each other.

Speaking them aloud makes something settle inside of me with a decisive click, as if a piece of me I didn't even know I was missing has found its way back and made me whole. Rory gives me his trademark devastating grin, and I can feel my stomach turn over and tighten with desire like it always does when he looks at me like this.

He's just too damned sexy for his own good.

Or mine.

He draws me into another kiss, and I go with it,

pressing my mouth to his and humming softly because it feels good. It feels right. We just *fit* together like this, even with his arm in a sling and the danger of what comes next hanging over our heads. It feels like this is how it should be, and I hope like hell that someday, we'll be able to have all of the good without the bad.

It's a sweet kiss to start, the kind of kiss that feels like a declaration all on its own, even though we just said the words out loud.

But of course, with Rory, things don't stay sweet for long. Just a few seconds into it, he's already sliding his tongue along the seam of my lips, trying to coax me into parting them and letting him in.

And of course I do. I can't help it. My jaw drops open a little, and he presses his tongue inside, swiping through my mouth like he belongs there. A soft moan of contentment spills from my throat before I can stop it, and I can feel Rory chuckling against my lips.

He pulls me closer, his free hand roaming over my body with greedy touches. He delves his fingers into my hair and then slides his hand down lower so he can grope my back and my ass before moving to my thigh.

I moan again, losing myself in the feeling of his hand on me and his mouth on mine, and all the different ways we're coming together. It's so easy to get caught up in it and forget that we're technically not supposed to be doing this.

Although... I guess that's never really stopped us before.

Still, once he starts grinding his hips up, making sure I can feel how affected he is by what we're doing, I pull back. We're both breathing hard, and I can feel my face warming with a flush.

"Rory," I say, trying to sound stern and not as breathless and turned on as I am. "We're not supposed to."

"Says who?" he asks with a pout.

"Your doctor. You know, the one who told you and us that you're not supposed to be too active while you're recovering? I don't want to risk hurting you."

"Hey, a little risk never killed anyone," he says, waggling his eyebrows.

It sounds teasing, but I can see the flash of disappointment in his eyes as he goes to settle back against the pillows once more. The fabric of his t-shirt stretches over his broad chest, and although the tattoos on one arm are mostly covered up by the sling, his full sleeve on the other side is as bright and vibrant as ever. The shapes of his tattoos shift a little as his arm muscles ripple, his hands clenching and then unclenching.

Seeing how hard he's trying to follow the doctor's orders makes my chest ache a little. I know he's doing it for me, and for Jen and Piper and his friends, more than for himself. If he didn't have a team of people worried about him and invested in his healing, he'd probably already be up and about, pushing through no matter what.

I'm glad he's taking it easy, but I want to make it better for him somehow. An idea hits me, and I smirk, letting my lips curve wickedly as I slide myself down his body.

I settle between his legs, and my fingers go to the waist-band of his sweatpants, tugging them down. He didn't bother with underwear when he got dressed this morning, so as I pull his sweats down over his hips, his cock springs free.

My heart stutters at the sight, warmth suffusing my entire body, and I glance up at him to see him looking down at me with the same heat in his gaze.

His cock is already flushed and hard, and I lick my lips as I gaze down at it. Then I ease my mouth over him, holding him there for a second to just enjoy the heat and weight of his hard cock on my tongue.

"Damn, Mercy. Holy fuck," he moans, and my smirk just widens around my mouthful.

I tease him for a bit, sucking at the head of his dick but not going lower, pulling off so I can swirl my tongue around the crown and dip it into the little slit that's already starting to leak the salty fluid of his precum.

Rory's free hand comes down to tangle in my hair, and he tugs a little, not really pulling me more onto his cock, but just showing that he's enjoying it. His eyes are so dark, so heated, and I look up at him while I work my mouth down lower and lower until I feel him hit the back of my throat.

There's just something about that look on his face, something about watching what I do to him in real time while I do it, that makes me throb at my core.

His cock pulses in my mouth, and I focus on it even more, bobbing my head and leaving slick trails of saliva that make the next slide up and down even easier. I can feel him getting almost impossibly harder against my tongue as more of the blood in his body surges south. He could probably come easily and quickly if I let him, but it's more fun to be a tease.

So I pull off before he can buck his hips up, leaving trails of spit connecting my lips and his dick. He groans at the sudden loss, his chest heaving a little from his harsh breathing.

"Tease," he accuses me, his voice a little hoarse.

I just grin and lick my lips, which I'm sure are red and shiny from going down on him.

"Oh..." I cock my head as if confused. "Did you want something?"

"You're a bad, bad girl. So mean," he says, but his grin makes it clear he loves me for it.

His cock bobs in the air, resting just above his stomach, mere inches from my mouth, and I can't keep the teasing up for long—not when I was enjoying that just as much as he was. So I seal my lips around him again, sucking him all the way down.

My tongue rubs against the underside of his cock in a little massaging motion, and I swallow around the head. Rory throws his head back against the pillows and moans my name, and I can tell from the way his hips twitch upward, like he's trying not to choke me by bucking all the way, that he's close.

So I don't let up, sucking fast and deep, until he comes undone in hot, salty spurts that coat the back of my throat until I swallow.

I pull off, licking my lips, and I can feel my pussy throbbing with the need to be touched. Sucking Rory off turns me on in a way that blowjobs never really did before I met these men.

His cock has softened a bit from his orgasm, but from the way he's looking at me like he wants to eat me, it sure doesn't seem like he's done. He tugs at my arm until I move up his body and drape over him, straddling his waist and feeling the heat from his large frame seep into mine.

"Get naked, Hurricane," he murmurs. "I want to see you."

There's no fucking way I'm going to say no to him when he asks like that, and I start pulling my clothes off, shucking my shirt and shimmying out of my pants with Rory's help. He's still got his sweats partway on, and I don't try to take off his shirt because of his sling, just shoving it up a little to expose more of his abs and chest. But having some of the layers between us gone makes me want him even more, and I shift my hips a little, positioning my throbbing core right over his still half hard cock.

The heat is incredible, and judging from the way Rory moans, he can feel it too. For a moment, I just sit there, the wet heat of me pressed against his hardness. Rory licks his lips, his good hand settling on my hip, and I let out a soft noise of pleasure and contentment.

But as good as this is, it's not even anywhere close to being enough. I have to start moving. I slide myself over him, grinding against his cock that's rapidly going from half hard to fully hard.

It feels so damned good, that velvety feeling of his shaft against my clit, the head of him catching that sensitive bud on the way down.

I don't bother to hold back my gasp and moans, and Rory grits his teeth and swears under his breath while he rocks against me.

It's not the same as having him hard and deep inside me, but it's a close thing. It's close enough that every time I grind my hips down to feel him press hard against my sensitive flesh, I get that ache of pleasure right at my center, spurring me on and building up until I can hardly breathe.

I try to be as gentle as possible, because as much as I want to get off, I also don't want to hurt him. It takes a bit more time this way, but before long, I can feel the tell-tale heat spreading out, catching me up in a wave of sensation and throwing me headfirst into the spiral of pleasure that means my orgasm is close.

"Rory," I pant, looking down at him as my fingernails dig gently into his pecs. "I'm close. Fuck. I'm gonna—"

Before I can even get the words out, I'm coming undone, shaking my way through an intense climax as I slide up and down his cock, trapping his thick length between our bodies.

Rory watches with a hungry look on his face, his green eyes turning almost black as his pupils expand. And he's right behind me, falling apart once more with a muted curse as he comes all over my stomach and his own.

We catch our breath for a bit, just breathing each other in, along with the smell of sex and arousal that fills the air around us.

"Oops," he murmurs after a minute or two, sounding incredibly amused. "So much for not having sex."

I laugh, shaking my head. "We didn't! We obeyed the letter of the law. And you didn't have to exert yourself too much."

"True. You did all the work. I'll have to pay you back for that when I'm back to full health." The gleam in his eyes promises that he means to make good on his word, and I shiver at the idea of what he might do.

He smiles and pulls me in for another kiss, this one soft and slow as he nuzzles at my lips.

"I love you," he murmurs again, as if he'll never get tired of saying it.

My heart swells, and there's no fear or apprehension at all as I echo the words back to him.

I love this man so much.

I love all three of them.

And even though I was raised to be a fighter, I'm done fighting that.

5

A FEW DAYS GO BY, and Rory's recovery is going well. He's out of bed more often than not, and even though we still won't let him go down to the gym and work out or anything, he's back in the kitchen and the living room, draping himself over counters and couches dramatically while he teases the rest of us.

It's nice to have things getting back to normal. Or as normal as they can be, I guess. His arm is still in the sling, which is a constant physical reminder that things are different.

And it's impossible to forget the reason why.

The tensions with the Jackals haven't lessened even a little bit, and while we're all keeping our eyes and ears open to make sure nothing like what happened to Rory and his family happens again, Gavin is trying to get a handle on the situation before it gets worse.

About a week after Rory's return home, we get called to a meeting with all the top players of the Black Roses. Of course this includes Sloan, as the leader's son, but it also includes Rory and Levi, as his right and left hands. Surprisingly enough, it also includes me.

I don't know if I'll ever be able to wrap my head around that one, but Rory cheerfully points out that even if I wasn't invited, they'd just come home and tell me everything anyway, so it's easier this way.

He does have a point.

Sloan is the one who delivers the news about us being called to the meeting, and it's clear he's not happy about it. His mood has been better now that it's clear Rory is recovering well from the gunshot, but there are dark circles under his eyes, and the way he's holding his jaw just shows he's still stressed and tense as hell.

I wish there was something I could do to help or at least take some of the stress off of him, but he hardly even talks about it. He's opened up to me a lot since I first met him, but there are some things he still holds back.

His stiffness and silence seem to be taking a toll on Levi and Rory too—although that could just be the situation itself. Being one of the higher-ups during a brewing gang war just means more of the work and blame and trouble falls in your lap, and I know all three of them are deep in it right now.

"We can't be late," Sloan says, ushering us all out the

door and into the garage. He strides ahead, focused on his phone while his thumbs practically fly across the screen, sending out rapid fire texts before he has to get in the car and drive.

I frown after him, and Levi comes up next to me with a little sigh. He leans down so he can speak in my ear, voice soft and breath warm as it fans across the side of my face.

"Sloan and Gavin are having it out, I think," he murmurs. "They can't come to an agreement on how to handle all of this."

"That's not really anything new though, is it?" I ask him just as softly. Almost every time I've seen Sloan and Gavin interact, it's been the two of them arguing over what should be done.

Levi shrugs a shoulder in response. "They've always had slightly different styles. Sloan's so head-on, you know, and Gavin likes to know for sure what he's getting into before he makes a move. But all this stuff with the Jackals recently is making the differences between them more obvious. I don't know what's going to happen, but it can't go on indefinitely like this. One of them is going to blow up at some point."

Worry tightens my stomach as I absorb his words, and the two of us hurry after the others to get in the car so we can drive to the meeting place.

I know Gavin hates me. Ever since I fucked up and sold out the Black Roses' accountant to the Jackals and then had the nerve to not die in the process of retrieving him, Sloan's dad has had a grudge against me. The fact that the new leader of the Jackals is my uncle just makes it all worse, probably. It would be so much easier for Gavin if I wasn't a part of this, or if Sloan hadn't decided to protect me, and I wonder if part of the reason the two of them have this rift is because of me.

Even if it is, there's nothing I can really do about it. Gavin seems like he won't be satisfied unless I'm dead or out of the way, and Sloan's not going to let that happen, obviously.

We get to the meeting place quickly enough and file in. It's another of those slightly abandoned warehouse type places that serves as a front for the Black Roses' interests. There are twenty or so other people here already, standing around and chatting while we settle in ourselves.

Gavin's already here, of course, standing front and center with that commanding presence he gives off. He glances at us as we come in, but the expression on his face doesn't change, giving nothing away.

"Now that we're all here," he says, casting his gaze over everyone in the room. His voice cuts through the ambient conversations like a whip, even though his tone is casual. "We'll get started."

He nods to someone standing off to the side, and the man steps forward. He's older, closer to Gavin's age than ours, with a scar down one side of his face. From what I can gather, he's been in charge of keeping an eye on Jackal territory, close to the line where Black Rose stuff bleeds over into theirs, so he and his team can try to find out if they're going to make a move and stop it before it happens next time.

"The Jackals are sneaky fuckers," the man says, his lip curling with disgust. "There haven't been any outright attacks, nothing burned down and no one hurt, but there have been several smaller infractions. We've gotten reports of businesses being vandalized, all in our territory, and some of our connections have been warned away from doing business with us."

"That jewelry shop on Sixth," someone else chimes in. "Our contact there says she's seen men in front of the shop three days out of the last week, looking like they were scoping the place out or something. They didn't come in or stay long, but she noticed."

A few others step up and give their own reports, talking about things they've seen or what they've heard from informants. The first guy's words seem to hold true though. Nothing too aggressive, nothing that could be seen as a direct declaration of war, but definitely no sign of the rival gang backing down either.

Gavin listens to all of it with a serious look on his face, taking it in. Once everyone seems to have said their piece, he nods and sighs. "Well, this can only be a good thing, then."

I nearly recoil in surprise because that was definitely not what I was expecting him to say. A good thing would be the Jackals slinking back into their den with their tails between their legs, not making moves against businesses and people that are connected to the Black Roses.

"We've been bracing for another full-scale attack," Gavin continues. "But they haven't moved to start one. The perfect time would have been while we were all still reeling from the last one, but nothing has happened. They've toned down their tactics, going back to the more petty shit they've always done. Tensions are going down."

"Bullshit."

Sloan's voice cracks through the room, even more tense and whiplike than Gavin's was at the beginning of the meeting. All the stress and anger he's been feeling seem to be in his tone now, and he's glaring at his father with his jaw set and his hands balled into fists.

"Sloan." Gavin shoots him a warning look.

"No. That's bullshit, and you know it. You're trying to make it sound like things are going back to normal, but they aren't. They *can't*. Hugh fucking tricked us. He baited us and he attacked us. And not just us, but people we care about. Places that matter."

I glance over at Rory when Sloan says that and touch his hand lightly. He gives me a little smile and then looks back to Sloan, giving his friend his full attention.

"This doesn't have to turn into a full-scale war, Sloan," Gavin responds. "No one wants that."

"And again, I say that's *bullshit*. It's obviously what Hugh wants. There's no de-escalation anymore. There can't be. The Jackals can't be trusted, and they won't let go of their vendetta against us. So they need to be dealt with. They need to be taken out."

My stomach ties itself into a tight knot as a rush of adrenaline floods my body. I don't know if anyone's ever said it so bluntly before. There's been talk of the gathering storm of this war and the deaths and damage it'll probably cause, but no one's ever just come out and said the Jackals have to be taken out. Leave it to Sloan to cross that bridge before anyone else.

The others in the room seem to be split in their thinking. Some are nodding along with Sloan, some look like they're waiting for Gavin to talk some sense into him, and some just look uncomfortable.

Gavin has a look on his face like he means to be obeyed, but Sloan isn't backing down. He stares right back at his father, jaw clenched while he waits for Gavin to say something. It's a silent stand-off, and the tension in the room ratchets up so high the air is thick with it.

It feels like something could pop off at any second, and even though there's no shouting or guns drawn, Sloan and Gavin are both stubborn and powerful, and everyone there knows it. They're the two most important members of this gang, and them butting heads seems to make everyone anxious.

"It would be a mistake to start something we can't finish," Gavin says finally. "We have to be smart about this."

"The mistake would be letting them get away with this shit," Sloan retorts angrily. "What the fuck kind of message does that send? They do this, and we just walk away? They'll never leave us alone. It's never going to go away."

"Sloan," Gavin snaps sharply.

Sloan bites his tongue with a frustrated noise, and his knuckles are white from how hard he's clenching his fingers. I want to touch him or do something to help relieve some of the awful tension that's settled into his posture, but I keep my distance. This is between the two of them.

"That's all for now," Gavin says to the others. "Stay on alert, and if anything changes, use the usual channels."

There's a murmur of agreement, and people seem more than happy to head out, leaving the brewing battle between Sloan and Gavin behind.

By unspoken agreement, Levi, Rory, and I stay put, backing Sloan up. As soon as the door closes behind the last person, the last of his restraint seems to evaporate, and he turns on his dad once more, fire in his eyes.

"We could have stopped this," he growls hotly. "We could have done something before anyone got hurt. I told you I didn't trust Hugh, that he was a fucking liar and a snake, but you insisted on meeting with him and trying to buy into his farce of a truce. He never wanted peace between us. He's *never* going to want that."

"So you blame this on me," Gavin replies, and it's not a question. "You think it's my fault things have reached this point with the Jackals."

"If you had listened to me, none of this shit would have happened—"

"If you had never brought *her* into this, none of this shit would have happened!" Gavin cuts in, talking over Sloan.

He looks at me, and there's cold dislike in his eyes. It's the same way he looked at me before, when he told me I was a member of the gang now, when I didn't die in the rescue mission like he expected me to.

Fuck. He *really* doesn't like me, and I don't know if anything Sloan says will change that.

My heart thuds heavily in my chest, but I hold my ground, keeping my face neutral as I look back at Gavin.

Sloan narrows his eyes and takes a step forward. Levi and Rory both react like they want to hold him back or keep him from doing something stupid, and the tension escalates so high it feels like I might choke on it.

Gavin turns his gaze from me back to his son, his face set in grim lines.

"Don't forget who sold us out," he says after a beat of silence. "Don't forget who gave the Jackals exactly what they needed to feel like they were powerful enough to start something with us. I didn't do that."

"No," Sloan replies. "But you sure as fuck didn't do anything to shut them down after the fact. You're so fucking scared of a war that you'll let them run all over us to prevent it, and it probably won't change shit anyway. Hugh's gonna go after what he wants, whether you hand it to him or he has to take it, and I'm not gonna let that happen."

Father and son stare at each other for another long minute, and it's almost like the argument has continued in some kind of silent language that only the two of them can speak. Even though the room is completely silent, I can feel the emotions lashing through the space like whips of electric energy.

When Gavin doesn't say anything else, Sloan finally scoffs and shakes his head. "Right. Of course."

There's anger and bitter disappointment in his tone, and Gavin clenches his jaw but still doesn't respond.

"Fuck this." Sloan's lips curl, and he grabs my arm and stalks out of the room, leading me out with Rory and Levi right behind us.

6

THE RIDE back to the house is quiet and tense. Sloan doesn't even turn on the radio as he drives, and no one seems to know what to say to him, so we all just sit in silence.

I can feel the angst from that meeting still lingering in me, making my heart beat faster than usual. I have to relax my jaw as it tightens up over and over again, and by the time we get back home, I know I need to get all of my excess energy out somehow.

We all head into the house, and I go upstairs and change into my workout clothes, figuring I'll slip down to the gym and work off some steam that way. Maybe it'll help me forget the way Gavin looked at me or how no one seems to know what's going to happen next.

I sure as fuck don't know what to expect, and it took a

lot of self-control not to insert myself in the fight between Gavin and Sloan and tell the older man to go fuck himself. Logically, I'm glad I didn't say anything, because speaking up like that would have only made things worse. It's not like Gavin was strictly wrong, anyway. I *did* have a part to play in all of this.

But he was still being a dick back there at the meeting, and I hate that it's looking more and more like he'll never move on from what I did to his gang, no matter how many of his "tests" I pass or how hard I work to prove myself.

Fuck. I need to hit something.

Throwing my dark hair into a quick ponytail, I glance in the mirror. My tank top shows off my sculpted arms and the ink that swirls over my skin, and I look forward to getting a bit sweaty and disheveled. Fighting is the best emotional outlet I've ever found, apart from sex.

I slip out of my bedroom and trot quickly downstairs, planning to head to the basement. As I step off the staircase on the first floor, I hear the low murmur of voices coming from the kitchen. All three of the men are gathered in there—I can hear each of their distinctive deep voices talking in quiet tones. Frowning, I change course and head in that direction instead.

As soon as I enter the kitchen, they all look up, their gazes finding me immediately.

That's not unusual, especially not since I've been

sleeping with all of them. I'm used to being the center of all of their attention, but there's no desire or playfulness in any of their faces now. They look grim and serious, and there's a heaviness in the air that tells me something is off.

I frown at them, trying to figure out what kind of conversation I just interrupted. It feels like someone just died.

"What's going on?" I ask, my brows drawing together.

None of them answer me at first, and that doesn't do anything to make me think I'm wrong about the whole "someone died" theory.

"Seriously, you guys," I say, resting my hands on my hips. "You're freaking me out."

Levi is the first to speak up, glancing at the other two before looking back to me.

"Sloan needs to marry you," he says matter of factly.

My eyebrows shoot up to my hairline as my heart skips two beats in a row.

For a second, it's like my brain is convinced I heard him wrong. It can't get the words he spoke to make sense in that order.

My jaw drops open when it finally hits me properly, and I laugh in shocked surprise.

None of them laugh with me.

I can't tell if they're joking or not, and their faces aren't giving anything away. I glance at each of the men in turn, waiting for one of them to spring the *gotcha!* on me or something.

"Wait... what?" I blink, trying to recalibrate my addled brain. Because if this isn't a joke, I don't know how the hell to deal with it. "What the fuck are you talking about?"

Instead of answering, Rory and Levi both look to Sloan, who clenches his jaw before he speaks.

"My father still blames you for all of this shit," he says. "Even the parts you didn't have anything to do with. You heard him at the meeting. He's decided that *you're* the cause of everything that's happened since the night of your dad's fight, and I don't know what he'll do."

"What do you mean?" I ask, my throat tight.

"I mean he's under a lot of pressure from the Jackals right now, and it's fucking obvious he doesn't want to escalate anything. We don't... we don't know if he'll try and sell you out or hurt you in some way. To 'smooth things over.'"

The air quotes in his words are vicious, and I swallow hard. I hadn't even really thought about that.

"But he won't do that if you're married to his son," Sloan continues. "To me. The family line and the sanctity of marriage mean too much to him. If you were my... my wife, then he'd have to back off."

His wife.

Become Sloan's wife so that Gavin will back off.

Even hearing it explained like that, I can't wrap my head around it.

My heart is racing in my chest again, beating hard enough that I swear I can hear it echoing through my body. I have no idea what the hell to say to this. I came downstairs to work out and get rid of some of the tension in my muscles, and now the strangest marriage proposal I've ever heard of is sitting at my feet.

It's too much.

All of it is just too fucking much.

The three of them are standing there, looking at me expectantly, and I know they want an answer. I know what answer they want.

I open my mouth and say the first word that comes to my head.

"No."

The men all react to that, their expressions shifting. They're all staring at me, just adding to the pressure that's building up inside me like a balloon stretched too thin. I start to back away from them, confused and fucked in the head, then turn and flee from the kitchen like the place is on fire.

I walk quickly down the hall and take the stairs down to the basement so fast it's a miracle I don't fall and break my neck. But it'll be quiet down there, and no one will be looking at me with unreadable expressions, expecting me to make major life decisions based on a gang's whims.

The gym feels as comfortable as it always does, and I let out a sigh of relief as I step inside the large basement room, trying to clear my head by shaking it, which doesn't do much.

With my mind still churning, I wrap my hands the way I always do before I plan to really wale on the heavy bag, then take a stance in front of it. More than ever, I need to get my emotions out, before they get so out of hand that they start to choke me.

So much has happened in the last few weeks, and I feel like I'm still reeling from it all, trying to find my footing and constantly failing to develop an equilibrium. This latest issue added to the stack isn't helping, and I try to block out the thought of it as I start to hit the bag, relishing the sounds my fists make when they slam into it.

It's easy to lose track of time like this, falling into a rhythm of moving my hands and shifting my body to follow the motions. The slight sting of pain when my knuckles make contact with the bag helps too, keeping me focused on the exercise and not the torrent of emotions that are all clamoring to be dealt with.

I push my body hard once I've warmed up, letting the heat of exertion settle into my muscles. My breathing comes in hard pants as I get worked up, and I keep hitting the bag harder and harder, going to my upper limit and then a little bit past it for a few seconds before slowing back down.

It's cathartic in a way, to be down here alone with just

the sound of my fists on the bag, my breathing, and the occasional grunt of exertion.

But after several moments, I become aware that there's somebody else in the space.

I didn't hear him on the stairs, but I can feel eyes on me, and I look up from my narrow focus on the bag to see him standing in the doorway, watching me.

Sloan.

7

I'M aware of him standing there, his broad shoulders filling up the doorway, but I ignore him for a while, continuing to punch the bag. Just seeing him after what happened in the kitchen is enough to kick up the emotions churning through my chest again, undoing all the calm I thought I had achieved.

It's always been like that with all the guys, but Sloan especially, so I don't know why I'm surprised. Whatever plans I have in place for how I'm *supposed* to feel go flying right out the window, and all I can think about is him or whatever fight we're having at the time.

I don't even think this is a fight, which doesn't really help because I have no idea what I'm feeling. Sloan's face is hard to read, like usual, so I don't know what he's thinking either. He did just suggest that we need to get married, and I did turn him down, so maybe he's pissed about that. Maybe he came down here to call me selfish and tell me I'm not thinking of the bigger picture or something.

I have a few choice things I could say in response to that—such as the fact that a decision like this shouldn't be made for the *bigger picture*—but I don't even know how to put it in words. I don't know anything.

It all just feels like too much. Too much, too soon, on top of everything else that's already going on.

So I just focus on hitting the bag, slamming my fists into it over and over again. One right after the other, the satisfying smacks radiating up my arms and making my shoulders burn.

Sloan just watches me, not saying anything, but after a little while, he comes forward. I brace myself for whatever he's going to say, but he doesn't say anything. He just steadies the bag, standing there like he's waiting.

I stop punching, breathing hard, sweat running down my face. I lift one arm and wipe the sweat away with my wrist and look at him, trying to see if there's anything I can tell about where he's at emotionally.

I can't tell if he's angry or hurt or what, but something unpleasant churns in my stomach, and I realize I can't tell if *I'm* angry or hurt either. All that punching was for nothing, apparently, because I'm right where I didn't want to be, in the center of all these emotions with no clear way to get out.

"Did you come down here to ask me again?" I ask him, panting softly between words.

"No," he says, and his voice doesn't hold any anger or resentment. He just sounds tired. "I just wanted to find out why you said no."

I clench my jaw and look away from him, avoiding his gaze. "I don't know, Sloan," I mutter, trying to get him to leave it alone.

"Yes, you do," he insists. His gray eyes churn like storm clouds as he stares at me. "You do know. You said it like there was no doubt in your mind that that was your answer."

"It was the first thing that popped into my head!"

"And I want to know why."

One hand lifts, and I run my fingers through my hair, feeling frustrated. Out of all the conversations I could have been having today, this is not one I ever expected. And I don't even know what to say. It all feels so strange and weird, but it's clear that Sloan isn't going to let up until I tell him something.

He still doesn't seem mad, just like he wants to understand what I'm feeling, and that's a pretty big improvement for him. The two of us are used to blowing up at each other whenever that spark lights between us, letting our emotions run rampant rather than talking shit out, but that's not what he's doing right now. It wouldn't be fair to blow him off when he's trying.

I sigh and look at him, trying to wrangle my racing thoughts into something that sounds vaguely like an explanation.

"I just... fuck, Sloan, I don't want to marry you out of an obligation," I say finally. "Just to keep your dad off my back or whatever. I get the point you guys are trying to make, but that just feels... gross to me."

There. That's the best I have, and it's actually close enough to the core of the issue.

I'm expecting him to tell me it'll be for the best in the long run or to say I'm being silly or something, but instead he just goes silent, saying nothing. The silence lasts for so long that I look up at him, needing to see his face.

Instead of a harsh glare on his face or that sculpted jaw being clenched in anger and frustration, there's something soft in his features. A kind of tenderness and realization all wrapped into one. It takes my breath away for a second, because I feel like I'm still getting used to seeing Sloan be open with his feelings and emotions.

He's definitely not hiding behind anything now.

"Is that what you think this is?" he asks me, voice soft. "An obligation?"

I blink at him, confused. "Isn't it? Isn't that the whole point?"

He steps around the bag and comes closer to me. There's an intense look in his eyes, but it's soft around the edges, different from anything I've ever seen in him.

"Mercy," he says, and it's a tone I've never heard either.

It makes my name sound like something precious, something to be cherished, and I have to swallow hard around the tight lump in my throat. Part of me wants to run away, and part of me wants to lean into him, to bask in the way he says that single word.

He pauses for a moment, just studying me with those gorgeous steel gray eyes of his. Then he shakes his head, letting out a soft breath that's almost a sigh.

"It's not an obligation. It's not a burden. Proposing to you was never a matter of *if*, but *when*," he murmurs. "From the first moment I met you, falling in love with you was inevitable."

My mouth opens a little, but no sound comes out. I have no idea what I could even possibly say to that, so I don't say anything. It's all I can do to keep my legs under me as I stare at him in a whole new kind of shock.

And still, he isn't done.

He takes a step closer to me, his eyes growing a little unfocused as he seems to search inside himself for the right words. "It was like... like a snowball kicked down a mountain, just getting bigger and bigger as it goes. My feelings for you are so big, so fucking powerful that they could destroy anything in their path."

He reaches out and takes hold of my wrist, and I don't stop him. The threads that have been weaving around us since the moment we met, binding us together heart and soul, seem so strong now that I almost believe I could look down and see them shimmering in the air between our bodies, connecting our chests like gossamer webs.

I'm powerless to resist when he pulls me toward him and tips my face up with his other hand so he can kiss me.

The feeling of his lips, hot and insistent on mine, is enough to shake me out of my shocked daze, but then I'm basically flung headfirst into another one by his kiss. It's consuming and deep, and he doesn't take his hand away from my face as his lips move against mine. Sloan grips my chin to hold me still and devours me with his mouth, nipping at my lips and plunging his tongue in when they part.

He kisses like he never wants to stop, and I cling to him, cupping the back of his neck as I kiss him back. It's impossible to deny the flow of emotions between us, and I don't even want to try anymore. So I just give into it, kissing him back with just as much passion and love as he's pouring into me.

I have no fucking idea how long we stay like that, wrapped up in each other, sharing breath as we kiss. It feels like it could easily go on forever, but eventually we break apart.

My head is spinning a bit, and I have to lick my lips and blink to try to get my balance back.

By the time I manage to focus on something other than

how warm I suddenly am and how good Sloan's mouth felt on mine, he's let me go and stepped back. I feel like I should say something, but before I can, he drops down to one knee in front of me.

My heart was already beating fast, but now it kicks into a breakneck rhythm, slamming against my ribcage like it's trying to force its way out.

Sloan looks up at me, and that tender expression is still there. He's still looking like I'm the only thing in the room that matters, and it takes my breath away.

"Mercy," he says quietly, beginning with my name again. It feels so significant when he says it, and I can't look away from him. "I love you. I want to be a part of your life, always. I want you by my side, and I want to protect you and take care of you forever. Will you marry me?"

I gaze down at him, my heart beating fast and hard as the world seems to blur around me.

Before, up in the kitchen, the idea of marrying him seemed like something crazy that I could just brush off.

This, though?

This is real.

This is Sloan on one knee, telling me he wants to spend the rest of his life with me.

It's significant, not a means to an end, and that matters.

What surprises me the most as I look down at him is that something seismic has shifted inside me. No part of

81

me wants to say no anymore. I'm still scared, and it's still a huge step, and it still probably doesn't make any sense.

But the one thing it's *not* is an obligation.

It's real. *We're* real, and I want this. I want everything he's offering, everything that could be in front of us if I can just be brave enough to reach out and take it.

I want the security and the safety and the love and the closeness.

I want the fierceness and wildness of the bond we share.

I want all of it. And I never want to let it go.

Something hot and sweet wells up in me, tightening my throat until there's nothing I can do but nod as he looks up at me, waiting for my answer. It takes a few tries for me to find my voice, and when I do, it's raspy and shaky, but I manage.

"Yes," I tell him. "Yes, I'll marry you."

Sloan's handsome face splits into a smile that lights up his eyes, and he stands up and hauls me into his arms again, pulling me so close that there's no distance between us. He leans down and captures my mouth in a deep kiss, and I can feel the love he pours into it all over again. His woodsy scent surrounds me, overwhelming me with *him* as he buries his fingers in my hair.

When we finally pull apart, Sloan is still grinning, and it makes him look younger than I've ever seen him, almost boyish in his excitement.

"We should go tell the others," he says, releasing me from his embrace and taking hold of my hand.

"Okay."

I nod, unable to keep myself from grinning back. He turns toward the door, and I thread my fingers through his as he leads me back upstairs. When we reach the main level of the house, we head for the kitchen, where Rory and Levi are still waiting.

They both look up as we walk in, and the anxiety melts from their faces as soon as they see me. Or rather, see *us*. Based on whatever they see in our expressions, they don't seem to need to hear the words to know what happened. They can probably read it in the dazed smile on my face and the pleased one on Sloan's.

Levi lets out a little sigh of relief, then crosses the kitchen to stand in front of me. He pulls me into his arms and kisses my cheek lightly before following the line of my face to press a kiss to my mouth.

When he pulls back, his deep brown eyes are warm and steady, and he looks happy and not at all jealous. Still, worry flares inside me anyway. We've just started navigating this four-way thing between us, and I don't know if any of us factored marriage into the plan. So it's hard to know how it will all turn out.

"Levi..." I chew my lower lip, trying to figure out how to broach what I need to say. "I agreed to marry Sloan, but

I don't want you to think that means I don't love you and Rory too. It's not about that, and I—"

He just leans down and kisses me again, cutting off my nervous babble before it can get too out of hand. I can feel him smiling against my mouth, and when he pulls back again, his eyes are bright.

"I know," he says simply. "I love you too, Mercy."

Rory comes around the kitchen island and steps in to take Levi's place when his friend moves out of the way for him. He's takes his turn pulling me into a hug and kissing me, peppering my cheeks with little kisses that make me laugh and scrunch up my nose before he kisses me just as deeply as Sloan and Levi did before.

"You don't have to worry," he says when he leans back to let me breathe. "We all talked about it, and we came to an understanding."

"You did?" I ask him, blinking in surprise.

"Of course. We're capable of deep shit like that," he teases. Then his expression grows more serious. "But yeah. We decided that, sure, you're marrying Sloan, but that's just a piece of paper. Really, you're binding yourself to all of us, right? We all know you're committed to all of us, even if only Sloan's name is on the paper with yours."

Hearing him say that feels like a weight off my shoulders, honestly. Throughout these last couple of weeks where we've been trying me being with all of them, I've worried about one of them feeling left out.

Sloan, mostly, because he was the one who had the hardest time with this in the first place, but it could have been Rory or Levi too. If one of them bailed, it would send the whole thing toppling down, and I never wanted that.

But with this, it seems like I don't have to worry. They want me, all of them.

Forever.

Maybe that should scare me, but it doesn't.

I wrap my arms around Rory's neck and lean up to kiss him again, letting him know just how much his words mean to me with the way I move my mouth against his. Judging by his low chuckle of amusement, he gets the message.

I can feel it as the other two move in to surround me. Levi's hands move over my back, rubbing gently as Sloan runs his fingers through my hair. I can tell which one it is just by the feel of their touch, even with my eyes closed, and a giddy sort of happiness rises in my chest.

This is so far from where I ever thought I'd get with these guys. So much more than any of us could have really expected when life threw us all together in a chaotic mess of violence and hate.

And it's so much more than an obligation or something only done for practical reasons.

Yeah, it might keep Gavin off my ass long enough to sort out the whole mess with the Jackals, but that's just a perk. It's not why we're doing this, not why we want it so much.

I can feel it in the way they all touch me.

It's *love*.

Pure and fucking simple.

8

LATER THAT NIGHT, when I'm alone in my room, I grab my cell phone from the nightstand and scroll to Scarlett's contact. There's only so much a girl can hide from her best friend, and being proposed to is definitely not one of those things. If she found out later, she'd hit the roof, and I think I'd almost rather deal with Gavin in a foul mood than with a pissed off Scarlett because she's been left out of the loop.

"Okay," I tell her when she answers the phone. "I have some news for you, but you have to keep the screaming to a minimum."

"Uh oh." She clicks her tongue against her teeth. "I can't tell if this is going to be good screaming or bad screaming. What's going on?"

I can tell she's bracing herself, which is fair, considering the fact that every time we talk these days, there's always some new drama that's kicked up for me to fill her in on. At least this isn't bad drama.

As insane as it is, the news I have to tell her is very good.

"So, we went to a meeting with Sloan's dad and a bunch of other Black Roses higher ups earlier today," I begin, filling her in about the meeting and the Jackals and what they've been up to. She already knows about what happened to Rory and how upset we've all been because of it, so when I tell her that Gavin just wants to move on from it like it didn't happen, she makes an appropriately outraged noise.

"They came to Rory's house and tried to hurt his family," she says, sounding indignant. "They could've killed him, or Jen or Piper, not to mention the other targets they hit. You can't just ignore that. Right?"

"Right," I agree. "That's Sloan's position, pretty much. He doesn't think the Jackals should be allowed to get away with this blatant attack, and he doesn't believe they're going to back off now. You should have seen how he was with his dad when they were arguing. I thought one of them was going to haul off and hit the other one."

"Jesus," she murmurs under her breath. "So what happened? Why am I supposed to be screaming?"

"Well..." I blow out a breath, remembering the awful tension that crackled through the room. "Sloan said it was Gavin's fault it all happened, because he's been so

88

goddamn eager to make peace that he's just letting the Jackals fuck us over, basically. And then Gavin said that, no, it's actually all *my* fault."

"Asshole." Scarlett snorts.

"Yeah. But the guys are all worried that he's going to do something to me."

There's a pause, and when she speaks again, her voice has a worried edge to it. "Do something? Something like what?"

"Like try to trade me to Hugh or use me for leverage. Or just kill me himself, I guess. So they were all talking about that earlier, and when I came downstairs, they'd come up with a solution."

"Smack Gavin in his dumb face?" she mutters.

I laugh at that, amused by her sass. "Nope. Their solution was for me to marry Sloan."

I wait a second for that to sink in, and my bestie does not disappoint. She makes a muted shriek that's probably lower than her top volume but still practically vibrates through the phone.

"What did you say?" she asks, and I can picture her now, sitting up on her bed like I'm sitting on mine, bouncing up and down with excitement.

"I said no," I tell her, drawing my knees up and tucking them beneath me.

"Wait. What? Why?"

"At the time, because I didn't want to marry Sloan just

out of an obligation. Just so his dad wouldn't try to fuck with me. That's not a good reason to get married."

"Oh," she murmurs, her tone softening a bit. "Okay, yeah. That's fair. How did Sloan take that?"

"He came down to the gym later to talk to me about it. And he told me that wasn't why he was proposing. That it wasn't just because of an obligation, and he loves me and wants to be with me. He proposed again, like with getting down on one knee and everything, and that time... I said yes. We talked to Rory and Levi too, and they basically said that even though the marriage on paper will just be to Sloan, it sort of stands for all of them. So I guess, in a way, I'm getting three husbands soon."

I brace myself for another screech of excitement, but it never comes. Instead, Scarlett is quiet for a second.

"Hey. Are you okay?" I ask her.

"Yeah," she replies. "I'm fine. Just thinking, I guess. I'm just really surprised when it comes down to it. Really excited for you too, don't get me wrong. That's amazing that Sloan actually proposed for real. But I'm partly super worried. I mean, it's my job as your best friend to worry about you, and you've been through a lot with these guys. I mean, a *lot*. From the beginning, where they basically kidnapped you, to thinking Sloan killed your dad and all. So many ups and downs, and it feels like it's been going on forever, but actually it hasn't even been that long. Isn't this maybe too fast? Is it too fast?"

I drag my lip between my teeth, considering her words.

I can see where she's coming from. She's right that it feels like all of this with the guys has been going on for longer than it actually has.

It's actually hard to remember what my life was like before I got involved with these three men and the Black Roses. Back when I was just going to school and watching fights and hanging out with my dad and Scarlett on the weekends. I feel like a completely different person than I used to be, and her point is a good one.

But at the same time, I can't remember ever being as sure about anything as I feel about this.

"It's not too fast," I tell her. "I know how I feel about Sloan—about *all* of them. I spent so much time trying to convince myself that I hated them for who they are and everything they stand for, because I thought I had a reason to. And even when I was so sure that I had more than enough reasons to hate them, I couldn't quite do it."

Keeping the phone tucked against my ear, I lie down on the bed, letting the words pour out of me.

"Who they are, and how loyal and strong and protective they are... it all just shone above everything else. Enough that I started falling for all of them even though I knew I shouldn't. But now I know there's no reason to hold back how I feel, and without those things in my way, I can admit how I really feel. And I love them, Scar. I love them with my whole heart."

Even as I say it, I realize how true it is. How deep my feelings run.

"So maybe it's happened a little quickly in the grand scheme of things," I continue, "but I don't think it's too fast. Because whether the wedding part happens now or later, I want to be with them forever. They've gotten under my skin, and I want to keep them there."

Scarlett goes silent for a minute after I finish speaking, and honestly, I don't know if she's *ever* been this quiet for this long. I'm almost worried she doesn't approve when she laughs softly and sniffles a bit.

"Damn it, you bitch. You're going to make me cry over here with all the mushy stuff," she says. It comes off like a joke, but I know that means she can tell I'm serious, that I really do love these guys.

"Sorry to get all rom-com on you," I tease lightly, and she laughs.

"Yeah, right. If they made rom-coms about this, I'd like them more. One woman with three gorgeous guys? Sign me up." I can hear her moving around on her bed, getting more comfortable and probably wiping her eyes. "Okay," she says. "Okay! So we have to make some plans then."

That's the Scarlett I know.

She's clearly over her doubt, convinced by what I told her, and now she's turned the corner to being fully supportive of this whole thing.

That's just the kind of friend she is, and I've always loved that about her. She looks out for me, worries about me, and isn't afraid to tell me when she thinks I'm doing something stupid, but she also supports me in that ride-or-die kind of way when I make crazy choices, as long as it's clear I believe in them.

Maybe tying myself to three guys who are involved in a gang and a looming war with another criminal organization is a crazy choice, but now that she's heard how much it means to me, I know she's on my side without question. It's just one more reason why I love the fuck out of her. She's like a sister to me, and I definitely couldn't do any of this without her support.

The small stretch of time when I was trying to keep her out of all of this mess was hard enough. I hated not being able to share things with her or talk openly about what was going on in my life, so I'm so glad I don't have to hide any of this.

"Have you thought about a date? A guest list? Cake? Dress? Flowers?" she asks, peppering me with rapid-fire questions.

"It's not going to be a big ceremony or anything, Scar," I warn her, already able to hear the gears grinding in her head as she plots out an extravagant celebration. "I mean, who would we even invite? The rest of the gang?"

"I'll be there!" she insists. "And that's not the point. You only get married once, assuming you do it right, and it's supposed to be special! You have to have a dress, of course."

"Really? For a courthouse wedding?"

"Yes! It's important. Don't you want to walk down the aisle—"

"There won't be an aisle," I cut in.

"Don't you want to walk into the courthouse in something so gorgeous it knocks all three of them out?" she continues, raising her voice to talk over me. "I mean, you only get that experience once. Well, with a wedding dress, at least. Something fancy and beautiful that will make you look like a princess, but like a badass one, you know. Plus, I need to have a maid of honor dress too."

I laugh, shaking my head fondly as I stare up at the ceiling. "Just nominating yourself, then?"

"Well, who else would you pick?" she asks, as if it should be obvious. Then she makes an excited noise. "We have to go shopping. Please, Mercy? *Please?* This is the only time we'll ever be able to do this. The only time my best friend will get married."

She's right. It's not like I'm planning to get married again, and it's not like either of us have a lot of other friends that would be walking down the aisle anytime soon. She sounds so insistent and excited that even though I don't really care about the fanfare of it, I can feel myself giving in.

"Okay, okay." I hold up my free hand in surrender,

even though she can't see it. "We'll go dress shopping. Although, with the way things are with the Jackals right now, we'll probably need an escort. I don't think the guys will want me out on my own."

"Wow, you're basically royalty at this point," she jokes. "An *escort*." She puts on a fancy, fake British accent for the last part. "It'll be like shopping with the queen."

"Not even a little bit," I reply, rolling my eyes. But at least she's not arguing about the guard. She probably knows as well as I do that it would be pointless because the guys wouldn't budge on it.

"Aw, you're no fun," she fires back. "Anyway, dress shopping this weekend? I know a place we can check out."

"Sure." I grin, unable to hold back my wide smile. "Why not?"

I WAS right about the guys wanting to send a guard to watch over us while we shop, so a few days later, Scarlett and I head to a little wedding dress shop, accompanied by a guy from the Black Roses.

My men wanted it to be one of them who came with us, but since I'm shopping for a wedding dress, I put my foot down on that. Rory bitched about it a little, but I told him the surprise would be worth it, and if we're doing the whole dress and fancy clothes thing, we might as well get on board with the rest of the traditions too.

The guy they chose is a chill dude named Andy, who seems fine to stand outside the dressing room area as Scarlett and I sort through dresses and try to narrow down our choices.

I don't shop for fancy clothes a lot, so I feel out of my depth, but Scar seems to know what she's doing, alternating between eyeing me like I'm a piece of meat and pulling things off racks.

"What do you think about a train?" she asks, looking at a dress that seems to have double the fabric it should. I realize the excess must be the train, held up off the floor while it's on the rack, and shake my head.

"Too fussy. There's no aisle, Scarlett."

She sticks her tongue out at me and goes back to looking. Now that she knows this is real and that the guys will take care of me, she's totally on board and is probably more excited about the actual wedding part than I am. I'm more interested in the end result, the part where the guys and I build a life together. Something real and lasting.

"What we really need is a dress that says 'yes, hello, I am the proud owner of my own personal harem,'" she teases, waggling her eyebrows as she looks over at me.

I roll my eyes, letting my hand trail over the dresses. "I don't own them, Scar. They're not *mine*."

"I bet that's not what they'd say if I asked them," Scarlett replies. "They'd tell me they're yours heart and soul, or something sappy like that. Or maybe something a little dirtier, but the message would still be the same."

I huff out a laugh, wincing when I find a dress that seems to be more beads and sequins that anything else. I put it back on the rack quickly. "You're getting a little carried away."

"What do you expect?" She pokes me in the ribs. "You're living the dream, and I have to live vicariously through you. And anyway, don't tell me you haven't been dying to dish about the three sexy as fuck guys you're sleeping with. I know you better than that, Mercy."

Dying to dish is definitely an overstatement, but she does have a point. Scarlett's the one person I tell everything to, and I've been holding back a lot of the details from her when it comes to all of this. Some of it was to keep her safe, and some of it was because I had no idea how to talk about it. Then there were the parts that I didn't talk about because it felt like saying it out loud would jinx it.

What me and the guys have is something we've had to fight for.

We've had to overcome our own stubbornness and the circumstances we're all in to make it work, and it felt fragile and delicate for a while. Like if it was held up to the light so someone else could see it, it would just crumble and break apart.

But standing in the middle of a wedding dress shop

with my best friend, picking out a dress that's supposed to knock the socks off the three men who love me, I can see that we're past the point where I have to worry about any of that.

Scarlett watches me while I turn the thoughts over in my head, a patient but excitedly expectant expression on her face. Her infectious grin is hard to resist, and I decide that yeah, it would be fun to dish a little.

"Okay, okay," I say, making it seem like I'm caving to her demands reluctantly, even though the grin stretching my face probably gives me away.

Scarlett grins back and claps her hands.

"Yes! What are they like?" she asks, leaning forward with a look of rabid interest on her face.

"You've met them."

She wrinkles her nose. "I mean, kind of. But I've never seen them when they're just relaxed and in love with you. There's always been a weird tension whenever I was around you guys before."

She's not wrong about that, so I nod. "Fair. They're... intense. All of them in different ways. I mean, Sloan's the most intense, and he's only recently started opening up and showing he has more emotions than just anger and more anger. He can be really sweet when he wants to be."

I think about the way he proposed, down on one knee, promising to be there for me and take care of me. It was a vulnerable moment for him, letting me see past the hard outer shell he wears and putting his heart on the line like that. I love that he trusts me enough to let me see *all* of him, not just what most people get to see.

"Levi and Rory are different," I continue. "More laid back. Levi's the level-headed one, and Rory never stops cracking jokes. Unless something is very, very wrong."

Like him bleeding out on the ground or being terrified for his family. I still don't want to think too hard about that, and Scarlett can either sense it with her best friend powers or she has other things on her mind, because she swoops in, handing me a bundle of white fabric and propelling me toward the door of the dressing room in the back.

The dressing room is big, with several plush chairs arranged around the space and large mirrors on the walls. There's a row of small changing stalls along one wall for putting dresses on and taking them off.

"They're all so *big*," she says, standing outside the door while I go into a changing room and start stripping out of my t-shirt and jeans. "Tall and buff, I mean. But I bet they're big everywhere else too."

I can just picture her waggling her eyebrows while she says it, and I laugh, hanging up each dress on the hooks on the wall. The changing stall is painted the same dusty shade of pink as the walls outside in the main dressing room area, and there's a little table in the corner with a bouquet of dried pink flowers sitting on it.

This is probably the girliest thing I've done in a while, and I don't hate it.

"They are," I tell her, grinning at my reflection. "It's all proportional."

"I knew it," she crows. "They don't make men like that with small dicks."

"Men like what?"

"You know, tall, dark, and handsome. Intense in just the right way. Ready to throw you over their shoulders and take you away to be ravaged because someone else dared to look at you."

That makes me laugh, and I take the first dress off the hook and shimmy into it. The silky material feels nice against my skin, but I only need to look in the mirror once to know this isn't the one.

"You've put a lot of thought into this," I say with a chuckle. Then I wrinkle my nose at my reflection. "Not this dress."

"Second opinion?"

I shake my head even though she can't see it. "Nah, definitely not this one."

"On to the next, then! Anyway, are you saying I'm wrong? Are they not the types who would do that?"

"No... you're not wrong," I admit, thinking back to how pissed Rory and Levi got when that guy was insinuating I needed to suck off all the rest of the Black Rose guys for what I did to the gang.

"Knew it," she repeats, sounding smug, and I laugh again.

The next two dresses are also not really for me, and I poke my head out of the dressing room to ask for a couple more, passing the rejects back to Scarlett.

She looks like she's having the time of her life, and she hands me back three more and then settles on one of the velvet lined chairs that are positioned around the main dressing room area. I close the changing stall door and start pulling on the next dress.

"It's funny," I say, smiling absently at nothing. "They're all so intense in their way, but they can also be surprisingly gentle. Sometimes Levi just holds me like I'm precious. Like I'm everything he ever wanted. Rory invited me into his family. Sloan would probably kill a man for looking at me, which might be his version of gentle, I don't know. They're *not* gentle in bed, which I like."

"Have you been with all three of them yet?" Scarlett asks. "I mean, at the same time?"

"Yeah." My skin heats just thinking about, and I bite my lower lip as a wave of remembered images and sensations wash through me. "Once, so far. It was..." I trail off, trying to find the right word for it. "Amazing. All of them had their hands on me as they kissed me and touched me. They all fucked me, one after the other, until I couldn't feel anything else but them. I felt like I was going to die, in the best way."

Scarlett makes a low sound of interest. "Holy shit. I'm jealous."

I step out of the changing stall in time to see her fanning herself, and she smiles as she looks at me in the current dress. It's an off-the-shoulder number with a skirt that hugs my hips and thighs before flaring out around my knees and down to my feet.

"I can't decide on this one," I say, turning this way and that so I can get a better view in the mirrors that are set up along the wall.

"Hm." Scarlett tilts her head, getting up so she can walk around me. "It's nice, but I don't know if it's the one, you know?" She smacks my ass with the flat of her hand and then laughs. "It does make your butt look fantastic, though. How do you feel in it?"

"Good, but not amazing."

"Then we keep looking!"

It's so easy to lose track of how many dresses I try on. There are a ton of them to choose from, and after an hour and a half, we've barely made a dent in the boutique's selection.

Still, there's always something just not quite right about each dress. Too high of a neckline, too many beads, too much fabric in the skirt. I've seen enough movies and TV shows to feel like there's supposed to be a moment when you put on the dress that you know is the one.

Where it just clicks and feels right and makes you sure everything is right with the world or whatever.

Scarlett doesn't seem to care how long it takes to get me that moment, and if I didn't already love her before, I definitely do now.

"Ooh," my bestie calls as she walks back into the dressing room taps at the changing stall door. "Try this one. I have a good feeling about it."

That's good enough for me, and I open the door to take the dress she hands me. It's become methodical by this point to unzip myself and carefully take off whatever dress I was already wearing, hanging it back up before I move to the next one.

This one is a bit different from the others I tried on. It's more sleek and less poofy, for one thing, skewing more sexy and sophisticated than fairytale princess. It fits perfectly when I get it on, and when I look in the mirror, I just know.

This is the moment.

This is the one.

It's off the shoulder, with a plunging neckline that draws attention to my cleavage in a subtle way. The three quarter sleeves end at my elbow, made of a soft, delicate lace that makes my skin look tanned and warm instead of washing me out. Little bits of my tattoos show through the lace, hinting at the ink on my skin.

The lace continues down the bodice, and then the dress

separates a bit. The skirt is long and brushes the floor above my feet, made of the same satiny material as the parts under the lace. It doesn't poof or flare when I twirl, but it feels good when I move, and there's a slit up the side that offers flashes of thigh when I walk around the changing stall.

There's an overskirt sort of thing, made of the same lace as the sleeves, that falls around the satin fabric in a couple layers, giving the skirt more body and just barely hiding the leg the dress shows.

It looks amazing on me, and I can already picture the way the guys will react when they see me in it.

"Okay, I'm coming out," I say to Scarlett, and I hear her clap in excitement outside.

I open the door and step out, careful not to step on the skirt of the dress since I'm not wearing shoes. As soon as I step out and see the reflection in the full length mirrors, I know I made the right choice.

Scarlett's eyes are wide, and she puts a hand over her mouth and looks me over before rushing to hug me, careful of all the lace.

"You look so fucking beautiful!" she gushes. "Like a badass warrior princess or something. God, those guys are not going to know what hit them. Do you love it? It only matters if you love it."

"I love it," I tell her, grinning like an idiot. "This is the one."

"Yes!" She cheers, bouncing up and down on the balls of her feet. "I knew it. Shit, I'm so happy for you, Mercy."

I don't know if she means about the dress or in general, but we hug again, and it doesn't really matter.

Since this dress is definitely the winner, I go back in the stall to change out of it and back into my regular clothes. As fun as it is playing dress-up, I'm ready to be done trying things on—now it's my turn to sit in one of the fancy chairs and watch Scarlett pick her maid of honor dress. Since we're not doing a big ceremony with a full wedding party or anything, I told her the color choice is up to her.

She's just as excited about choosing her own dress as she was for mine, and she tries on dresses in a rainbow of colors and styles, modeling them for me and for herself in front of the mirrors.

I give my opinions, limited as they are, but there's a part of my brain that's not totally focused on the shopping.

As happy as I am to be getting married and to have found a dress that's perfect, I can't help thinking about how sad I am that my dad won't be there to see me walk down the aisle. He won't be there to give me away or make a speech or tell the guys they'd better be good to me, or else.

I don't know, maybe it's for the best that he's not here right now. I honestly have no idea how he'd react to the idea of his daughter with three men, especially ones in a powerful gang. It's not like his disapproval would change anything. I'm not leaving them, and there's no one on earth who could make me. But even if he was confused or pissed off by my decision, I still wish he could come to the wedding. I wish he could be a part of this moment in my life.

At the end of the day though, I know the most important thing is that he's safe. Hugh thinks he's dead, and that's how it has to be for now. Once we deal with the Jackals, he can come back and reclaim his life. He won't have to be in hiding anymore.

A few minutes later, Scarlett comes out of the dressing room in a red dress that matches her name. It's not too over-the-top, but it looks amazing on her, and she smiles at her reflection and then at me.

"Too much?" she asks.

I shake my head. "Nah, I think it's perfect. I'd be so honored to have my brilliant, bright best friend next to me in that."

Scarlett looks like she's going to cry, and she turns one more time in front of the mirrors. "Okay, I think this is the one, then. Now I'm going to change at the speed of light and then go see if they have a bathroom in this place, because I have to pee like a racehorse."

I just laugh and gather my dress and hers once she's gone, pulling the plastic back over them so we can take them home with us. I hunt down my shoes and jacket and am just starting to pull them back on when the changing stall door opens.

"That was fast," I say as I turn around, expecting to see Scarlett there. Instead, there's another woman standing in the doorway. I don't recognize her. She definitely doesn't work here, as we met all the staff already, and they were a trio of chirpy blonde women. They've mostly left Scarlett and me alone as we've tried stuff on, which I think Scar might've requested when she made the appointment, knowing that the two of us would rather spend time just with each other.

But even if I hadn't met the boutique staff, I don't think I could mistake this girl for one of them.

She's about the same height as I am, with silver hair, pale skin, and dark blue eyes. She's wearing skintight jeans and a leather jacket that's zipped all the way up, but I can still see hints of tattoos peeking out from the places her clothes don't cover.

"I think you've got the wrong room," I tell her, instantly on the alert. It's always been a pretty basic instinct not to trust anyone I don't know, and with the shit that's been going on in my life recently, that impulse is stronger than ever.

She doesn't look flustered or embarrassed as if she walked into the wrong changing room, and she doesn't leave. Instead, she strides up to me and leans in close.

My fight response kicks into high gear, my hands

curling into fists. I've been in too many scrapes lately to trust some random girl coming up and getting in my space. I almost punch her, figuring I'll hit first and ask questions later, but before I can let a fist fly, she speaks.

"I have information about the Jackals," she murmurs in a low voice.

I blink in surprise and take a step back. "What?"

She just shakes her head, a look of vague annoyance crossing over her features. Instead of repeating herself, she just takes another step forward to close the distance between us. Leaning in, she starts rattling off a series of words and phrases that don't make any sense.

"They're codes," she says afterward, talking quickly as draws back to meet my gaze. "Secret phrases that Hugh uses with his high-level captains. To make sure no one has been compromised."

"Codes," I repeat slowly, my mind scrambling to keep up.

How the hell does she know these codes? And how does she know I might need them?

"Listen," she says, her voice hard and insistent. She reaches out and grips my arms tightly, pulling me in closer. She says the words again and then once more for good measure, then stares at me expectantly until I repeat them after her.

Only then does she let go and step back.

"I hope you and the Black Roses destroy them," she

says, her expression turning hard. "Burn the Jackals down to the ground."

Before I can ask her anything else, she turns on her heel and slips out of the changing stall just as quietly as she came in, leaving me blinking in shock after her.

What the fuck?

9

SCARLETT DROPS me off at the house a little while later, taking both dresses with her when she drives away so that there will be less chance of any of the guys getting a glimpse of mine.

The house is quiet, and Rory and Sloan don't seem to be here. Levi's in the living room when I step in, watching something on TV, but he mutes it when he sees me.

"Hey! How'd it go?" he asks, grinning.

"I found something perfect," I tell him. "You guys are going to love it."

His grin goes sharper around the edges, and there's heat in his deep chocolate-brown eyes. "I can't wait to see it."

I cross the room to him, and he pulls me down onto the couch and wraps an arm around me. I lean into the embrace gratefully, letting my body melt against his as I rest my head on his shoulder.

"Something weird happened though," I murmur, dragging my fingers absently up and down his muscled thigh.

"Weird how?"

I tell him about the strange girl with the silver hair and blue eyes—what she told me, and how insistent she was. I describe her as well as I can, and Levi frowns, thinking about it.

"I don't think I know anyone who looks like that," he says. "Not in the Black Roses anyway."

"Makes sense, I guess, since she had information about the Jackals. Maybe she's an ex-girlfriend of one of their members or something."

"Yeah, maybe. We should tell Sloan and Rory about it when they get back," Levi says. "And remember what she told you. I don't know how we can use it right now, or even if it's viable information, but write those codes down somewhere, just in case."

I nod. "I already did on the way home."

"Ah. Of course you did."

"Part of me is scared maybe it's Hugh fucking with us somehow, but that's not the vibe I got from her at all. I don't know where she got her info from, but she definitely seemed to hate the Jackals."

"Well, I'm glad you told me," Levi says. "We'll fill the other guys in and figure out where to go from here."

He drops a kiss to the top of my head, and I shift my position, climbing into his lap. I straddle him as he settles his hands on my hips, looking up to meet my gaze. Whatever he was watching on TV is forgotten as he leans up to capture my mouth in a kiss, and I hum into it, kissing him back.

Like all the kisses I share with the guys, this one is heated, but it's also comfortable. Not necessarily going anywhere, but hot in its own right.

It's just nice to kiss and be kissed, and even if it's the middle of the afternoon, I don't give a fuck. There's nothing else we need to be doing right now, and nothing else I'd rather be doing.

Levi slides a hand up my back, tangling it in my hair, and I make a soft noise of encouragement, resting my hands on the broad expanse of his shoulders while we make out.

Once upon a time, I would have hoped the others didn't walk in and see the two of us making out on the couch, but now I wouldn't mind if they did, and I don't think Levi would either.

There's nothing at all to hide, and we just go with it, happy to kiss and touch as we please.

I smile against his mouth when I feel his hand start to dip under my shirt and slide up. I don't have any issues with him getting handsy on the couch, and I make a soft noise of encouragement, grinding down on his lap a little to make sure he gets the point.

Instead of continuing, though, Levi pulls away, looking at me with a little smile on his kiss-swollen lips.

"I want to show you something," he says. "Upstairs."

Half of me thinks this is just an excuse to get me into a bedroom so we can have more room to maneuver. But we've had some pretty hot sex on the couch, so it's not like he doesn't know it's possible.

Intrigued, I nod. "Okay, sure."

I get off of his lap, and he takes my hand and leads me upstairs to his room. He pulls his sketchbook from the desk and flips a few pages before handing it to me.

At this point, I'm familiar enough with his sketches to know it'll be a good one, and I look down at the page he's opened the book to. I'm not really sure what I'm expecting to see, but the shaded pencil drawing on the page takes my breath away for a moment.

It's a beautiful sketch of me, Levi, Sloan, and Rory all together. I'm wearing a dress that isn't too far off from the wedding dress I picked out, actually. The guys are clustered around me like protective guardians, and it's so obvious that we're all in love.

It's gorgeous and sweet, and it hits me right in the chest with a million feelings. All I can do is stare down at it, taking in the details. We're all smiling in the picture, and each of my three guys is leaning in toward me, like they'll never let anything bad even get close.

When I glance up at Levi, he looks almost shy as he watches me, his full bottom lip dragging between his teeth.

"This is what I want," he says softly, gesturing to the sketchbook. "This is what I see for the future when I think about it. Just all of us together, happy. That's all I want, Mercy. It's so simple, but it's everything."

I lean up and kiss him, resting one hand on his chest and feeling the steady thud of his heart beneath my palm.

When we break apart, I look back down at the sketch, and something catches my eye. My brows jump upward, then pull together.

"Is that... a *baby bump*?" I ask, noticing the roundness of my stomach in the dress.

Levi doesn't answer, but there's a grin on his face that's both sweet and sinful at the same time.

A flutter passes through my belly even as I swat at his arm. I've never really thought about kids, if I'm being honest. I've never considered myself all that maternal, since my mom died when I was pretty young and I was surrounded by a lot of male energy growing up.

But the idea of these three men as fathers makes my heart warm. I've already seen how Rory is with Piper, and I know that all of them would be so dedicated to any child we ever had.

A child.

Holy shit, it's *way* too soon to be thinking seriously about that. We've got so much other shit on our plates right now, and even though I have no doubts or hesitation about the wedding, I know I'll want to have the guys to myself for a little while before we add another tiny person to the mix.

Still, even knowing all of that, the thought of watching my guys shower all of their love and affection on a little baby lights a fire inside me. I never thought I'd be the type to get turned on by that image, but fuck, my ovaries might've just exploded.

I take the sketchbook and set it down on the desk once more so our hands are free. Then I move toward Levi and wrap my arms around him, kissing him deeply.

He smiles and reciprocates, cradling my face in his hands as he kisses me back with feeling.

I'm not sure which one of us steers the kiss toward the bed, but we end up there after a few stumbling strides and fall onto it, the soft sheets and mattress welcoming us.

Levi rolls us over so he's on top, still cradling my face as he tugs me up to meet him in kiss after kiss. My hands roam down his back, over his shoulders, across his ass, just needing to touch him and feel how warm and solid he is on top of me.

I grab the hem of his shirt and tug it up insistently, and Levi gets the message. He parts from my mouth for long enough that we can get his shirt off, and then he's back on me, devouring me with his lips.

His mouth finds my neck, and I gasp softly, tilting my head to the side to give him more room to explore the sensitive skin there. I shiver under him, getting more and more turned on by the second.

That's how it always is with these guys. They barely have to touch me before I'm panting for them, desperate to have them on me and in me.

Levi chuckles, his warm breath huffing against my skin, and it's almost like he knows what I was thinking. Maybe he does. Either way, his hands make their way down to my shirt, and we get that off too.

Both of our pants and underwear follow shortly after, leaving us gloriously naked in his bed. Levi eyes me hungrily for a bit, taking in the sight of me spread out and bare against his pillows and sheets. Then he lunges for me again, kissing my neck and my collarbones before heading lower.

His mouth finds my nipples, and I arch into the sensation of it, the sweet, wet heat of his lips and tongue sending jolts of pleasure right down to my core.

He latches on to one of the hard buds, grazing it with his teeth and then swirling his tongue around it to soothe the sting.

"Fuck! Levi..." I moan, writhing on the blankets.

My pussy throbs with the desire to get the same attention, but Levi just grins, moving his head to the other side so he can do the same to my other nipple.

By the time he lets up, I'm practically dripping with need. He makes his way slowly down my chest to my stomach, pressing those hot, open-mouthed kisses along the way, and then finally settles himself between my legs.

They spread automatically to make more room for him, and I gaze down the line of my body, entranced by the sight of him with his head between my thighs. Levi's fingers spread me open, and I know he can see how my folds glisten with wetness. I can smell the scent of my own arousal as he tilts his head up to meet my gaze for a moment.

The look he gives me is hungry, and whatever he sees on my face must inspire him to stop torturing me, because he finally buries his face between my legs just like I need.

His tongue slides out, beginning to lap at my slick pussy in long, confident strokes.

"Oh, fuck," I gasp, reaching down to thread my fingers through his hair just to have something to hold on to. My other hand tangles in the sheets, and I arch against his face, practically humping and grinding against it in my need for more.

His tongue knows all the right places to lick at, and I can feel a fierce, needy heat burning in my gut.

It's perfect. It's so damn perfect, and if he keeps it up, I'm going to come all over his face in less than a minute.

But that's clearly not Levi's plan. After a few more strokes, he pulls back with a wicked grin, lips shiny from my wetness. It gives me a chance to catch my breath, at least, and I watch him as he sits back on his heels.

His cock is hard and flushed, bobbing lightly between his legs. He reaches for me, turning me onto my stomach, and my stomach tightens with anticipation. I love this position.

With exaggerated slowness, I get up on my hands and knees, pushing my ass out for him to see. I don't need to be facing Levi to know his eyes will be dark with the lust he's feeling, and I can practically feel the way he looks at me like his gaze is a physical thing, sweeping over my body with burning heat.

He grabs a handful of my ass and spreads me open once more, sliding his cock into my pussy with his other hand. He's thick and hard and perfect, and I hang my head, trying to breathe through how good it feels.

It *always* feels so fucking amazing, and we fit together like we were made for this.

Levi's clearly not in a hurry, and each thrust is deep and slow, making sure I feel every single inch of his cock as he buries it inside me again and again. My fingers clench in the sheets, and I don't hold back the moans and gasps that spill from my lips. We're alone in the house, and even if we weren't I'm past the point where I don't want the other two to know when I'm having sex with Levi. Or with any of them. Now it's just hot to think of them hearing and wanting to join in.

That thought just makes me even hotter, and I start pushing my hips back, meeting Levi halfway through each thrust. His hands are tight on my hips, and he pulls when I push, our bodies meeting in the middle with the echoing slap, slap, slap of skin hitting skin.

His breathing is rough and harsh, and I can feel the way he grinds into me, hitting that spot so perfectly that I see stars and feel the heat of my orgasm starting to build already.

"Are you gonna come for me?" he asks, his voice rough and breathless.

I nod eagerly, because I'm already so close, and I can feel myself edging even closer with every thrust he makes. He loses some of that slow pace and starts battering into me, making sure there's no time for me to catch my breath before the power of my orgasm hits me like a ton of bricks.

I moan loud and long, going down to my elbows when my arms give out. Wave after wave of pleasure crashes down on me, threatening to steal my breath while my vision goes white around the edges.

It takes a good few seconds before I can breathe properly again, and I can feel my heart hammering in my chest as I come down.

Levi's still rock hard inside me, and he stays still for a long moment, grunting as I clench around him. Then he pulls out slowly, making sure I can feel the hard drag of his cock against my sensitive walls.

His hands cup my ass, splaying me open once more, but this time, he doesn't go for my pussy, even though it's soaked from my orgasm and how turned on I still am.

Instead, he traces the rim of my ass with the tip of one finger.

My eyes fly open wide in surprise, and the noise I make seems to burst out of me in a guttural way that I can't control. Levi just chuckles under his breath and keeps teasing me there.

He drags his fingers through the slick wetness of my pussy, collecting it before he goes back to my ass, using my own juices to lubricate his finger enough that he can work the tip of it into the tightly furled hole.

"Oh my god," I breathe out, shuddering hard. It feels so much better than I would have though, and that burning glow of arousal that was banked a bit when I came a moment ago flares hot and bright again.

I've never done this before, not with anyone, but I like the way it feels.

"You're so tight back here," Levi murmurs, sounding almost reverent. He reaches over to the nightstand and fumbles around in a drawer for a second. I can't see what he fishes out, but when I feel the cool drizzle of something slippery against my hole, I know it must be lube.

There's no rush here, and I'm grateful for it. He takes his time, dipping that finger in and out of my ass until he can move it smoothly, with no resistance.

By the time he starts working toward two fingers, I'm practically a puddle on the bed. I had no idea it would feel like this, and the nerves are firing like crazy. My pussy throbs all over again, but it's not just that. My ass feels so sensitive, like it's craving being stuffed and filled, and when Levi works that second finger in along with the first, I let out a sound that's almost a sob.

That stops him for a second, and he strokes his clean hand down my back in a soothing motion. "Are you alright?"

I nod against the covers, too overcome to say words at the moment. It's hard enough to remember to breathe, dragging air in through my mouth while I tremble under Levi's touch.

He chuckles softly and pets my back for a bit longer before pushing those fingers back in, twisting them in a way that makes me nearly scream with pleasure. I'm not even sure what it is that does it, but the sensation is enough to send me flying over the edge into another orgasm, shaking and teary eyed as I struggle to breathe.

"Beautiful," Levi murmurs. "You're so fucking beautiful like this. So tight and hot for me. I bet you're gonna feel amazing on my cock, baby."

He keeps stroking my back while he talks, the gentle touch a strange contrast from the reality of him talking about fucking my ass.

"Can I fuck you here?" he asks, pulling his fingers free

with a wet noise that goes right to my core. He goes back to tracing my rim, stretched and ready for him now. "Can I push into you and see if I can make you come again?"

"Y-yeah," I manage to choke out this time, and I feel proud of myself for manage words finally. "Fuck me."

That's all the urging he needs, clearly. His fingers disappear, and there's a moment of me feeling empty and needy. I can hear Levi fumbling with the lube, coating his fingers once more and slicking up his cock, before the blunt head of it finds its way to my ass.

He's never been small, but somehow his cock feels even bigger against the tight rim of my ass. Like he could split me open if he wanted to, and I'd probably thank him for it.

I drag in a deep, ragged breath as he presses inwards, and the smooth head of him manages to slide inside me. I nearly choke on my next breath, overwhelmed and over-come. It's electric, like lighting shooting through my veins, and every little movement is amplified times ten.

Levi keeps going slow, working into me with little thrusts of his hips. Whenever I tense up, he pauses and touches me, murmuring reassurance and urging me to relax. It gets easier every time, until eventually, his cock is fully seated in me, and I'm panting out little shuddering breaths at how full I am.

The thought of having one of the guys in my ass and one of the others fucking my pussy flashes across my mind, and I moan, low and loud. It would be so much, maybe too much, but there's only one way to find out.

Levi seems to be having his own struggles with control, and he holds himself still, fingers digging into the flesh of my hips while he holds me steady. I can only imagine what it feels like for him, tight and intense, and I'm surprised he can hold back.

"Fuck me," I tell him again, wiggling my hips as much as I can with him holding on to me. "Levi, please."

He growls a bit under his breath, and it's such a sexy sound that my pussy throbs. I never would have thought my ass would be as sensitive as my pussy, but when Levi drags his cock out, every nerve ending fires, making me shiver and press back against him, seeking more of that feeling.

I don't have long to wait, and he pushes in again and starts a deep, slow rhythm, fucking into me with long strokes that make sure there's no way I'm not going to feel every inch of him.

I'm already so oversensitive from coming twice before, and I can feel that heat burning, signaling it won't be long before I'm falling apart again for him.

Our bodies move together, and Levi groans my name over and over again, leaving finger shaped bruises on my hips from how tightly he holds on. I nearly tear his sheets in return, fingers clenched so hard in them that my knuckles are white.

It feels like I'm burning alive, and it's possibly the most intense sex I've ever had, if you don't count the time I had all three of them fucking me. Everything is sensitive and I can't keep up with everything I'm feeling.

Levi loses the rhythm of his thrusts in due time, going from slow and measured to fast and erratic, slamming into me hard and taking my breath away.

I open my mouth, maybe to beg for more or to tell him I'm close, but no sound comes out. All I can do is hold on and try to breathe, and when he fucks into me just right, I do scream his name, the sound echoing around us as I fall apart again.

My whole body goes tight, and the hiss from Levi tells, through the haze of my orgasm, that it's enough to get him off, sending him spiraling into his own pleasure.

It takes nearly a minute before I can breathe properly again, and even longer before Levi pulls out, leaving me open and dripping. I'm going to need a shower after all this, but at the moment, I don't even care.

As soon as he lets go of me, I flop down on the bed in a heap, chest still heaving and heart rate just about slowing down. My skin is damp with sweat, and my thighs are smeared with my juices. Levi doesn't seem to care as he pulls me into his arms, pressing me against his bare, sweaty chest.

"You know," I say. "If you're trying to get me pregnant, that's definitely not the way to do it."

Levi laughs and then groans, and it's hard to tell if it's because the joke was bad or he's turned on by the idea of me being pregnant.

But then he pulls me even closer and kisses me deeply, and there's no doubt about the reaction. Hearing me talk about it turned him on all over again.

It feels like one of those things that should scare me, but weirdly, it doesn't, and it hits me all over again how deep I'm in it with these guys.

They're it for me.

They're *everything*.

10

SEVERAL DAYS GO BY, and by the end of the week, we're set to go to the courthouse for the wedding. As excited as I am for it, and no matter how many times I think about it, it never stops blowing my damn mind.

I'm getting married. Holy fuck.

There's no fear when I think about it, no regret. Just a giddy little rush of excitement and anticipation.

It's a hell of a lot better than the feelings I've had for most of the week. Things are still a fucked up mess between the Black Roses and the Jackals. No matter how much Gavin wants to pretend and hope that things are settling back down, it's clearly not the case. They've been stepping up their "small acts of aggression" and "petty bull-shit," as Gavin calls it, and it's obvious they're testing our weaknesses, pushing to see where they can hurt us most.

But Gavin still refuses to see that.

For the past few days, Sloan has been trying to do some things on his own, not just relying on his father to deal with this shit show. From conversations I've heard Sloan have with Rory and Levi and on the phone, I know he's been having people he trusts in the Black Roses gather info on the Jackals, finding out more about their top people and their operations, preparing to go after them if necessary.

According to him, it's probably going to be necessary.

I've seen him agitated, pacing in his room with his hands balled into fists and his jaw clenched tight enough that the muscles in his cheeks are probably as well developed as his biceps. He feels like a war is inevitable, and Gavin's refusal to face that fact only making it more likely that we'll lose when the war does break out. It's like Sloan's compensating for his dad's lack of preparation by trying to go above and beyond, and I can tell it's been weighing on him.

Hell, it's weighing on all of us.

We're all a part of this, our futures hanging in the balance while we wait to find out what's going to happen.

Sometimes I wake up in the middle of the night, heart pounding and mouth dry, shaking from a nightmare I can barely remember about losing one or all of the guys I love.

It's a lot to deal with, and the waiting just makes it worse.

But today, I don't want to focus on any of that.

Shaking my head, I push those thoughts out of my

mind and look at my reflection in the mirror in my bedroom. There will be plenty of time to stress about what may or may not happen with the Jackals, but for now, I'm ready to be happy.

I'm ready to get married.

I'm wearing my dress, and it looks just as good on me now as it did at the shop. Scarlett came over to help me get ready, and she did my makeup, making me look radiant and pretty, but also hot enough to catch anyone's attention. My hair is done in loose curls, pinned up on one side with a spray of white flowers tucked behind my ear, while the rest of my locks cascade over my shoulders.

Scarlett puts the finishing touches on her own hair, then comes over to stand with me in the mirror, smiling bright at our reflections. The red dress she chose for her maid of honor outfit is killer on her, highlighting her curves and long legs, and we look gorgeous together.

"Damn. You're so beautiful, Mercy," she says, her eyes going suspiciously shiny. She dabs at the corners of her eyes with her fingers.

"Keep it together. You're going to ruin your makeup if you start crying now," I tell her, nudging her gently.

She flaps a hand at me, grinning. "Waterproof mascara, babe. I'd never go to a wedding without it. I'm just so happy for you!"

She's so sincere, and her smile is so bright, that I can't help reaching out and hugging her. I hold her close, relishing how solid and steady she is in my arms. Through everything that's ever happened in my life, she's been there. Growing up without a mom, getting in fights all the time, breakups and letdowns and trying to figure out who the hell I wanted to be. Everything with the guys and the Black Roses in general would have been so much harder without her there to steady me and be my voice of reason and second opinion. Today is a day for love, and I love her so fucking much.

"Thank you," I murmur, smiling even though she can't see it.

"For what?"

"For everything. For being you. For being here. For always being there for me, even when I'm doing something stupid or impulsive or reckless."

"Or all three," she teases, and I can hear her sniffling. "Always and forever, babe. That's what best friends are for."

I squeeze her tight one more time and then let go, pulling back to see her dabbing at her eyes again.

"Okay, okay," she says, shaking it off. "Enough of that. You don't want to be late for your own wedding!"

I laugh and follow her lead, grabbing my shoes and putting them on and then doing one last check to make sure everything is in place. "They're not going to start without us," I remind her.

"Still. Let's get a move on."

She prods me in the side, and I poke her back but follow her out into the hall and toward the stairs. I can hear the guys talking in low voices in the living room, already ready to go, and my heart flutters a bit as I come down the stairs and catch sight of them.

All three of them are dressed to the nines, and I stop on the last couple of steps to take them in.

Unless someone knew which one of them was the groom for this affair, you wouldn't be able to tell from their outfits.

They're all in nice black suits with crisp white shirts underneath, and each of them has a different colored pocket square to add a little vibrancy. Rory's is a rich crimson, which makes his eyes seem brighter and goes well with Scarlett's dress. Levi's is a teal-ish blue, which stands out with his dark hair and eyes and suit. Sloan's is more jade, and after looking at it for a second, I realize he's tried to match the color of my eyes.

The doctor gave Rory the all-clear to stop wearing his sling recently, so that lingering reminder of his gunshot wound is gone.

Dressed up and fancy, they all look taller than usual and so damn handsome. Good enough to eat.

I'm momentarily rendered speechless by the sight of them, but Scarlett lets out a low whistle that draws their attention to us.

For a split second, I have a fluttering of nerves,

wondering what they're going to think about how I look. This is different from how I usually dress, even if I'm getting fancy, and they've never seen me like this before.

One by one they turn, then stop and stare, gazing at me with varying expressions of dazed awe and open hunger.

"Holy shit," Rory says, breaking out of the spell first and coming over to me. He holds out a hand and helps me down the last couple of steps, even though I hardly need it. "You look gorgeous," he breathes.

"Doesn't she?" Scarlett says, sounding giddy.

Rory barely seems to hear her. His gaze doesn't leave me as he uses his grip on my hand to drag me forward so he can kiss me deeply. I make a low sound of approval against his lips, and when he finally lets me go, I feel a little dazed myself.

Sloan and Levi aren't far behind, and they both take their turns, kissing me until I'm practically seeing stars.

"Holy goddamn. Is it just me or is it getting too freaking hot in here?" Scarlett teases, fanning herself dramatically.

Her teasing voice breaks the spell, and the guys step back, even though none of them take their eyes off me.

"We should get going," Levi says, checking his watch. "We don't want to be late for this."

"That's what *I* said," Scarlett puts in as we all start heading for the door. "But no one listens to me. I can understand why though, in this case."

I roll my eyes and stick my tongue out at her, and she just grins.

For the occasion, Sloan has procured a big black SUV for us to ride to the courthouse in. It's roomy enough that there's space for Scarlett, and that our dresses won't get crushed under our feet.

"Less conspicuous than a limo too," Rory points out as we pile in. He doesn't elaborate, but we all know why we don't want to draw too much attention to ourselves right now.

Sloan drives, as usual, and we make our way to the courthouse with our very small wedding party. It's just the five of us—a tiny affair, since this has to happen fast so Gavin will back the fuck off of his vendetta against me.

Honestly, I didn't expect to think of it so much like a real wedding, just a formality to get the piece of paper we need. But as we get to the courthouse, I realize it really does feel real.

Sloan parks, and we all head in, drawing attention from people on the street as we pile out dressed in our wedding finest. It's not a busy day, so we only have to wait about ten minutes before our names are called and we're shown into the small room where the ceremony will be performed.

There are no bells and whistles, no flowers or garlands or fairy lights or whatever else most people have at their weddings. There's just a Justice of the Peace and the people I love most in the world. I spare a wistful thought for my dad, wishing so badly that he could be here, but as I stand across the makeshift aisle from Sloan, I'm feeling like I have everything else I could possibly want.

The justice doesn't have anything fancy to say, just a very basic pronouncement of what we're here to do today. Then comes the moment where Sloan and I can say our own short vows.

Sloan goes first, looking a little nervous, but mostly like he's exactly where he wants to be. He looks so fucking gorgeous standing there with Rory and Levi at his back, the three of them forming a unit that I somehow fell into. I gaze at all of them, trying to cement this imagine in my mind.

"Mercy," Sloan says, and his voice is deep and soft, like even though there are other people here, the words he's saying are just for me. "From the minute you walked into our lives, kicking and fighting and so fucking determined, you've been undeniable. No matter how rough things have gotten, you've been here. You're one of the strongest people I've ever met, and I know when it comes down to it, you'll do anything to protect the people you love."

I think of how many times Sloan and I have clashed because we were each trying to protect the other, and I bite back the smile that curves my lips. I know we won't stop fighting, won't stop trying to protect each other, but I love that passion in him.

"That's one of the things I love the most about you," he continues, as if echoing my thoughts. "How fierce you are. How you never give up or give in. But I swear on my life, you'll never have to do that alone. You'll never have to be afraid because I'll always be here for you. Keeping you safe. Giving you what you need. Loving you. Your place is here. Right by my side—by *our* sides. And I'm going to make sure you never have any reason to doubt that, for as long as I live."

I'm not sure if the justice notices Sloan's little correction, where he included Rory and Levi in his vows, but the man doesn't say anything, and I don't look over to see his reaction.

I'm too busy looking at the man I'm about to marry, not even bothering to restrain my smile anymore.

That's such a *Sloan* way to make a declaration of love. Not flowery or over the top, but strongly worded and full of promises that I know he'll keep. They're perfect, and the emotion and dedication in them are so strong that tears burn the backs of my eyes while he talks.

Rory and Levi watch me with intense expressions, and I know that even though Sloan is the one speaking the words, everything he's saying goes for both of them too.

The justice motions to me next, and I have to take a second and clear my throat before I can speak.

The vows were the hardest part of all this. I've never been good at putting my emotions and feelings into words, but for this, I knew I had to try. Trying to write stuff down didn't help, so in the end, I just decided I would speak from the heart and hope that's enough.

I lift my chin and look at Sloan, holding his gaze. His ash-blond hair is combed back from his face, and his chiseled, symmetrical features look softer than I've ever seen them as he waits for me to begin.

"From the moment we met, I tried so hard to hate you," I say. "Everything about you, from your attitude to the way you drive to the way you're so damn stubborn. I really wanted to hate you, and for a long time, I thought I did. But that's how I know this thing between us is right. The love we have for each other, the way I feel about you? It overcame hate."

He chuckles at that, but there's something burning in his gray eyes that tells me he feels it to. That inevitability he talked about when he proposed to me. The chemistry that can turn hate into love.

"My feelings for you are as undeniable as yours are for me. The pull between us is more powerful for all the other bullshit we've been through, and that makes me certain that it can weather anything in our future. Anything that comes at us is going to have to get through us—and we're so strong together that it won't stand a chance."

I take a deep breath, blinking back tears as I try to distill everything I'm feeling into the final words of my vows.

"That's what love means to me," I murmur. "That we're stronger together. And that's how I know I love you. Now, and always."

Sloan hasn't looked away from me once as I've spoken, and as soon as I'm done, he reaches across the small space between us and pulls me into a kiss before the Justice of the Peace can so much as get a word in.

The man just laughs under his breath and clears his throat. "Then by the power vested in me by the state, I now pronounce you married. You may... continue kissing your bride."

Everyone laughs at that, and Sloan doesn't need the permission, but he takes it.

I can tell from the looks on Rory and Levi's faces that they're waiting for their turns, and we thank the justice and head out of the courthouse. They at least wait until we make it back to where we parked a little way down the street, and then Levi takes me into his arms and kisses me hard before letting Rory step in.

Rory's kiss is dramatic, just the way he is, and he ends up dipping me a little before pulling me back up and holding me close. He nips at my ear, and the warmth of his breath puffs against my skin as he whispers, "One of these days I'm going to find some way to say wedding vows to you too, Hurricane. I've got some great ones. They'd blow Sloan's right out of the water."

I tip my head back and laugh, feeling giddy and happier and lighter than I have in a while.

We pile back into the SUV quickly. Now that the formalities are over, it's time for the fun part. Scarlett took care of finding a nice bar for us to have a little "reception" at after the fact, and the five of us head over.

It's a nice place—nothing like the dives Scarlett and I got used to faking our way into over the years—and one of the private rooms in the back has been reserved for us.

"Wedding present," Scar says with a grin when I glance at her in surprise. "I had to do *something*, and you didn't exactly have a registry. So I thought I'd throw the five of us a little party instead."

"You're the fucking best," I tell her.

"You know it, bitch."

It's been a long-ass time since I let go of everything else and just had fun, and I didn't realize how badly I needed this until now.

There are so many drinks that I lose track, and somehow I manage not to spill anything on my dress. We eat huge burgers that the bar is famous for, and split platters of wings and fries that are hot and fried to perfection.

Rory gives a series of silly toasts that go from sweet and cute to ridiculous and dirty in a matter of minutes, and we all laugh and throw napkins at him until he sits back down.

Levi challenges me to a game of pool, and even moderately tipsy and with a rum and coke in my hand, I manage to obliterate him easily and with grace, toasting him with my glass after I sink my last shot.

He doesn't even look mad about losing, just impressed and a little turned on, if the glimmering heat in his eyes is any indication.

A little while later, a song comes on over the speakers, and Scarlett grabs my hand and spins me into a dance. I laugh as we twirl around the floor, the skirts of our dresses whipping around our ankles.

This whole thing is nothing like what I might have expected for my wedding if I was the kind of person who thought about things like that as a little girl. But as I look around at the people I'm with, I realize it's perfect.

The guys are laughing, toasting each other with their beers and watching as Scarlett and I dip and twirl. When Scar lets me go, she turns to face Rory, Levi, and Sloan and gives them her best impression of a stern look.

"She'd better *always* be this happy with you guys, you hear me?" she says. "Always."

It's the sort of thing my dad would probably say if he were here, and I wish he could see it.

He will one day, I promise myself. *He will.*

My men and I will fix things, and we'll make it safe for him to come out of hiding.

Because what I said in my vows was true. We're stronger together.

So the Jackals better watch the fuck out.

1 1

It's late at night by the time the four of us make it back to the house. We dropped Scarlett off on the way, the two of us exchanging more hugs before she went inside her apartment.

Now it's just me and the guys again, a little buzzed and very happy. I'm still giddy with excitement and disbelief that this is real, and I can tell the guys are in high spirits too.

But as we cross into the living room, something seems to change in the air.

The pleasant warmth between us shifts to something different, and heat pools in my stomach as goose bumps prickle over my skin.

I turn around and see all three of the guys coming toward me, surrounding me in an instant. One of them reaches out, and I barely have a chance to register that it's

Sloan before I'm wrapped up in the feeling of it all. There are so many hands and mouths on me everywhere, each man's touch a perfect counterpoint to the others as they share me seamlessly between them.

I kiss whoever I can reach, letting my hands roam over the smooth material of suits and shirts, and then lower down, groping at growing bulges and trying to press myself against them.

My head is spinning from the drinks and the attention, and it's hard to focus on any one thing. It's all a mishmash of feelings and sensations, and it feels a bit like I'm floating.

I close my eyes and let it happen, mouth open on soft moans and whispered pleas for more.

When I open my eyes again, there's a flash of a teal pocket square in my vision, and I drag my gaze upward to see Levi in front of me. He grins and grabs a handful of the front skirt of my dress, easing it higher and higher until his other hand finds my panties.

He drags a finger over the lace, and I know I'm already getting wet through the underwear, which are white and lacy to match the dress.

My clit is throbbing with the need to be touched, and when Levi drags the lace against the sensitive bud, I shiver and melt a little, moaning his name.

Rory moves in behind me, hitching up my dress from behind. He moves the lace of my underwear aside, exposing my ass, and before I can even really register that, his fingers are probing and exploring that tight hole, teasing around the rim in a way that makes me yelp.

Sloan moves in to kiss me, and I bite his lip as my knees almost buckle.

Levi's hand finds its way into my panties, and he dips his fingers into my pussy, teasing my clit directly before finding my wet hole and pressing in there. Behind me, Rory is doing a similar thing, but slower, working me loose enough that he can dip one finger into my ass and tease me, sending shocks of pleasure through my body.

My mouth is occupied by Sloan's kisses as his hands cup my breasts through the lace of my dress, and I feel like it's all I can really do to stay upright. I could come like this, just from their fingers in me, but it's not what I want.

I don't want to be teased.

Not on a night like this.

I break away from the kiss to pin Levi with a look, and then try to turn my head enough to see Rory.

"Don't joke around about shit like this," I tell them, trying to sound stern, even though it just comes out sounding breathless. "If we're gonna do this, I want your cocks, not just your hands."

"Fuck," Rory groans, and Levi's eyes have that flaring heat in them again. Despite my words, they don't let up with the teasing at all, and Levi thrusts his fingers in deeper, adding a third when two just aren't enough.

I bite back the whimper as pleasure roars through me,

not sure whether to work my hips forward to get more from Levi or press back and take Rory deeper.

Rory chuckles, even though it does sound a bit strained. He leans forward enough to press himself against my back and breathe against my ear, speaking loud enough for us all to hear him.

"Are you saying you want one of us to fuck your pussy and another one to fuck your ass?" he asks.

I moan just from the way that sounds, remembering the flash of a thought I had about exactly this when Levi was fucking my ass before.

"Yes," I pant. "I want you all at once."

"What about Sloan?" Rory asks.

"That's what my mouth is for," I quip back. "That, and giving you sass when you deserve it. Which is basically always."

I know I sound flippant as usual, but even I can hear the edge of desperation in my own tone, proof of how much I want this.

Sloan chuckles, and his voice is rough with desire. He grabs my chin in firm fingers, forcing me to look at him for a second before he leans in to devour my mouth in a hard kiss that leaves me even more breathless.

"Well, *wife*," he says, and the emphasis he puts on that word is enough to have me going weak in the knees all over again. "Your mouth is perfect for doing both of those things, and I fucking love it. I can't think of a better way to end the night, than fucking your face while my brothers claim your ass and pussy. We'll make you ours. Completely."

Fuck.

I think I just came a little.

The heat in his voice and the raw desire in his eyes drive me crazy. He sounds so confident and sure of what he wants. For so long, he wasn't sure if he could share, but there's no hesitation in him now. He wants this. Not just to be present while the other men fuck me, not just to watch, but to be part of it.

To share me in the most raw, primal way there is.

And god, I want it too.

Levi and Rory haven't let up their teasing, and their fingers in me combined with Sloan's words are enough that I can't stop the rush of pleasure that bears down on me, tipping me over into the first orgasm of the night.

I come on their fingers, trembling and rocking between both of them.

They're both smug about it in their way, and I kiss them both and then pin all three of them with a hot stare.

"More."

That's all they need to hear.

Levi and Rory pull their fingers out of me, and the whimper that falls from my lips makes them both groan. Then Sloan picks me up bridal style, which makes me laugh as I wrap my arms around his shoulders. It's like I barely weigh anything to him, and he carries me up the stairs to his bedroom with Levi and Rory right behind us.

Rory closes the door, and as Sloan sets me back on my feet, I watch his two best friends strip out of their wedding finery. The jackets come off first, ending up in a heap on the floor, like they could care less about them now that they've got their sights set on me.

Shirts come untucked, ties get loosened and pulled off, and Sloan joins in quickly, not bothered about undressing in front of his friends.

At first, all I can do is stare. All three of them are so fucking sexy, and even though I've seen them naked plenty of times, it never gets old. I never stop wanting to see it. It takes me a second to realize I should be getting naked too, but before I can make a move to undress myself, they're on me again.

Hands find the zipper of my dress and drag it down, exposing my bare back and the band of my strapless bra that matches the white lace of my panties.

They ease the dress down over my shoulders, and I shimmy out if it, letting it pool on the floor around my feet. It leaves me standing there in just my underwear, and I can feel their gazes on me, taking in every inch of the newly revealed skin.

Mouths find my shoulders, my neck, my collarbones, sucking and biting and sending shivers up my spine as hot tongues drag over bite marks. They take off my bra with ease, flinging it somewhere in the room, and then hook fingers in my panties to drag them down as well.

Standing naked in front of them has become second nature now, but the way they're looking at me is just so intense. It's ownership and love and desire in a way I've never felt before, and it goes both ways. The four of us are a unit, a group, unbreakable. We promised as much today, and it's going to last. I can feel that. I believe that every time they see me like this, they'll react the same way. With hunger and want, taking me to new heights of pleasure.

I run my hands over their bodies while they touch me, sliding over muscles and warm skin. Every time one of them is close enough to kiss, I do so, whimpering softly whenever they pull away.

Configuring how four people can have sex at the same time isn't easy, but we manage it. Rory picks me up around the waist and throws me onto the bed with a laugh, following me up. He motions for Levi to join us, and he does, laying down so I can straddle him.

I'm soaking wet at my core, and I don't waste any time climbing on top of him and seating myself slowly on his cock. It's so big and filling, the way it always is, and I tip my head back and moan, breathing quickly through my nose.

Even just from this, I'm already so close, and we've barely begun. Sloan and Rory just watch for the moment, and I try not to move too much on Levi's dick, not wanting to get him off before the other two have a chance to join in.

Rory produces lube from somewhere I don't have the presence of mind to notice at the moment, and I can feel how slick it is when he slides a lubed up finger back into my ass. It's not as intense as when Levi did it, since I'm more used to the sensation now, but it still makes me throb with pleasure.

Being full of Levi's cock while Rory opens me up for him is just so fucking good, and the sensations ping pong around inside me, making it impossible to sit still.

I'm squirming on Levi's cock, and he holds my hips firmly, keeping me in place. He doesn't move, doesn't thrust up into me, and it's like I'm sitting there, warming his cock, keeping it ready until the moment is right.

That thought just mixes with all the others, and when I look up at Sloan, he's looking right back at me. His gray eyes are stormy and dark, and the naked hunger on his face takes my breath away. He has one hand wrapped around his cock, holding it tightly like he's trying not to stroke himself.

I lick my lips subconsciously, and he groans, stepping forward and grabbing my chin.

"You look so good like this," he murmurs, voice heavy with the desire and heat he's feeling. "Getting full of our cocks. So perfect. Like you were made for it."

"Sloan, please," I whine, looking up at him. "Need

you."

He chuckles. "Don't worry, you'll get as much as you can handle."

Rory pushes in another slick finger, and I moan out loud, jerking forward more into Sloan's hold and clenching around Levi's cock. Levi lets out a hissed breath, and his fingers dig into the flesh of my hips even more while he holds himself back.

My breath comes in desperate little pants, and Sloan reaches down to trail fingers over my erect nipples, pinching and squeezing them roughly. He pulls them out from my body, forcing me to rock forward even more, and then Rory adds another finger to my ass, and I'm done for.

The moan comes out on a sobbing breath, and I don't know which name to say, so I just settle for swearing as my orgasm rushes over me. It's just a prelude for what they have in store for me, but I'm already trembling, mouth open and skin shining with the first traces of sweat.

Rory pulls his fingers free and slicks up his cock, and I yelp when he smacks my ass.

"Ready, Hurricane?" he asks, sounding amused but also like he's barely holding himself back from slamming into me.

"Yeah," I manage. "Fuck. Give it to me."

He laughs and does what I say, lining the head of his cock up with my loosened hole. Just like before with Levi, it feels bigger back there than it does when he's in my pussy, and I gasp sharply when he starts to push in, stretching me almost past the point of comfort.

He goes slow, inch by inch, and by the time he's halfway inside, I'm panting for air and trembling all over again.

Sloan grabs my chin once more and makes me look at him. He's got one hand around the base of his cock again, and it's close enough that I can smell the musk of his arousal. He's the only one not inside me at the moment, and I want to change that as soon as possible.

"Open up for me, baby," he growls, and I do, opening my mouth so he can have access to it. He promised to fuck my face, and I want that.

His skin tastes salty and clean when he pushes into my mouth, the hard heaviness of his erection dragging over my tongue. He pushes all the way in, hitting the back of my throat, and then just like that, all my holes are filled.

Levi's in my pussy, Rory is nearly all the way in my ass, and Sloan's claimed my mouth, making me theirs completely. My head spins with the thought of it, the way I'm airtight for them, worked open and ready for them to fuck each of my holes until we're all satisfied.

Just having them in me is enough to make me dizzy with pleasure, but then they start to move, and it gets even better. Levi and Rory move in a sort of tandem, with Rory's thrusts rocking me forward and pushing Levi's cock deeper in me. Levi rolls his hips, snapping them up a bit so he can bury himself in me, making me almost choke on Sloan's cock.

Sloan wasn't kidding about fucking my face either. He buries a hand in my hair and uses it to hold me in place. His hips snap almost in time with Rory's, and he works his cock in and out of my mouth, using it like the others are using my other holes.

It's a good thing they're doing all the work, honestly. My head is spinning too much too fast to be able to do anything but take it. I can't concentrate on any individual sensation because they're all blurring together too quickly, morphing into a raging storm of pleasure. I just feel full and a bit like I'm on fire, and it takes about two minutes before I'm tipping right over into another orgasm, crying out around Sloan's cock in my mouth and going tight around both Levi and Rory.

Rory hisses and slaps my ass again. "Fuck, Mercy. You're so goddamned tight," he gasps out. "Jesus Christ."

I can't even get out a response to that, half because my mouth is still full of cock and half because any words other than *yes*, *please*, and *more* have left my brain. I'm just a vessel for all of this, being filled up over and over again until I'm nothing but raw, unbridled pleasure.

The room is full of the sounds of us fucking, the wet noises of them moving inside me, and the grunts and groans of how good it feels.

Sloan starts pushing in deeper, working himself into

my throat, and I gag a little but don't pull away. He can have anything he wants from me, anything at all, and I know he'll give back as much as he takes.

It doesn't take too much longer before I can feel another orgasm rising, and if my brain was working, I'd be surprised I can even still keep coming. Three orgasms in a night is already a good number, but the fourth comes bearing down on me before I can do anything but notice it, and I scream around Sloan's cock, choking enough that drool and precum spill down my chin.

"Goddamn," Levi grunts, and I know he's feeling how my pussy keeps clenching every time I come, like it's trying to milk him dry while I'm in the throes of pleasure.

All of them have crazy stamina, still going, while I'm basically limp between them all. If it wasn't for them holding me up, I would have collapsed already, and my body seems to be humming with sensation and exhaustion. Each new burst of pleasure borders on pain from how sensitive I already am, but they don't stop, and I don't ask them to.

It won't be over until they all come, until we've fulfilled this thing like it's some kind of ritual to bind us all together.

Before they even get close, I'm spiraling into yet another orgasm, and this time I don't even have the breath to scream. I just whimper and suckle Sloan's cock, letting him keep working it deep into my mouth.

He's the first to lose the measured pace of his thrusts,

pushing into me faster and harder, hard enough that I gag and more drool comes slipping out of my mouth.

"Fuck," he hisses, fingers tightening in my hair almost to the point of pain. He fucks my mouth hard, and when he comes, he slams into my throat, unloading right into it, sending the hot, salty jets of his cum right down my throat.

When he pulls out, my face is a mess of tears and spit, and I gasp for breath, feeling raspy from having him so deep in my throat.

Rory and Levi have to be close as well, because they also pick up the pace, hammering into my pussy and ass with forceful thrusts that rock me back and forth.

Levi jams his hips up, hitting that spot that takes my breath away, and my fifth orgasm is smaller, but no less intense. I shake against them, and Rory slams into me hard, swearing a blue streak as he fills my ass with his cum.

Levi's right behind him, fingers so hard on my hips as he pumps into me three more times and then loses it himself, coming with a gasp of my name.

None of us have the energy to move at first, but when they draw out of me, my body feels oddly empty. I'm a mess of sweat and fluids and all the evidence of what we just did, but I don't even care. I feel complete and happy.

I've tied myself to these guys, and they've tied themselves to me.

But I don't feel bound at all. I don't feel caged.

Instead, I feel *free*.

12

THE FIRST FEW days of married life are pretty much the same as the days that came before the wedding. Sloan hasn't told his father yet, but in the middle of the week, we get the perfect chance to make sure Gavin knows where we all stand.

There's a swanky party being thrown and a lot of the Black Roses will be there. Some guy who's a leader of a gang in another city is visiting to make possible connections with us, and the party is a way for Gavin to try to woo him.

He uses those words, with air quotes around "woo," and it makes me giggle just thinking about Gavin trying to be personable enough to woo anyone. The man is all hard edges and blunt anger, a lot like his son. They're like two sides of the same coin, I guess, considering how much they butt heads.

The long and short of it is that we're all going, and just the way they used to when I first got here, a fancy dress magically appears on my bed on the day of the party. That trick used to bug the fuck out of me, but now I just grin and pull it on, eager to see what the guys picked for me this time. It's a gorgeous, flowy dress in a dark gray color, and I wonder if Sloan chose it to match his eyes. It makes sense, since it'll help drive home the fact that we're connected now, that our fates are entwined.

The party is being held at a venue downtown, and when we get there, the event is in full swing. Soft music plays, and there are champagne flutes and little finger foods laid out. Everyone glitters in their fancy clothes and jewelry, so different than the other Black Rose parties I've been to, or the casual hangouts at the warehouse where I fought Baldy.

Sloan, Rory, and Levi nod to several people as we walk in, and I stick close to the guys as we make our way through the crowd. No one from the Black Roses has given me any trouble lately, but I don't want to chance it by wandering too far away.

Gavin stands a little way away, holding court in the middle of a group of people. There's a glass of whiskey in his hand, and he lifts it in a makeshift toast to the group.

Sloan not so subtly steers us in that direction, and eventually he catches Gavin's eye. In a show of determination, he lifts my hand, making sure the light catches the silver band of the ring on my finger, and kisses the back of it. Once he lets me go, he lifts the drink in his other hand, which I know gives Gavin a chance to spot the ring on his finger as well.

The older man makes a face for a split second, his lips pressing together angrily. But he doesn't say anything, instead beckoning us over to meet the people he's talking to.

It's clear that Gavin got the message, and although he's obviously not going to make a big deal about it now, I can tell that he's got a lot of fucking feelings about me being married to his son.

He keeps up his "gracious host" facade though, introducing Sloan to the other man before they fall into a discussion about how a partnership could benefit both of their organizations.

Sloan keeps one hand on my back as they talk, and Rory and Levi don't go too far, mingling with the other members of the gang and trading information on the down-low.

My stomach growls after a bit, reminding me that I skipped dinner, and I lean up to kiss Sloan's cheek before slipping away from the group and heading for one of the tables with all the food spread out.

There are little finger sandwiches and crab puffs and something involving shrimp wrapped in a pastry and drizzled in sauce. I load up a small plate and sample one of everything, impressed with whoever Gavin got to cater this affair.

Rory comes up and snatches a shrimp thing off my plate, grinning teasingly as he pops it in his mouth.

"Mm, shrimp."

"You're a pig," I tease, taking another from the tray and eating it before he can get any ideas.

"Eh. I'm just hungry. Mingling takes energy, you know. And this is the second time in too long that I've had to be all pressed and fancy. I miss my sweatpants."

He makes a face that's dejected and absurd, and I laugh softly.

"I miss your sweatpants too," I murmur, shooting him a suggestive look.

He chuckles. "What is it about women and sweatpants? *Gray* sweatpants, right? You all love that shit."

My look turns dirtier, and I cock an eyebrow at him. "You really need me to explain this to you?"

"Explain what?" Levi asks as he joins us.

"I think Rory needs the birds and the bees talk," I say teasingly, and the green-eyed man laughs.

"I know plenty about birds and bees." He dips his head, letting his lips brush the shell of my ear. "I'll show you how much I know later. About all kinds of wildlife."

Pleasurable shivers run up my spine, and I suck in a breath. "Fuck. How can you make *anything* sound like dirty talk?"

He straightens, looking pleased with himself. "It's a gift."

The music shifts to something more upbeat, and people start taking to the dance floor in pairs and little groups. Sloan is still deep in conversation, but Rory waggles his eyebrows at me and holds a hand out.

"Dance?"

"Should we?" I ask him. "Is it a bad idea?"

He shrugs. "What's anyone here gonna do? Burn you at the stake for not dancing with your husband? Everyone knows we're all close."

It's a fair point, so I put down my empty plate and let him lead me to the dance floor.

Of course, he's a great dancer. He's bigger and broader than my other two men, but he has a grace about him that proves he knows how to move his body. He spins me and then pulls me close, and I laugh breathlessly, trying to keep up with him and his energy.

Partway through the dance, I feel eyes on me, and turn to see Sloan smiling as he watches us move around the floor. Gavin's following us with his gaze as well, still looking like he sucked on a lemon and doesn't want anyone to know.

I just smile back at Sloan and ignore his father.

For now, at least, Gavin won't touch me, and that's going to have to be good enough. I don't give a shit if he hates me, so long as he doesn't try to kill me.

When a new song starts, Levi heads toward us, clearly intending to cut in and take his turn dancing with me, but before he can, there's a clatter from the doorway.

A group of guys come stumbling in, and I recognize them as other members of the Black Roses. They don't match the swanky elegance of the party at all, dressed in jeans and jackets and looking roughed up like they've been in a fight. One of them has a trickle of blood moving down the side of his head, and another is holding his side and wincing with every step he takes.

People move out of their way, parting like the Red Sea as they move from the door to where Gavin is standing. Most of them hang around the fringes of the little circle of people gathered around Gavin, but one moves in and murmurs in his ear, looking insistent.

Gavin's face remains neutral, and he listens, nodding every once in a while. When the man leans back, Gavin waves him away in a clear dismissal.

For a second, the man blinks at him, but then he walks away, motioning for the others to follow.

Like nothing even happened, Gavin turns smoothly back to the tall, handsome man that I gather is the one he's trying to schmooze with, and keeps talking.

Rory and Levi watch from my side, and Sloan sees it from his spot near his dad. Almost in unison, all three of them start walking toward the corner of the room where the group of newcomers are huddled.

I hurry to follow, my heart climbing into my throat.

Sloan takes the lead, turning to face the men as soon as we're in the room. "What happened?" he asks, getting right to the point.

"We just told Gavin," one of the guys mutters.

"Yeah? Well, now you tell me," Sloan insists.

The one who did the talking before clears his throat. "It was the fucking Jackals, of course. Who else would it be? We were doing a drop—should've been simple and straightforward. Woulda been, except three motherfuckers jumped us. There was a shootout, and we got away, but the deal was fucked."

Rory and Levi look at each other and then Sloan, and we all brace for the oncoming explosion.

"You told my father that, and he didn't do anything about it?" Sloan asks. His jaw is already clenched, and his hands are curling into fists.

The guy shrugs, jerking his head toward the other side of the room. "He seemed like he was more interested in whatever he's got going on there."

"Sloan." Levi's voice is tight as he sets a hand on his friend's shoulder. "Maybe we should—"

But it's too late. Sloan shrugs the hand off and strides away from the little group of Black Rose members, making his way back over to where Gavin is laughing at something the tall man is saying. Gavin glances at his son for a second, and there's something like warning in his eyes, but it doesn't stop Sloan for a second.

"We need to talk," my husband says, and it's not a polite request. There's a demand in his voice, and Gavin doesn't appear to like it one bit.

He glances at the guy he's trying to get in good with and forces a smile. "Just a moment," he murmurs. "I have to go handle something."

The guy nods, gesturing with his half-full glass. "Never a dull moment." He chuckles.

Gavin smiles back, but as soon as he steps away from the other man to go with Sloan, that smile drops, and it's clear he's pissed off at being interrupted.

Levi, Rory, and I follow the two of them into a little room a short way down the hall from the large space where the party is happening, and the three of us keep bracing for the clash we know is coming.

"How many times are you going to let this happen?" Sloan demands. There's fire in his eyes, and his arms are folded. He looks unyielding, and only someone like his father would dare to stand against him when he gets like this.

But Gavin is just as damn stubborn, and he looks back at his son, unimpressed.

"I didn't *let* anything happen. The Jackals have always done what they can to disrupt our business. These little skirmishes happen all the time. It's not a cause for alarm. We have to—"

"Not a cause for alarm?" Sloan interrupts, sounding incredulous. "Not a cause for fucking alarm? When are you going to wake the fuck up and see what's happening here? They're making a fucking mockery of you! They already stole from us, and now they're sabotaging our deals, and you're just letting it happen! You're letting our people get hurt because you're too much of a fucking coward to do anything about it."

Levi sucks in a breath as that harsh condemnation rings out in the room. Luckily, the music playing in the main area of the party is probably loud enough that no one outside this room heard Sloan call his father and the leader of his gang a fucking coward, but it still hit hard.

Gavin narrows his eyes, looking like he's about to go off on his son, and it's like all the air is being sucked out of the room by the mounting tension. It's like watching a car crash that you know is going to be grisly and terrible, but somehow, you still can't look away.

When they face off like this, it's so easy to see how similar they are in some ways. They're both headstrong, and when they get it in their heads that their way is the right way, they don't want to yield to anything else.

But it's the differences between them that are driving them apart now.

Sloan's not one to let things fester. He's all about

action, especially when people he cares about are in danger. Gavin's more measured, preferring to look at things from every angle and try to find a solution that will keep the most people from getting hurt. To Sloan, it just seems like stalling, while to Gavin, Sloan's way must seem like being too impatient and reckless.

Neither one of them wants to give an inch, so they keep ending up in these standoffs with the rest of us caught between them.

"We can't do nothing," Sloan growls. "The Jackals aren't going to go away, and the more we let them get away with, the more they'll take. Where's the fucking line, Dad? When do we say enough is enough and deal with this bull-shit head on?"

Gavin sighs and pinches the bridge of his nose. This is definitely not what he was planning on dealing with tonight, I'm willing to bet.

"I'll think about it," he says finally. "But I can't deal with this right now. I have to get back to the party."

Before Sloan can get another word in edgewise, his father turns on his heel and leaves the room, letting the door close behind him.

We watch him go and then turn to Sloan, and my stomach clenches as I wait to see what he's going to do. For a long moment, he just stares at the spot where his dad last stood, his jaw clenching and his nostrils flared wide. Then he curses under his breath, turning away.

"Let's get out of here," he mutters.

He doesn't wait for any of us to respond, just follows his dad out, so we follow him.

Gavin's already gone back to talking with that guy from the other gang, and no one really notices as the four of us leave the party and head home.

It's pretty late when we get back, and I go upstairs to shower and change into my pajamas. Rory isn't the only one who prefers comfy clothes to formalwear, and it's nice to get out of the dress.

Once I'm clean and comfortable, I go to Sloan's room to check on him and make sure he's okay. It's got to be hard when you're not being taken seriously by someone you respect, especially because I know Sloan wouldn't argue so hard for taking a head on approach if he didn't believe it was the only way.

His room is empty when I ease the door open, and I frown and go downstairs to the gym to see if he's there. It's just as empty as his room, and he's not in the living room either.

When I walk into the kitchen, Rory's there, sitting at the island with a bottle of beer. He smiles at me and then nods in the direction of the garage.

"Sloan's out there."

"How did you know I was looking for him?" I ask.

Rory snorts and grins. "Because I know you. Levi and I

usually keep our distance when he gets like this, but he'll probably talk to you."

I can only hope he's right. I walk into the garage, and there's Sloan, still in his suit from the party. He took off the jacket at least, and it's flung over a stack of cardboard boxes in the corner. His sleeves are rolled up, and he's tinkering with something under the raised hood of his car.

There's still so much tension in his body, and it's obvious he's not working on his car this late at night because there's something wrong with it, but because he's using it as a kind of stress relief.

I lean against the side of the car and clear my throat to get his attention. "So is this normal for you?" I ask him. "Late night mechanic projects?"

He shoots me a look. "No."

"Do you want to talk about it?"

"No."

That's usually a complete sentence when Sloan says it, and I sigh internally, trying to think of another angle. But then to my surprise, Sloan starts talking anyway.

"I'm just tired of trying to get him to listen to me," he says, and it bursts out of him like he's been holding it back for so long that he really needs to get it out.

"He just... he never does enough."

"Enough for what?" I ask gently.

"Anything," he snaps, but I know he's not mad at me.

"He just lets things happen. Just watches the losses pile up until it's too fucking late."

I tip my head to one side, watching as he keeps tightening something with the wrench in his hand. "You're not just talking about this stuff with the Jackals, are you?"

Sloan sighs and shakes his head. "No. It was the same shit when my mom died. He didn't do enough, and I always told myself that he probably tried his best when I was younger, but seeing him now, I know he probably didn't."

I remember him talking about his mom back when we had that disastrous date weeks ago. The pain in his voice is much more apparent now than it was then, and I wonder how long he's been carrying this around.

"He was just complacent," he continues. "Like he didn't think it was going to be that bad or he didn't need to act and the whole issue would take care of itself, and then she was just... dead. She was gone. It's just like how it is now. He's not doing enough, and it feels the same, especially with you in the picture."

"Me?"

Sloan looks up at me with those haunted eyes. "They're a threat to *you*, specifically. Hugh's your damn uncle, and he's obviously not giving up on having you in his shitty gang or killing you if he can't get you on his side. They're a threat to all of us too, and it feels like my dad is going to protect us all too little too late. He'll only step up when the losses are so great that it'll leave us broken."

There's pain in his voice like I've never heard before, and I can tell he's not just angry with this father, but actually worried about what could happen as a result of his negligence.

I reach out and set a hand on his shoulder, feeling like I should do something to show him he's not alone in this.

His eyes find mine again, and he puts the wrench down and pulls me into his arms, holding me close. His head rests on top of mine, and I stroke my hands up and down his back, trying to be soothing.

"Have you thought about telling your dad all of this stuff?" I ask softly. "Letting him know how you feel?"

"What would be the point?" Sloan mutters. "His mind's made up."

"I don't just mean the stuff with the Jackals, Sloan. There's the stuff with your mom too."

"I don't know. Back when I was kid, it was just like... like he shut off when she was killed. He took care of me and everything, but he didn't want to hear about her or think about her. I thought it was just him missing her as much as I did, but now I wonder if it's just guilt. He knows he didn't do enough to save her, and he can't face it. But he's doing the same thing now, so it's not even like he learned anything from it. Even if I did say something, it's not like he'd understand."

That's probably true, honestly. "Yeah. He is pretty stubborn," I agree. "But maybe you guys should hash it out anyway. Maybe it would help. At the end of the day though, I'm always on your side over Gavin's. He's not the one I married, after all."

Sloan groans, probably at the mental image of that, but I can feel him smile against the top of my head all the same. He pulls back enough that I can look up to see his face, and he looks a little less riled up than he did before.

I lean up and kiss him, arms around his neck. He leans into it gratefully, melting into the embrace and the kiss with a soft sigh.

"You're my husband, and I'll always be here for you," I murmur against his lips when we part for breath, and that sparks heat in Sloan's gray eyes.

He pulls me in even more, going for another deep kiss, and I surrender to it, not caring that we're in the garage of all places or anything. It's definitely not the first time something like this has happened out here, and it won't be the last I'm sure.

"And you're my wife. Fuck, I'm so glad you're here," Sloan replies. It's a sweet sentiment, but that heat is behind it, making it clear how much he loves the sound of it.

I grin, and he slides his hands down, cupping my ass through the shorts I threw on earlier.

"You know," I murmur huskily. "There's a way I might

be able to help relieve some of the stress you're under. Make it a little easier for you to get some sleep tonight."

"Oh yeah?" One hand roams upward, squeezing my breast through my tank top and plucking at my nipple. "What's that?"

With a mischievous grin, I pull away from his arms and sink down to my knees in front of him. The concrete floor of the garage is cold and hard against my knees, but it doesn't stop me from honing in on what I want.

Reaching up, I palm Sloan's cock through his dress pants, and he moans and looks down at me, stroking a hand over my hair.

"That would probably do the trick," he says, his voice hitting that low register it drops to when he's turned on. "Fuck. Put your mouth on me, baby. I want to see your lips wrapped around my cock."

My grin just grows, and I start undoing his pants, eager to get to work.

Maybe I can't fix everything for him, but I can at least take his mind off of it for a little while.

13

A FEW DAYS LATER, I take the opportunity to get out of the house and meet Scarlett at our favorite coffee shop. We haven't had time to do this in a while, with everything that's been going on, so it's nice to get a coffee and a muffin and sit in the window with her to talk.

We've been making an effort to spend more time together since I married Sloan and all, and I want her to know that even though my life has changed a lot in the last few months, she's still my best friend, and I'm always going to have time for her.

Every time we go out, we're accompanied by someone from the Black Roses that the guys trust if they don't have time to come themselves, and this isn't an exception. I've gotten the lecture about how dangerous shit is right now, with things being so tense with the Jackals, and how there's a target on my back because of who I am to Hugh.

I don't want to put Scar in danger because Hugh's after me, and I know it's important to the guys that I'm safe, so I don't push back on it.

All the guys my men send with us are usually chill and content to just hang out while we do whatever, so it's not that big of a deal.

Scarlett stirs her iced coffee with her straw and gazes out the window at the cars going by. "So Gavin knows all about the marriage now, huh?"

"Yeah, he does." I grimace. "He's definitely not happy about it, but I guess that was kind of the point. It makes it harder for him to fuck with me or give me a hard time, since I'm bound to his son."

"And how's that going?" She cocks an eyebrow. "The being bound part?"

"It's..." I think about it for a second and then grin. "It's good."

We talk about married life for a while, and she teases me about being a wife and asks if I've taken up ironing the guys' clothes for them, which makes me throw a napkin at her.

"You're terrible," I tell her, shaking my head. "Even if they wanted me to do that, I wouldn't. Mostly everything's just been the same."

"I guess that makes sense," she says. "Since you were basically already married to them to begin with."

"I'm pretty sure most marriages don't usually start the way this one did, Scar."

She shrugs, sticking her tongue out to chase the straw in her drink. "So you took an unconventional path to get there. What's wrong with that?"

Nothing, I guess. She's got a point. I snort and take a bite of my coffee cake muffin, chasing it with a sip of my latte.

"So how's school and everything?" I ask her. It doesn't seem fair that every time we meet up, we always end up talking about me and my life. I guess I do have the most life-and-death going on, but that's no excuse.

"Ugh." Scarlett grimaces, putting her elbows on the table and dropping her chin into her hands. "It's the same old. Midterms and papers and bullshit. I have a project due next week that I'm mostly done with, but I don't know how it's going to turn out."

"Probably incredible, because you always do well on that stuff," I point out.

She shrugs. "I guess so. I'm just burned out, I guess. I wish I was in your shoes so I didn't have to go anymore."

"I didn't really have a choice, babe," I tell her. "And I definitely want to finish at some point. I've been thinking about what I want to study, trying to work it out in my head. Before, I wasn't quite sure, but now that I'm part of this group with the guys, I have more sense of direction in my life and more ideas about how I might shape it." I shrug and take another sip of my coffee. "I want to do something that could be helpful to the Black Roses, I guess. So I could contribute to the gang."

Scarlett studies me for a second, her lips pursing to one side as she cocks her head.

"What?" I ask.

"Nothing. It's just weird how big a part of your life this has all become," she says. "How it's all... *normal* now. At the beginning, it was like you were waiting for it all to be over so you could escape and get on with your life, but now it *is* your life."

She's not wrong about that, and I nod in agreement. "Yeah, it is pretty insane. I never saw it coming, but I'm really happy with where I'm at in my life now."

"I'm happy for you, then," Scar says, grinning. She swirls the ice in her cup, tapping her lips with the fingers of her other hand. "Now I just need to find my own reverse harem. Are there any of the other Black Roses out there looking for a girl to share?"

I laugh and roll my eyes. "I'll ask around. Maybe some of them are jealous when they see me and the guys together and would like to get in on that for themselves."

"Thanks. Just give 'em my number and talk me up, would you? Mention all my good qualities."

"Short list," I tease, and when she kicks me under the table, I know I deserve it.

Scarlett puts on a wounded face, pressing her palm to

her chest. "Ouch! Betrayed by my best friend, I can't believe it. I know you just want to be the only one with a trio of sexy guys at your beck and call. You can just say it. This is a safe space."

"You're absolutely right, Scar. I want to be the special one with the three boyfriends, and there's nothing you can do about it."

"Two boyfriends and a husband, technically," she corrects me.

I toast her with my coffee cup. "Yup. Two boyfriends and a husband. Which is really more like three husbands when you get down to it. It's not like I'm planning on dumping any of them."

"Thank fuck. How awkward would that breakup be?"

She gives an exaggerated grimace, and I laugh. There's no one else I can talk to like this, and I love that she's stuck by my side when other people might've bailed or gotten too weirded out. But not Scar. She's right here like she's always been, teasing me about the three men in my life as if it's the most normal thing in the world.

I love her even more for that.

We finish up our coffee date and Scarlett sighs and heads home to finish working on her project and what she describes as a "literal mountain of homework." I wish her well and go to the car with the assigned Black Rose guard of the day—a guy named Malek.

We don't make much small talk on the drive, which is

fine by me. I've gotten to know more of the Black Roses since I've become an official member, and no one gives me shit like Baldy tried to that one time, but it's not like I'm best friends with any of them yet. The silence is comfortable though, and Malek drops me off back at the house with a little wave before he drives away.

I let myself into the house, poking my head into the kitchen and living room as I head toward the stairs. The place seems empty. The guys are probably out handling business, and I can only hope that for all of their lectures about me staying safe, they're doing the same themselves.

I reach for my phone to text them and see what time they plan to be home, but it's not in my pocket where I'm pretty sure I left it.

Fuck. That means I either left it at the coffee shop, in the car, or it fell out of my pocket somewhere in between.

The sun's already going down, and I don't really want to go back to the coffee shop or call the Black Rose guy back to the house, so I hope it's outside. I think I had it on my lap in the car, so it probably fell when I climbed out of the seat.

I head back out the front door to check, scanning the ground near where Malek dropped me off.

Luckily, my guess was right. I spot it after a few seconds of searching and scoop it up, pressing the button on the side to turn on the screen and check for messages as I head back toward the house.

But before I reach the front door, the back of my neck prickles.

Something is... off.

A quiet sound behind me makes my adrenaline spike, and I whirl around quickly, my hands already curling into fists as I drop my phone. I lash out instinctively, my arm snapping out in a quick right hook.

The man behind me rears back, just barely dodging my punch. He's closer than I thought, and fear surges in my chest as I realize how close he came to grabbing me.

Where the fuck did he come from?

He's tall and dressed in a hoodie, and with the setting sun backlighting him, I can't get a good look at his face. Not that it fucking matters.

I punch again, and this time, my shot connects. He staggers back, and I turn and sprint for the house. But he tackles me with the full weight of his body before I make it three steps, bringing us both down in a heap and knocking the wind out of me. He grabs my hair, and I fight back, kicking out and writhing beneath him, trying to get a good shot at a vulnerable area.

He's much bigger than me though, and with me face down on the grass, he has the advantage.

I can't get the right leverage to buck him off me, and when he yanks my hair back so hard that something in my neck pops, I yelp in pain. He flattens his chest against my back, keeping me pinned in place while his free hand fumbles for something.

It's a cloth, and he brings it toward my face, pressing it over my mouth and nose and gripping my face so tightly that his fingers dig into my jaw.

I've seen enough movies to know where this is going, and I try not to breathe in, but I can't help it.

The scent of something pungent and sharp fills my nose and lungs, and angry tears sting my eyes as I try to fight off the darkness that follows.

It's no use.

The world blurs around me, and blackness swallows me up.

14

I HAVE no idea how much time has passed when I slowly come back to consciousness. For a second, I don't know *anything*.

My head hurts, and my thoughts are slow and hazy while my brain tries to catch up. I remember being at the coffee place with Scarlett, and I remember going home. I remember searching for my phone, and then—

It hits me with a bolt of adrenaline that I got basically kidnapped in front of the house, and I jerk my head up, looking around frantically.

I don't recognize the building I'm in. It looks generic enough that it could be anywhere. I also realize that I'm tied to a chair, my arms bound behind me.

My breathing comes in fast pants, and my heart is racing, but I try to make myself calm down. Getting frantic and starting to panic won't help here. I have to figure out where I am and what happened before I can do anything to try and get out of it.

Although, considering the situation at hand, I have a pretty good idea of who the fuck is behind this.

Someone clears their throat, and the image of Hugh striding toward me comes into focus as my vision clears. I clench my jaw, shoving away the nausea that grips my stomach as he comes to stand over me.

He's smiling, but there's nothing friendly in it at all. His brown eyes are cold as he looks at me, and I glare right back. The fact that he looks so much like my father pisses me off. My dad is in a safe house somewhere because of this man. He missed my wedding because of this man, and that just makes me hate Hugh more. He's a fucking asshole, a *monster*, and I wish he looked like one on the outside.

"Mercy," he drawls, and his voice is like cold oil, slimy and gross. "Mercy, Mercy, Mercy. You really thought this was over?"

"It's supposed to be over," I snap back. "It's not my fault you can't fucking let shit go. We had a deal. I beat your guy fair and square, which I *know* you didn't think I could do. Sorry to disappoint you."

My uncle's eyes narrow, and the smile drops from his face, making him look even more dangerous, like a predatory animal. It's clear he's pissed off, still holding a grudge that he didn't get what he wanted before.

"You chose the Black Roses over me," he bites out. "Over your *family*. Over your *blood*. And I know I said that I wouldn't retaliate, but... well." He chuckles darkly. "I've never taken rejection very well at all."

His smile is pure cruelty, and it sends a spike of fear shooting through my chest.

He could do anything to me right now. I have no idea where we are or if anyone even knows how to find me. Hugh could shoot me in the fucking face, and I couldn't stop him. I'm tied to a chair, still woozy from whatever knocked me out and completely unable to defend myself.

Just the thought of that makes me struggle against the ropes holding me to the chair, and I try to swallow past the fear gripping me. My instinct to fight is surging through my veins, and the fact that I can't raise a fist makes panic beat against my ribs.

"What do you want?" I demand. "Why the fuck are you so obsessed with me?"

"I already told you," Hugh tells me, speaking slowly as if explaining it to someone very slow. "I want my family to be together."

I draw back and spit in his face, a grim sense of pleasure filling me when the gob of spit hits him square in the eye.

Good. Fuck you, you asshole.

"You're not my family," I hiss. "I didn't even know you

178

existed until a few weeks ago. You're just some crazy uncle I barely know."

Hugh wipes the spit from his eye, and a strange look passes over his face. It's angry and bitter all at once, and he shakes his head, smearing his spit covered fingers down his pants.

"That's where you're wrong," he says softly, his voice dropping low. "Clearly Oscar never told you the truth, but I will."

I stop struggling when he says that, a different kind of fear rising inside me, even though I don't quite know why. There's something about the way he talks to me that makes me feel like a mouse being batted around by a cat. Like he wants me to be dazed and bruised before he sinks his teeth in for the killing blow.

"What truth?" I whisper. I don't even think I want to hear the answer, but the words fall from my lips anyway.

Hugh smiles, his gaze tracking my face as leans a little closer. "Oscar isn't your father. I am."

He might as well have hit me.

He might as well have stuck a dagger in my heart.

The words hang there in the air for a second, and it's like my brain doesn't want to process them. I can feel myself reeling back in shock, and the only thing I can think is that it has to be a lie.

It has to be.

As if he can pluck the thoughts right from my head, or

more likely, read them on my face, Hugh continues, a malicious grin twisting his features. "It's true. You want me to explain? Lay it out for you?"

The last thing I want him to do is explain. I don't want to hear another word out of his mouth. I'm still struggling to understand what he's talking about, struggling to believe he could possibly be telling me the truth. But that doesn't stop him, and it's clear he's taking a sick sort of pleasure from telling me this and using me as captive audience for his story.

"I joined the Jackals when I was young," he says. "To become one of them, you have to do something as an initiation. Something that proves you're made of strong enough stuff to be in the gang." He tilts his head, looking almost nostalgic as he contemplates some memory in his mind's eye. "I always had a thing for your mother. She was beautiful and smart and funny. The most stunning woman I'd ever seen."

His face hardens, his gaze sharpening as his jaw clenches. "But she didn't want me. I asked her to be mine, and she rejected me. So I figured I could kill two birds with one stone, to turn a phrase. I wanted her. I deserved her. And she should've known better than to say no. So I took her by force as my initiation. I let a few of the Jackals watch, so they could verify that I'd done what I set out to do."

My stomach drops as he speaks, disgust filling me.

He says it so easily, the same way someone else would talk about going to the store and deciding to buy a different brand of laundry detergent or something. Like it's something to be proud of, something normal and not horrifyingly fucked up. My skin feels too tight and too hot, as if my blood is on fire, and I can't stop picturing my sweet mother being held down by this man. Being forced to—

Fuck.

Jesus fuck.

I don't even know what to say, but Hugh doesn't wait for me to speak anyway.

"Oscar was furious with me afterward. He cut me out of his life. Called me a monster. Asked what could be worth doing that to another person." Hugh snorts, his lip curling. "He took care of your mother when he found out she was pregnant. He wouldn't let her suffer alone. Eventually they fell in love, I guess, and Oscar raised you as his own. He never told you about me, obviously. He wanted to keep you as far away from me as possible."

I can understand why. This man is a fucking psycho.

Once again, it's like Hugh can read what I'm thinking, and that disgusting smile creeps back over his face.

"That's how I got Oscar to agree not to throw the fight like he was supposed to, all those weeks ago," he says. "I threatened to find you and tell you the truth. And Oscar would do anything to keep you away from me, so he agreed to go against the Black Roses and win the fight after all." He barks a harsh laugh. "What a fucking hero."

My tongue feels like it's glued to the roof of my mouth. It's hard to swallow, hard to breathe around the feelings that are rising up and choking me. There are so many emotions that it's hard to distinguish one from the other, or tell which one is the strongest.

Horror is pretty high up there, along with anger, so I latch onto those because they're easier to deal with than the rest of it. There's also a soul-numbing sadness that the man I've thought of as my dad for my whole life isn't actually my dad. That the father I never knew about raped my mother. That my conception was bathed in blood and pain.

The anger is strongest though, rising above the heartbreak and shock.

Fuck this asshole.

I'd rather have no dad at all than have this man for a father.

"You're a fucking psycho," I snap. "Fuck you! You want me to join you? You really think I would *ever* do that after what you just told me? I'll never join your sick fucking gang, and I'll do everything I can to help the Black Roses bring you down."

Hugh just keeps smiling, full of cool satisfaction, like this is exactly the reaction he wanted to get out of me.

"Sorry, kiddo. You're not going to have that chance," he says.

Almost on cue, a door opens and other men start to come into the room. It's just a few guys, but they're all looming behind Hugh, watching me. I'm outnumbered, still tied to a chair, and my heart starts racing all over again.

Hugh gestures for someone to come forward, and a man steps up. He looks... eager, for lack of a better word. Watching me with hungry eyes.

"When I took over the Jackals, I expected some resistance," Hugh tells me calmly. "Samuel was very popular, and people mourned him when he died. But there were some members of the gang who were loyal to me from day one. And I need to reward their choice to stand by me. You understand?"

The man next to him stands up straighter, and it's clear my uncle—my *father*—is talking about him.

"You can have her, Niko," he says to the man, not looking away from me.

My stomach goes sour, and I know immediately what Hugh means. He's going to recreate his initiation, replaying it with this guy and me. He's going to let this fucker rape me as a way of proving his loyalty and to punish me for rejecting him the way my mother did.

I start to hyperventilate, and I force myself to slow my breath before I pass out. I can't afford to lose consciousness right now.

Hugh reaches down, resting his hand on the top of my head in a gesture almost like a benediction. It might even be soothing if I didn't know that the hand is attached to a goddamn psychopath.

"When I took your mother, it was in front of others," he says gently. "But I'm not a complete monster. I won't watch." He strokes my hair, and a shudder runs down my spine. "We'll talk later. After you've had a chance to reconsider."

With that, he turns to the other men who entered the room with Niko and snaps his fingers. They nod in unison, heading for the door with the man who claims to be my father behind them.

Hugh glances back at me one more time as he stands in the doorway, and the expression on his face terrifies me more than the thought of what's going to come next.

He looks almost... proud. As if I'm fulfilling some sick sort of legacy right now.

Me and my mother, both victims of the Jackals.

Both victims of Hugh.

He meets my gaze for a second, his too-familiar brown eyes burning into me, then nods and turns to go.

The heavy door slams closed behind him, leaving me and Niko alone together. The big man's eyes go from eager and hungry to dark and lustful, and I hate the way he's looking at me. He's several inches taller than I am, and probably has a hundred pounds on me, but I keep reminding myself that I fought the bruiser Hugh put me up against and won. I can take down this guy too.

But you weren't tied up then, a voice whispers inside my head. *You weren't woozy from drugs. And you almost lost.*

I grit my teeth, willing that part of my brain to shut the fuck up so I can function. So I can *think.* Maybe I won't win, but there's no goddamn way I'm going down without a fight.

"You're a real stunner, you know that?" Niko croons, walking toward me with his head cocked to one side. "I thought so even on the day you fought Hector. I bet half the guys in the room had a boner from watchin' you roll around on the floor with him. Although..." He makes a face. "You weren't quite so pretty with your face all bloodied and bruised. So let's not do that today, huh? Don't make me hurt you."

My hands clench into fists instinctively, itching to rearrange this asshole's face, and I strain against the bonds tying my wrists together.

Niko laughs. "Yeah, I thought maybe you wouldn't be reasonable. It's okay, sweetheart. I've got ways to make you be a good little girl and take it. You can't fight all the time, right?"

With that, he pulls out a wicked looking knife, twisting it in the air in front of my face so that light glints off the blade. He licks the steel, and my stomach churns so violently that I think I might hurl all over his shoes.

"There you go," he says encouragingly, a sly grin spreading over his features as he reads the look on my face. "Now you're starting to get it. Come on, little girl. Let's get you out of that chair."

He uses the knife to cut the cords tying me to the chair, leaving my wrists bound. As soon as I'm free, the blade of the knife is at my throat, digging in hard enough that I'm afraid I'll cut myself if I even swallow.

"Up," he says sharply, grabbing my elbow to drag me out of the chair.

My legs almost buckle, barely able to support my weight as I shake off the remnants of whatever they knocked me out with. I struggle to stay upright, but Niko doesn't seem to give a fuck, dragging me over to a large wooden table on one side of the dingy, barren room. I still have no idea where the hell we are—probably some random building that the Jackals own, given how rundown and abandoned this place looks.

Niko practically throws me against the table, and I grunt in pain as my hips slam into the wood. I double over, and he adjusts his grip on the knife, keeping it pressed to the side of my neck as his free hand roams over my hips and ass.

"I'm gonna enjoy this. I'm gonna take my fucking time, and I promise you'll be screaming by the end, sweetheart," he groans, squeezing my ass cheek with a meaty hand. The knife blade digs deeper into my neck, and I feel a sharp sting that makes me hiss. "One way or another, you'll scream."

My body is shaking, shivering from head to toe as if I'm freezing.

But I don't feel cold. I just feel numb.

Niko's upper body bends over mine, and my mind flashes to the moment when Sloan fucked me in the supply closet at the hospital. He curled himself around me the same way, but in that moment, I felt so safe and protected. So loved.

Like he was a barrier between me and everything awful in the world.

As Niko's broad chest presses against my back, an overwhelming rage fills me, pushing away everything else.

Fuck this asshole.

Fuck him for being nothing like Sloan. For being nothing like Levi and Rory.

Fuck him for trying to break me.

My body moves before I consciously decide to act, years of fight training taking over as I sense an opening and take it. As Niko bends over me, trapping my bound hands between us, I throw my head back as hard as I can.

The back of my head catches his face, and pain explodes inside my skull as I feel the crunch of his nose breaking.

He lets out a harsh yell, staggering backward in shock as his grip on me loosens. I throw my bodyweight backward, knocking him back another step before slipping out from between him and the table. I turn toward the door, trying to force my wobbly legs to move faster.

"Oh, no, you don't, you fucking cunt."

Niko grabs me by the back of the shirt, hurling me sideways. I hit the wall with my shoulder, stumbling and nearly going down to my knees.

He's on me a second later, pulling me away from the wall and throwing me again, sending me down to the floor this time. I land hard and roll, and he stalks after me, the knife still in his hand and a pissed off look on his bloodied face.

"You'll pay for that," he snarls.

My heart is beating so fast it feels like it's going to burst. My hands are still bound, and my arms twist painfully beneath me as I roll onto my back. I kick out at him as he nears me, and he dodges backward, cursing.

Next time I kick, he's ready for me, and he manages to shove my leg aside and throw himself on top of me.

I aim my other knee for his crotch, but he twists so that the blow lands on his thigh instead. Then he rears back and slaps me across the face hard enough that I see stars and my ears start to ring.

"Bitch." He bares his teeth, wrapping his thick fingers

around my neck. "You keep making this worse for yourself."

His grip is bruising, and my lungs heave as I struggle for air, writhing and bucking beneath him. When he releases me, I drag in a ragged breath, and he presses the knife against my neck right beneath my chin, forcing me to tip my head back.

Niko is breathing hard as he glares down at me, red in the face with blood pouring down over his mouth and chin. His teeth are coated with it, and it makes him look like a monster. Like a fucking animal.

But there's a savage, triumphant grin on his face, and it sparks a primal fear inside me.

Because I'm out of options.

"Maybe you didn't get it the first time, you fucking slut," he grits out. "But you're mine."

His free hand grabs my face, squeezing so hard that my lips purse awkwardly. Even with a broken nose and out of breath from having to fight with me, the asshole on top of me looks pleased with himself. He leans down a little, looking like he's going to say something else, but a sudden burst of noise outside the room interrupts him.

Pop! Pop! Pop!

My heart jerks in my chest, my eyes widening.

Shouts follow the gunshots, and Niko's head whips around to follow the sound. The pressure of the knife on my neck eases, and I renew my struggles beneath him, trying to get out from under his bulky weight.

"Not so fast." He growls, turning back to me and grabbing a fistful of my hair, lifting my head to bash it against the hard cement floor.

But he never gets the chance.

Time seems to slow to a crawl as the door bursts open, and Levi, Sloan, and Rory run into the room.

There's a fleeting moment where I think I have to be hallucinating—that there's no way they can really be here, that my disoriented brain must've conjured them up as the last people I want to see before I die.

But then Rory aims his gun at Niko and shoots him right in the head.

The big man topples sideways, the knife slipping from his hand as he hits the floor. His lower body is still on top of me, and I can feel from the way his weight goes slack that he's dead already.

"Fuck! Mercy!" Levi shouts, rushing over to me. He shoves Niko's body off me before cradling my face with his hands. "Jesus. Are you okay?"

I can't find my voice at first, so I just nod, feeling shaky and out of it. He helps me to my feet, and Sloan steps forward quickly to cut the ropes that held me, using the knife Niko dropped.

"Come on," he says, his voice hard. "We're getting you out of here."

15

Levi and Sloan help me out of the room, and Rory takes the lead as they hustle me quickly through the abandoned building, past two dead bodies on the floor. A quick glance tells me what I already could've guessed.

Hugh's not among them.

He must've already left before my guys showed up—or maybe he ran like a fucking coward when they broke in, not even bothering to stick around and fight with his own men. So much for goddamn loyalty.

Given how obsessed with me Hugh is, I'm sure he'll be pissed as shit that his plans for me failed, but I can't even think about that now. I don't know what he could do that would be a worse kind of retaliation than what he's already done, and it makes me sick to even try to imagine it.

We pass one more body by the building's entrance, and once we get outside into the night air, I feel like I can breathe again. I drag in gulping breaths, feeling them burn in my chest. I want to clear my head, but I still feel so out of it, and I know that has to be the shock of everything that's happened tonight settling in.

"How... how did you find me?" I ask as we practically run down the street, presumably toward the guys' car.

"It was pure fucking luck," Levi says, his gaze darting around the darkened street as he holds my arm to steady me. "Rory was home when they..." He trails off, looking sick. "When they took you. So he was able to follow the fuckers part way. He called Sloan and me, and we hunted until we found you."

The firmness of his tone makes it clear that they wouldn't have stopped hunting until they did find me, and I feel a rush of gratitude so strong that it makes my already weak legs wobble again.

Thank fuck they found me when they did. Even another few minutes, and I might've been dead. Or worse.

Sloan's car is parked at the end of the block, and the men hustle me toward it, guns still drawn as they keep an eye out for any Jackals lying in wait.

Even when we reach the car without being attacked, I can't quite wrap my mind around the fact that I'm safe. My stupefied mind can't believe it.

The guys have me, and they're going to take me home. Hugh and his twisted fucking plans can't touch me right now.

Rory and Levi help me into the back seat of the car, and Sloan slides in behind the wheel to drive as usual. Rory hesitates, looking like he wants to climb in back with me, but then he seems to decide to give me some space and gets in the front passenger seat instead, leaving just me and Levi in the back.

Sloan practically floors it, and we peel out quickly, just in case any more Jackals were hanging around and decided to follow us or something. But I can't see any sign of them, confirming my earlier guess that the building Hugh took me to was one the Jackals don't use very often.

As Sloan drives, I lean my head back against the seat and close my eyes.

Bad idea.

As soon as my eyelids close, I can see Niko looming over me, that sick grin on his face like he just won some prize because he gets to do horrible things to me. I can see Hugh, standing there looking proud of himself as he talks about raping my mother and holding the knowledge that he's my real father over my dad's head.

It makes me sick to my stomach, and all the feelings and stress hit me all at once.

"Wait. Stop," I croak, reaching for the door handle as bile rises in my throat.

We must be far enough away from Jackal territory that the guys feel relatively safe, because Sloan does what I ask, pulling over quickly by the side of the road. I open the door and stumble out of the car, going down to my hands and knees as I vomit on the sidewalk.

Warm hands pull my hair back gently, and Levi murmurs soothing words as I throw up again, my stomach heaving until there's nothing left inside.

When I sit back, he wraps his arms around me, the warmth of his solid body bleeding into mine. I swallow down the coppery taste in my mouth and allow myself two deep breaths before I try to stand.

He helps me, and we climb back into the car where Rory and Sloan are waiting silently.

Sloan starts driving again, and I sink into the seat beside Levi. My cheek hurts from being smacked so many times, and there are bruises on my arms and side from being thrown into the wall and onto the floor. My wrists burn from struggling against the ropes, and I feel shaky and queasy, even though my stomach is empty now.

I'm still reeling from everything I learned tonight. None of it feels entirely real, like this is all a bad dream or a fucked up movie of someone else's life.

I let out a shuddering breath, and Levi reaches out to touch me gently.

"Is this okay?" he asks, stroking a hand over my arm.

I swallow hard and nod, reaching out my hand across the seat. He takes it, lacing our fingers together and holding on tight. Maybe some people wouldn't want to be touched after something like what just happened to me, but all I want is the reminder that I'm safe now. That nothing can hurt me when I'm with these men.

"You're safe." Rory's voice is firm as he twists around to look at me, like he knows I need to hear those words. "It's over."

Sloan glances at me in the rearview mirror. His eyes are concerned, but his jaw is clenched, and there's a vein pulsing in his forehead. In true Sloan fashion, he's super pissed off.

I can relate.

"We're going to find whoever's responsible for this," he says. "It's never going to happen again."

There's promise and threat in his tone, like he'd tear someone limb from limb if they tried to come near me right now.

"Hugh's behind it," I say, surprised that Sloan would think it could be anyone else. It's not a mystery who's been after me all this time, although I didn't fully understand why until today. "It was him."

"He's not the only one." He shakes his head angrily, catching my gaze in the rearview mirror. "How did they know you'd be coming home then? And that the rest of us wouldn't be with you? Usually, we all leave the house together, and if someone had been tailing you, Malek would have noticed and said something."

"What are you saying?" Rory glances at Sloan with concern in his eyes. "You think one of ours sold her out?"

"Yes. And I think it was my father."

It's a heavy accusation, and I can tell Sloan knows it. His fingers grip the steering wheel, knuckles going white from how hard he's holding on.

Levi sucks in a breath. "That would be…" He shakes his head. "Fuck. You really think he sold her out?"

"Or used her as a bargaining chip or something. You saw how much he didn't want to talk about the Jackals and their bullshit before. How he'd do anything to make it go away so we don't have to deal with this war. He's always been able to justify the deaths of a few if it means keeping the peace he wants so fucking badly."

Sloan sounds disgusted to even be saying it, and my heart hammers in my chest. I don't want to think Gavin could be capable of something like that, but if tonight taught me anything, it's that people can be fucking monsters. And that the worst kinds of monsters are good at disguising what they are until it's too late.

Maybe my marriage to Sloan wasn't enough to keep Gavin off my back after all. Or maybe it backfired, pissing him off and making him that much more determined to get rid of me.

"So what are you going to do?" Rory asks, glancing over at Sloan with a worried expression on his face.

"I'm going to have a little chat with my father," Sloan declares grimly. "Right fucking now."

Instead of going home, we head to the Black Roses

headquarters where Sloan knows Gavin will be. I'm still feeling banged up and emotionally frayed, but when everyone piles out of the car, I go with them. I don't want to be alone, and we have to present a united front. If Gavin really is behind this, I want to look him is his goddamn eyes when Sloan confronts him.

There are other members of the Black Roses in the building, including a few standing guard near the entrance, but we bypass them and march right into Gavin's office, bursting in uninvited.

He's behind his usual desk, typing something on a laptop, and he looks up in surprise to see us there. The surprise shutters into something more neutral quickly, but Sloan doesn't seem to care.

My husband is in full-on confrontation mode, and the only thing the rest of us can do is step back and watch. There's no deference for his father at all, no effort to restrain his anger or try to hold himself in check.

He's more furious than I've ever seen him, his body practically vibrating with it.

"Too. Far," he snaps. "You son of a bitch. I know you'd do almost anything to head off a war with Jackals, but this is too fucking far. She's my *wife*."

Gavin frowns, his heavy brows pulling together. "What are you talking about?"

"I'm talking about Mercy!" Sloan shouts. "And how some Jackal asshole kidnapped her right in front of our goddamn front door this afternoon! I'm talking about how we had to go looking for her, and when we found her in the old *Jackal* building on Hubbard Street, there was some slimy motherfucker with his hands all over her. I want to know what you had to do with it."

Gavin's head jerks, his eyes widening before they narrow. "What *I* had to do with it? What would I have had to do with it?"

"I don't know! You sold her out or made a deal or something. You told them where she'd be. I can't believe you're so desperate to keep us from going toe to toe with the Jackals that you'd sink this low."

"I'm *not*," Gavin snaps, and his voice cracks through the room like a whip. I almost flinch, still on edge from everything that's happened, my fight or flight instinct raging through my veins.

The older man pushes away from the desk and gets to his feet, coming around it to stand in front of Sloan.

"I don't know who you think you are, barging in here and accusing me of something like that. I let you get away with a lot of shit because you're my son, but that doesn't mean you can throw accusations around with no evidence."

"What more evidence do I need?" Sloan demands. "You hate Mercy. You want the Jackal problem to disappear without actually lifting a fucking finger to do anything! I'm sure you thought giving her over to them would solve both of your problems, you fucking coward."

Gavin glares at Sloan, and the taut animosity thickening the air ratchets up another notch. Levi, Rory, and I just stand back, letting the two of them have it out, although I can feel the tension in the two men by my side.

If this turns into an actual fight between Gavin and Sloan, if things get violent, I don't know what the fuck will happen. I know Levi and Rory will back their friend up, but it would mean going against the leader of their gang. And there would be no coming back from that.

Sloan takes a threatening step closer when Gavin doesn't respond to his words, and my throat closes over my next breath.

"Admit it," he snarls. "Fucking admit it. Tell me you arranged this. Or that you knew about it and did nothing. Like fucking always."

"I won't admit to something I didn't do," Gavin barks, fury overtaking his features. He looks like if Sloan wants to make this physical, he's more than willing to go there. "And what do you mean, 'like fucking always'? You think I sit behind this desk and do nothing? Who's out there coordinating deals? Trying to expand our reach? Trying to keep our people safe?"

"Fuck off, and fuck you," Sloan snaps back. "You don't give a shit about keeping people safe. If you did, there wouldn't be Black Roses dragging themselves back from deals bleeding, only to have you turn them away because you're too busy playing party host to give a shit. Your people are out there dying and fighting for you, and you do *nothing*. Just like always. Just like when it came to mom."

Gavin's whole body goes still, as if Sloan hit him or something.

Rory and Levi both take subtle steps forward, blocking my body with theirs, and I have to remind myself how to breathe as all the oxygen seems to evaporate from the room.

"What does your mother have to do with this?"

Gavin's voice is low and hard. His face is expressionless, but his eyes aren't. A million different things seem to flash behind them, although I can't tell what he's thinking.

"Everything!" Sloan explodes, the words bursting out of him like he's been holding them in for way too fucking long. "She has *everything* to do with this. You didn't protect her. You couldn't even keep her safe. She trusted you, I know she did. She thought you'd never let her get hurt, and now she's dead."

There's something broken in his voice underneath all the rage, and it breaks my heart. I wonder how many nights he's lain awake at night thinking about this. Feeling heartbroken and bitter because his dad couldn't save his mother. Because he lost her too damn young.

"You didn't do enough," Sloan bites out, shaking his head as his jaw clenches. "You never do. You just sit back and wait until things are too bad to recover from, and *then* you decide it's enough and try to clean up the damage."

He laughs harshly, gesturing around to encompass the whole building and the people within it.

"It's already happening. We're losing people. We're suffering. Mercy was fucking kidnapped. Rory's family lost their house. We have members dragging themselves back here bleeding and hurt because the Jackals are walking all over us, and you're not doing a damn thing about it. It's like what happened to Mom all over again, and I'm not letting that happen to Mercy. I made a vow to protect her when I married her, and even if vows don't mean shit to you, they do to me. I won't let her get hurt again, no matter what I have to do to stop this."

He practically spits the last words at his father, his chest heaving and his hands fisted.

The silence seems very loud when Sloan finally stops ranting, and I glance at Gavin, trying to gauge his reaction.

The older man's face is still as blank as a goddamn block of ice, but the storm behind his eyes is raging. His jaw clenches, making the muscles on the sides of his face pop out.

Then he closes his eyes, cutting off my view of the turbulent emotions churning in his eyes. When he opens them again, instead of looking angrier than before, I see his expression turn sad. He slumps a little, the rage and frustration draining from his posture and his face.

"I never meant for her to die, Sloan," he says, his voice very soft. "I would have done anything to keep her safe. I loved her."

"You could've saved her," Sloan insists.

"Maybe." For a brief second, I can see a sharp flash of raw emotion pass over Gavin's face. He lifts a hand to smooth back his hair, shaking his head. "I tried. I thought I was making the right choices. I thought I was doing what was best for her."

Sloan seems to be holding his breath, like he's bracing for something, but as Gavin speaks, a little of the tension drains from him too. Instead of firing off some sharp comment in return, he nods jerkily. "I know you did. But you have to look around, Dad. We're going to be in that same situation with the Jackals if we don't do something."

Gavin looks up at his son, and there's something in his expression that makes me think he's seeing two versions of Sloan right now. The boy and the man. The little kid who lost his mother so long ago and the warrior who's determined to protect his people—to protect his wife.

But whether Gavin can see it or not, those two versions are one and the same. I don't know if I fully realized until this exact moment how much the death of Sloan's mother shaped who he is. Who he's become.

My gaze darts back and forth between the two men as they stand off, their eyes locked. Finally, Gavin drags in a deep breath and lets it out before nodding.

"You're right. Fuck. You're right."

It's clear that the leader of the Black Roses is a very proud man. I've seen it in everything he does, from the way he holds himself to the way he does business, but right now, I can also see the weight of the guilt that's been hanging on him for so long. I know Sloan doesn't believe Gavin cares enough about the loss of his wife, but I think he's wrong.

Maybe that moment defined Gavin as much as it did Sloan—just in a different way.

"I didn't have anything to do with Mercy's abduction," Gavin says, speaking each word clearly. "I swear it. I may have misplayed things with the Jackals, but I would never give up one of our own."

I blink, shocked to hear him refer to me in that way. I know he was pissed about my marriage to Sloan, and I know he only inducted me into the gang so he could keep an eye on me more easily. But my membership in his organization clearly means more to him than I thought.

Sloan nods, studying his father as if looking for the lie. When he doesn't seem to find it, he lets out a breath. "We killed a few of Hugh's foot soldiers getting Mercy out tonight. There's a chance they'll use that as an excuse to try to retaliate, even though they started it. We can let this war play out in a hundred little cuts, or we can do something big and end this before it gets worse. What's it gonna be, Dad?"

Gavin hesitates for a moment, shifting his gaze from his son to me, Levi, and Rory. Then he looks back at Sloan.

"All right. We'll try things your way." He lifts his chin in a sharp gesture. "You can take point on this. I'm elevating you to that level, starting now."

Sloan blinks in surprise, looking taken aback.

But his surprise only lasts for a second. Then he nods, and I can see a grim determination flooding his face. He's a man who gets things done, and this isn't going to be an exception.

"I'll do it," he promises firmly. "I'll end this."

16

My legs feel shaky as shit as we walk out of Gavin's office and head back through the main part of the building to go back outside.

There are still other Black Rose members gathered around, and it's hard to know how much of that altercation they overheard, because none of them do more than nod as we pass by. Sloan nods back, his expression hard and unyielding.

It's still hard for me to process everything that just happened. It was a better outcome than any of us were probably expecting, and it's a relief to know that Gavin didn't have anything to do with what happened to me. I do believe him on that. He may not like me much, but I think Sloan was wrong in his assessment of what his father is capable of—there's so much anger and baggage between the two men that I think it's hard for Sloan to see past that, but Gavin has more honor than Hugh ever will.

I feel a little better as we get back in the car and start the drive home, but I'm still on edge. Flashes of Hugh's and Niko's faces keep bursting behind my eyelids every time I close my eyes, and I clench my hands into fists.

We get a few miles away from the Black Roses head-quarters before Rory swivels in his seat to look back at me.

"What happened, Mercy?" he asks, voice soft. "Will you tell us?"

They only know the basics—that I was abducted by the Jackals and almost raped by one of Hugh's henchmen—but they don't know more than that.

I know I'll have to tell them sooner or later. They'll want to know the whole story, and it's important that they do. Hugh probably didn't plan on me being able to escape to tell anyone that he's my real father, and it could definitely be something he plans to use against me later. I wouldn't put it past him. I wouldn't put *anything* past that son of a bitch.

Even thinking about it now makes me sick to my stomach, but I swallow past the nausea and try to figure out where to start.

"A man attacked me when I got back from having coffee with Scar," I tell them. "I dropped my phone outside and went to go get it, and he snuck up on me and jumped me. He knocked me out with something, and when I woke up in that building, Hugh was there. He's pissed because he can't have me in his gang. He said it was important for family to be together."

I swallow down a wave of nausea. There's nothing left in my stomach for me to throw up, but my body seems plenty willing to try anyway.

"He... he told me the truth," I say quietly.

"About what?" Levi asks, reaching out to take my hand again. He's in the back seat with me like before, and all the guys are listening intently as I speak, their focus entirely on me.

"About my dad. About... about the man I *thought* was my dad for my whole life. But I was wrong. Oscar isn't my father. Hugh is."

I tell them the whole story of the initiation and how my mother rejected his advances. How that didn't matter at all to Hugh.

The guys react in disgust, and Levi squeezes my hand tighter, giving me something like a lifeline to hold on to while I keep talking. Even saying it now, it's still hard for me to believe it's real.

How could the man who raised me so well and loved me so unconditionally only be my uncle, while the man who was ready to let one of his loyal soldiers rape me tonight be my real father?

It's beyond fucked up.

"My dad—the man I've been thinking of as my dad—

wanted to keep Hugh away from me. Hugh knew that, and when it came time for Dad to throw that fight you guys paid him off to lose, Hugh threatened to come find me and tell me the truth if Dad didn't win. That's why he double-crossed you."

"Fuck." Sloan curses, hitting the steering wheel with his palm. "I never understood why he did it, but... Jesus, something like that didn't even occur to me."

"Yeah, me neither," I mutter bitterly.

"Mercy." Levi strokes his knuckles down the side of my face, catching my attention. "I'm so damn sorry. That's... shit, that's awful. But you're safe now. Hugh's not going to lay a fucking hand on you again."

"He'll be dead if he fucking tries," Sloan promises. "I'll kill him with my bare hands."

Rory's still turned around in the front passenger seat so he can look at me, and he smiles a little. "And don't worry about Oscar not being your biological father, Hurricane. Family is what you make of it. Oscar raised you. He took care of you when your mom died. He was even willing to face the wrath of Gavin and the rest of us for going back on our deal about the fight to keep you safe. That's what makes someone a dad. The rest of it doesn't matter."

Hearing those words, especially from Rory, does make me feel a little better. Because he's right. My dad has always been there for me. He's always been willing to do whatever it took to keep me safe. He raised me and cared for me and never let me doubt that I was loved.

That's what matters.

"Thanks." I nod, giving him a small smile.

He squeezes my knee and then turns back around. The car grows quiet, and a few minutes later, we finally pull up to the house.

I don't think I've ever been so glad to see this place before, and it's kind of amazing to me that a house I once saw as a prison and a punishment has come to mean safety and love. There's nowhere else on earth I'd rather be than here.

We get out of the car and walk into the house, and as soon as we're inside, Sloan pulls me into his arms. Instead of waiting for their turns, Rory and Levi just step in either side of me, wrapping me in their arms too. I'm surrounded on all sides by strength and warmth, and I close my eyes for a second, pushing back the tears that sting behind my eyelids.

"What can we do to help?" Levi asks as they step away a little to let me breathe. He's always the one to ask that sort of thing first, but I can tell they all want to know the answer to his question. They want to do whatever they can to make me feel better.

"Nothing, right now. You did enough by coming for me," I tell them. "I'm okay. Really. I'm alive, and I'm not even hurt that bad, only banged up a little. I just want a shower so I can wash all this shit off of me."

"Okay." His dark brown eyes are soft with worry. "If you're sure."

I can feel how reluctant they are to let me go and be alone, but none of them try to stop me as I go upstairs and head into my bathroom.

I strip off my clothes and throw them in a pile on the floor, seriously considering burning them or something so I don't have to look at them ever again.

Once I'm naked, I open the shower door and turn the water on. As I straighten up, I catch sight of my reflection in the mirror above the sink. There are bruises on my sides from where that fucker threw me into the walls, and my face is starting to bruise too. My wrists are red and streaked with blood.

I don't want to look at the fucked up girl in the mirror for too long, so I just crank the water in the shower hotter than I would usually like it and step inside.

The spray beating down on my skin feels good, easing some of my soreness even as it makes my cuts and raw skin sting. Ignoring the bite of pain, I soap up my loofah and start washing myself clean.

I can almost imagine that the slimy feeling left behind from Niko's hands on me is being washed away, left to swirl harmlessly down the drain along with the water and suds, and that helps for a bit.

But as soon as I think about his hands on me, I start to feel it. The way he grabbed me and pulled me around like I was nothing but a toy to him. Something he could use and then throw away. I can't stop thinking about how vulnerable I was. How even though I fought with everything I had to get away, I wasn't even close to escaping. It makes me feel sick.

My mind flashes through all the things that could have happened if the guys hadn't shown up when they did, and it freaks me out.

I'm not used to feeling helpless.

I stare down at the white surface of the shower floor, and it suddenly seems very far away. Spots and stars flit around the edges of my vision, and I realize that I feel light-headed because I'm not taking full breaths. Instead, they're short and shallow, barely filling my lungs. I feel shaky and a little dizzy, and I have to reach out one hand to brace myself against the wall so my knees don't give out.

A short knock on the bathroom door startles me into looking up, and through the fogged-up glass, I see Rory ease the door open and step in, closing it again behind him.

He takes one look at my face, and whatever he sees in my expression makes him give me a soft look.

"I thought it had been awhile since I'd gotten some tat," he says.

His words make me smile, even though I still feel shaky and sick. The reference to that long-running joke between us is grounding, making me remember that I'm here and I'm safe.

"Come here," I murmur. "Please."

He nods and starts to get undressed, leaving his clothes on the floor so he can step into the shower with me. Then he pulls the shower door closed, enclosing us in a little haven of hot water and steam.

The water runs over his arms and down his chest, making little rivulets that draw my gaze over his body. It soaks into his hair, and he reaches up to push the wet golden brown strands out of his face so he doesn't get water in his eyes.

"I had a feeling you might need someone to be with you right now," he tells me.

"I do," I admit, my throat tightening. "I thought I was going to be fine if I could just get clean, but..." I shake my head. "I just can't stop thinking about how fucking helpless I felt."

Rory nods, beads of water trickling down his face and over the tattoos on his chest and arms. "You know, after I got shot, I had that same problem. I kept replaying it all in my head while I was laid up in the hospital. All I ever want to do is protect the people I care about, and in that moment, laying on the ground bleeding out, I couldn't protect anyone. Not you, not Jen and Piper, not Levi and Sloan. Hell, I wouldn't even have been able to protect myself if I needed to."

I reach out and rest a hand on his arm, feeling his skin warming beneath the hot water as it beats down around us.

"I know what it feels like to be powerless, Hurricane," he murmurs. "But even though you felt like you were helpless in that moment, you're strong. You fought back. You're the strongest person I've ever met."

I don't know what to say to that, so I just lean in and close the distance so I can kiss him instead. He's warm and solid, the way he always is, and it's so easy to melt against him.

Rory kisses me back, gathering me into his arms and holding me close like he's promising with every touch that he's going to keep me safe.

It starts off as just a kiss for comfort, just me seeking out the touch of someone I know would never hurt me. But then Rory's hands start to wander, and it gets heated. He pulls back for a second, searching my face like he's looking for permission.

Instead of words, I just drag him back down and into another messy kiss.

That seems to be all he needs.

He kisses me in the way I've come to expect from Rory —with a hungry energy that heats my blood and leaves me desperate for more. His tongue tangles with mine, our slippery bodies pressed tightly together as he slicks my wet hair back from my face.

Before I'm ready to let go, he's easing back once more, a

wicked grin curving his lips. I don't have time to ask him what he's planning before he's sinking down to his knees in front of me and reaching for my hips to drag me closer.

"Oh," I breathe, spreading my legs instinctively.

Rory leans in to press a kiss to my wet inner thigh, and I can feel him smile against it. He licks his way up, catching drops of water on his tongue as he goes, and then finds the heat of my core.

I'm not wet yet, not from arousal anyway, but Rory seems plenty ready to change that. He laps at my folds first, not dipping inside, and my clit throbs with anticipation.

I suck in a soft breath and let one hand tangle in his wet hair. The other comes to brace myself against the wall because I know I'm going to end up going weak in the knees for a completely different reason soon.

It's so much better than just the shower. It was like the hot water and soap could wash off the surface layer of the pain I was feeling, but not touch the parts of it that have already rooted inside of me.

Having Rory on his knees in front of me, working his tongue slowly past the outside of my pussy and into the sensitive inner bits makes me feel more normal than I have in hours.

It washes all the bad stuff away and gets down to the middle of it, chasing it out with a burning heat that feels amazing.

I close my eyes, and I don't see Hugh. I don't see that fucker he sicced on me, either. I just see Rory. I feel him, parting my pussy with his fingers and licking over my clit, teasing it until it's a firm bud that's practically trembling for his touch.

His flicks his tongue over it a couple of times, and I moan his name, the sound of it echoing around us in the shower.

"Feels good," I murmur, and I can feel him smiling again. He keeps working my clit, licking it, circling it, sucking at it lightly until I'm nearly seeing stars, and then he trails his tongue to my hole, licking a teasing circle there as well.

"Please," I gasp out, pushing my hips forward to bury his face a little bit deeper between my legs. "Rory, please."

He hums teasingly, and keeps up that shallow licking, not giving me what I want for a few seconds. Until suddenly, he does. He plunges his tongue deep into me, and I cry out at the surprise of it.

My body clenches, like it's trying to trap his tongue where it is, and Rory moans, muffled by my wetness. My fingers in his hair tighten, and I grind against his face, unable to help myself.

Judging from the way I can see his cock getting hard and bobbing between his legs, I don't think he minds too much.

He draws his tongue out and then spears it back in

slowly, his fingers making up for lost time as they flick and tease at my clit. It all goes to my head so quickly, and I'm shaking a little and teetering right on the edge of an orgasm in no time.

Rory seems determined to push me the rest of the way over, too. He doesn't let up, continuing to fuck me with his tongue, using his fingers to work me up even more until I'm just a gasping, moaning mess. I tip my head back, feeling the water from my hair run down my spine, caressing me like a lover's hands.

It's enough, and I cry out, the sound of my pleasure echoing around us as my legs shake and that heat curls through me.

I don't need to be able to see Rory's face to know he's smirking, and it's clear neither of us is done yet.

He's a man on a mission, and I'm along for the ride, down to do anything to keep my mind from swinging back down dark paths.

I half expect him to get up and kiss me, let me taste the sweet salt tang of my own pleasure on his lips, and then turn me around and fuck me against the shower wall or something like that.

But he doesn't let up from where his mouth is, pulling his tongue out of me so he can lick slowly along my sensitive folds.

I shiver, even under the hot water, and catch myself just in time before I stagger backward and end up falling.

My body protests the extra stimulation so soon after coming, but not too much. Not enough for me to tell him to stop.

The discomfort doesn't last long anyway. It's only a matter of seconds before the heat is washing through again, taking anything that isn't pleasure and gratitude and burning it out.

Rory switches to doing loops and swirls with his tongue, probably doing that old trick people used to talk about in high school about spelling the alphabet with your tongue to get a girl off.

It's a trick for a reason though, and each looping letter jolts through me like a bolt of lightning. He starts around my hole and then works his way up, curling his tongue over my clit as he dots an I or crosses a T.

I have no idea what he's spelling, and I don't really care one way or another if I'm being honest. All I can focus on is how good it feels and how wet I am. Between the shower and my pussy, Rory is going to be drenched by the end of this, and there's something so fucking hot about him just diving in anyway, because he wants to and he can't get enough.

That thought just makes it even easier for Rory to work me up into a second orgasm. I practically yank at his hair when I come this time, biting down on my lip hard enough that it almost bleeds.

Rory doesn't seem to mind, because of course he

doesn't. He just keeps going, lapping up everything I give him like it's the most delicious treat he's ever had in his life.

He works his fingers into me next, now that I'm open and loose for him, and he fucks me with them slowly and deeply, taking his time while he sucks at my clit.

At this point I'm an overstimulated mess, and it's all I can do to stay standing. Every pass of his tongue makes me quiver, and every time his fingers curl into me, I want to sob his name.

The third orgasm comes easier than the other two, just a rush of feeling and a tightening of my pussy before I'm wailing once again, curling over at the waist a little while my hips buck forward. I feel like I'm on fire, the heat of the shower and the heat of the pleasure searing me from the inside out, making it impossible to focus on anything else.

I'm breathing hard, and my heart races. My vision is blurry from coming so hard, and I don't know if I have it in me to come again.

This time though, Rory does pull back, grinning that grin of his while he watches me try and come down from that orgasm. Like I expected, his face is drenched with my wetness, and it's a good look for him.

"Oh my god," I pant, shifting so I can lean back against the shower wall and let it support me while I try to remember how to breathe.

"Feeling better?" Rory asks.

All I can do is nod.

"Good. Because I'm not done yet."

I open my mouth to tell him I'm not sure I have more in me, but then he stands up, and I get to see how hard he is. His cock is flushed and juts out from his body impressively, a thin thread of precum dripping from the head.

I swallow that protest because, actually? I can probably go again with him looking like that. As soon as I remember how to move.

Rory doesn't make me work for it though. He shuts the water off and steps out onto the bath mat, grabbing my towel from the hook on the wall and opening it for me.

I step out on wobbly legs, and he wraps the fluffy fabric around me, gently toweling me dry. It feels so nice to be taken care of. To be handled gently, like I matter, after everything that happened earlier tonight.

I'm in a daze from that last orgasm, so I just let Rory take the lead, lifting my arms when he urges me to and turning when he presses gently at my shoulder.

Once we're both dry, he picks me up and carries me to the bedroom. Just as gently, he lays me down on the bed and then climbs up after me.

His cock bobs between his legs, and I fixate on it, spreading my own legs instinctively.

That makes him smile, and he slides into me in one smooth move. I'm so wet that it's easy enough to do, and so sensitive that just that motion is enough to have me arching up off of the mattress a little.

Usually, sex with Rory is all about teasing and flirting and him trying to make me scream. This is just as hot as it always is, but I can tell he's being sweeter now, trying to comfort me and remind me that he's here for me.

I graze my fingers over the scar left by the bullet that Jackal put through his arm, silently thanking whatever forces of fate allowed Rory to live through that and stay with me. Stay with *us*. We've all be through hell together, but we're still together.

And that's all I need.

Sliding my hands up, I wrap my arms around his neck and look into his eyes as he moves inside me, focusing only on Rory and how good it feels to have him on top of me like this.

He dips his head and kisses me deeply, working his hips in deep thrusts that push his cock into me over and over again. I moan into it, pulling back every few seconds to pant for breath as the kiss turns messy and heated.

I breathe his name into his mouth, and he smiles against my lips, fucking me a bit harder as he starts to chase his own pleasure. I can feel mine rising again, and apparently there's still another orgasm in me because he hits that spot just right, and I go tight around him, writhing on the bed and moaning desperately into the breathless kiss.

"Mercy," he moans, hips snapping faster and hard. "Mercy, Mercy, Mercy."

He's just saying my name, but it sounds like a plea, and

I clench around him again, like I want to milk him of everything he has. Maybe I do.

Finally, he spills inside me, and it feels almost like completion in the best way.

In the aftermath, Rory pulls me into his arms and holds me close. I snuggle against him, ready to drift off to sleep, worn out from the day I've had and the excellent sex.

I realize as I lie in his embrace that Rory was right.

I *am* strong.

Not only in my own right. Not only because I'll fight until my last breath for the people I care about.

But because I'm not alone.

I have three strong men who will stand beside me. Always.

17

A FEW DAYS LATER, Scarlett comes over to the house to hang out.

Jen finally got tired of being cooped up in the safe house with nothing to do and nowhere to go and insisted on running her own errands with a guard, so we have Piper with us while the guys are off handling something.

Sloan hasn't wasted a second since his father gave him the go-ahead to finally take decisive action against the Jackals, so we've barely had a minute to breathe since the night of my attack. Being given babysitting duty is a welcome relief from all the heavier shit that's hanging over my life these days.

For the last couple of days, Scar's been coming over after she gets out of school, since we're not really allowed to hang out outside the house anymore. It was dangerous to begin with, but after what happened with my abduction, the guys aren't willing to risk it. Unsurprisingly, my friend is one hundred percent on board with that, because she's worried too. When I called her to tell her what had happened after our coffee date, she rushed over immediately to see with her own eyes that I was okay.

As much as I hate being cooped up like this, I understand the reasoning behind it. The last thing I want is a repeat of what happened with Hugh, and it's not like I hate being at the house the way I used to.

Piper, Scarlett, and I spend some time playing with the toys the little girl brought over, then settle down in the living room to watch a movie about a princess who can talk to animals. Rory's daughter is completely engrossed in it, sitting in front of the TV and mouthing along with most of the lyrics to the songs.

Scarlett and I sit on the couch, keeping an eye on her and talking quietly.

I told Scar about Hugh being my real father when I told her about the rest of it, and she was furious on my behalf, calling him every name in the book and insisting that the guys take her with them when they finally make a move against him because she has some things she wants to say to him.

Since then, though, we haven't talked about it much. It's still a raw wound for me, knowing that my life has been a lie and someone so horrible could be a part of my DNA in such a big way.

Scarlett can tell, I know. She's always been able to read me better than almost anyone else, and she keeps things light as we talk, trying to distract me from the heavier things that have been weighing on my mind.

Her current crusade is insisting that the guys and I have to go on a honeymoon.

"You've *earned* it," she says. "I mean, after all the fighting and shit is done, you'll have doubly earned it."

"Aren't honeymoons for people who have fancy weddings in the first place?" I ask, wrinkling my nose.

She shakes her head. "They don't have to be. And, I mean, the fact that you had your wedding in a courthouse just means you have to go all out for the honeymoon. It's the best part!"

"Because it's a glorified vacation?"

"Because it's a glorified vacation where the expectation is that you're going to be—" She cuts herself off and glances down at Piper. "You know."

I don't need her suggestive eyebrow waggling to understand what she means, and I laugh and roll my eyes. "Trust me, we don't have to go to Hawaii or whatever to do lots of that anyway."

"That's not the point. The point is you deserve a getaway. Why do it here when you could be doing it on a beach with cocktails and handsome men everywhere?"

She sounds so dreamy when she says it, and I laugh and punch her in the arm.

"You know I have handsome men everywhere here, right? And that sand is terrible and itchy? Especially if you get it in the wrong places, if you know what I mean."

"You're no fun. You have no sense of romance."

Scar throws one of the pillows from the couch at me, and I catch it and whack her with it. It's the way things always are between us. Easy and fun. She makes me laugh even when I'm feeling crappy, and this is exactly what I need after the shit show certain parts of my life have turned into lately.

Piper looks up at us, her green eyes wide. "Can we have a snack?"

"Yeah, sure."

I grin at her and offer my hand, which she takes happily. We go to the kitchen to make sandwiches and chips and smoothies, then bring them into the living room to eat as we start the next movie in the singing animal princess trilogy.

It's a good way to pass the afternoon, even if Piper does insist on making us learn the words to the songs in the movies. Scarlett goes for it with gusto, turning on the flair and drama, one hand over her heart as she muddles through the lyrics to a song about how the prince she's supposed to be with just doesn't understand that her heart belongs to the woods. Or something.

The sound of the garage door opening interrupts the sing-along, and I hear the muffled voices heading our way. I look up as the guys enter the living room, expecting to see Rory dart forward to scoop his daughter up and twirl her around a bit.

But as they step into the room, someone else comes in behind them, and everything else seems to fall away.

For a second, I think I'm hallucinating.

But even after I blink and shake my head a little, the sight is still the same.

"Dad?" I whisper, my voice hoarse.

18

I STARE at the man I once thought was my father, my mouth hanging open as I take him in.

At first, I'm frozen, just gaping at him with no idea how to react.

But then my brain catches up—or maybe it's my heart that reacts first—and I jump off the couch and run to him. He meets me halfway, and I slam into him, wrapping my arms around him so tightly that my muscles ache.

He hugs me back just as hard, burying his face in my hair.

"Mercy. I'm so sorry. I'm so damn sorry about all of this," he murmurs, and it takes me a second to realize he's responding to the fact that I'm crying into his shoulder.

I just hold on to him, not ready to deal with any of that yet. All I want to do is bask in the fact that he's here, that he's solid and real and alive in front of me.

That thought makes my brows pull together, breaking through the surge of happiness at seeing my father. It hits me then that it's actually weird that he's here in front of me. He was sent away because he's supposed to be dead.

I look at Sloan, who's standing off to one side watching us.

"Why did you bring him back here?" I ask. "When things are so dangerous right now."

"Because we need him," Sloan replies. "My father gave me the chance to take the lead in bringing down the Jackals, and we need to act fast. This has to stop before anyone else gets hurt. I'll protect you with everything I have in me, and Oscar is the only other person I know of who would do as much to keep you safe as we will. We have to end this, so we brought him back to help."

Dad puts his hands on my shoulders and steps back, gazing at me with serious eyes. He looks tired, more so than I can ever remember him looking before all of this started, but he also radiates determination.

"No matter what the risks are, I want to help," he tells me, his voice strained. "My brother has always been a monster, and now that he has this much power, it's only giving him chances to fuck up more people's lives."

A look of pain passes across his face as he says those words, and he grips my shoulders, looking down at me seriously.

"Mercy... I need to talk to you about something. Alone."

Rory steps around us and squats down next to Piper, who's been glancing up at us curiously in between watching the action play out in her movie.

"Come on, squirt. Tell me all about what you did with Mercy and Aunt Scarlett."

He swoops her up and takes her into the kitchen. Scar gets up to follow, and Sloan goes with them, pausing to share a look with me as he goes.

I have a question in my eyes when I glance at him, and he looks back and shakes his head subtly. Even though no words are exchanged, I know what the gesture means. He didn't tell my dad that I know about Hugh being my real father. I appreciate that he gave me the chance to be the one to say it.

Once the room clears out and we're alone, Dad takes another step away from me. We settle on the couch together, and he looks down at the carpet for a second, like he's trying to figure out where to start and what to say, and when he takes a deep breath and looks up, I cut him off before he gets the chance to say anything.

"I already know," I tell him.

He blinks in surprise. "You know... what?"

"About Hugh. The truth about him."

He looks even more surprised at that, and I sigh, preparing myself to relive the shitty memories all over again. But if anyone has a right to know what happened, it's the man who raised me. I can't stop thinking of him as "Dad" in my head, and I realize in this moment that I don't want to. Fuck the DNA. Fuck the paternity.

"He told me he's my real father," I explain. "After he had me kidnapped and dragged to some abandoned building so he could gloat about it in my face."

I explain everything in a little more derail, leaving out the worst parts about my fight with Niko and how Hugh wanted to let someone rape me, because Dad doesn't need to have to deal with that on top of everything else right now.

"Did he hurt you?" Dad demands, looking me over like he'll be able to tell. The bruises on my face have faded, at least, and the cut on my neck is scabbed over and healing, so there's not really too much to see.

I shake my head, and it's not really a lie. Hugh wasn't the one who put his hands on me or put a knife to my throat, after all.

"Not physically, I guess. He just had a lot of fun telling me what happened with him and Mom and how you stepped in. Why he made you go against the Black Roses and double-cross them on the arrangement with your fight. It answered a few questions, but mostly, it just sucked."

Dad's expression breaks a little as I talk.

"I'm so sorry, Mercy," he says. "Maybe I should have told you this a long time ago, so he wouldn't have been able to hold it over either of our heads. But... fuck, I wanted to protect you from one of the worst people I know. My own goddamn brother."

He sounds pained when he says it, like he blames himself for who Hugh is. For the kind of person his brother has become. Before I can tell him that it's not his fault his brother is a monster, he keeps talking.

"Hugh was... furious when your mother turned him down. He walked around all the time with a chip on his shoulder, like the world owed him something, and when he didn't get it, he lost his fucking mind. She wasn't the first woman to see past his looks to his personality and tell him she wasn't interested. She was just the first one he felt like he could do something to punish for it. It was horrible."

He sighs, running his fingers through his hair.

"He wasn't even ashamed of it, after it happened. He bragged about it, saying he'd managed to show her what happened when someone said no to the wrong person and prove to the Jackals that he was worth their time, all in one go. I was disgusted, and I told him I never wanted to see or hear from him again after that."

My dad's expression softens, and he rests his elbows on his knees, looking down at the carpet as he relives the memories.

"I wanted to do the right thing, since it was obvious Hugh didn't give a shit anymore. I reached out to your mom to see if there was anything I could do to help her.

Someone had to. And even after what Hugh did, and after she found out she was pregnant, she was still just so... bright and full of life. She was upset, of course, but she never let it break her. She just talked about how she wanted better for her baby, for you. How she wasn't going to live her life in fear or hide from the world because of what Hugh did."

He turns his head to look at me, his eyes shining as he lets out a soft, sad laugh.

"I never meant to fall in love with her, and even after I developed feelings for her, I never thought she'd fall in love with me."

"Why not?" I lean forward to match his posture, my brows furrowing. "I mean, you're a good guy."

That's an understatement. Compared to Hugh, it's night and day. My father is one of the best men I know.

And from what I remember of my parents together, they were always happy. My mom was always smiling, always kissing my dad in the kitchen or the living room or the car. Wherever and whenever. Even when they had arguments, it was worked out quickly, and they always seemed to have the best relationship in my childish eyes.

"Hugh and I look a lot alike," Dad explains, his voice tight. "And I thought... I figure she would always see him in me. Always suspect that on some level, I was like him."

Jesus. My heart clenches, and I realize in a rush how much my mother truly did love this man, to be able to see past his resemblance to the man who hurt her so badly.

"But she ended up falling for me just like I fell for her." Dad smiles, and it's wistful and full of so much emotion it makes my chest ache. "We both agreed not to tell you the truth and to let you just believe I was your father. It seemed easier than having to explain it all, and I didn't have the heart to drag her through the pain of what she went through all over again. And then when she died, I..."

His voice breaks a little, and he trails off. I can see how hard this is for him. Years and years of secrets, something he's been carrying alone since my mother died. It's so much, and maybe if I'd learned this all at a different time, I would've been mad at him for keeping it from me. But in this moment, I can't be.

He tried to protect me, just like he tried to protect Mom.

Dad takes a deep breath and starts again. "When she died, you were all I had left. I didn't want to ruin our relationship by telling you. I didn't want to risk you wanting to meet Hugh or going after him. I just wanted to keep you safe."

The tears I saw glinting in his eyes earlier are streaking down his face by the time he finishes speaking, his voice heavy with emotion. I sniffle a little and realize I'm crying too.

It's been a while since we've talked about my mom at

all, and hearing about what it was like for her, how Hugh just used her and threw her away, hurts. Seeing how much my dad obviously loved her and misses her just makes me miss her too.

And it makes me grateful to have him in my life. Because I know he cares about me too. That he loves me enough to do anything to keep me safe.

I straighten up and wrap my arms around him again, holding him tightly.

"*You* are my father," I say in a hard voice. "I don't care about Hugh or anything that asshole says. You're the one who's been there for me my whole life. You're the one who's protected me and loved me and taught me how to be the person I am. No matter what, you're my dad."

"I love you, Mercy," he tells me, his voice thick. "I always have."

He hugs me back, and we stay like that for a long while.

19

IT'S SO FUCKING nice to be back with Dad and to have him hugging me after so long of just wishing I could hear his voice, but eventually, we remember that there are other people in the house, and we break apart to go to the kitchen where everyone else is waiting.

Rory has Piper sitting at the table, giving her a snack, and Levi showed up at some point while we were talking too. He smiles at me when we walk in, and I smile back.

Scarlett hops off the stool she's perched on and comes over to give Dad a big hug.

"Look at you," Dad says, hugging her tightly. "When did you get so grown up?"

Scar laughs and rolls her eyes. "It hasn't been *that* long since you've seen me," she says. "I'm still the same."

He shakes his head. "No, you've grown. I can tell."

I grin as I watch them interact. It's like being a

teenager again, with Dad teasing us when we came in from school, treating us both like we were his kids. I guess when it comes down to it, neither of us really were, but that never stopped him, and it's not stopping him now.

It's nice, to have so many people I care about in the same space. Scarlett banters with the guys while Levi grabs food out of the fridge, and Rory recruits Piper to help him fix up some snacks for all of us, carrying her around on his back as he rifles through the cupboards.

Dad watches all of it with amusement and something like wonder, and I'm willing to bet he never thought this would be the result of me getting taken as collateral by these guys when Gavin gave him that second chance. No one could have predicted it, but I'm grateful as hell that things worked out this way.

This little haven, in this house with these men, is the one shining bright spot in a sea of darkness.

Scarlett tells Dad about school and her mountain of homework, and then she sighs, glancing at the clock. "I'd love to stick around, but this damn paper is due tomorrow, and I'm only about halfway done with it."

"I'll be here for a while," Dad says. "You'll see me again."

"I'd better," she replies, putting her hands on her hips. "You stay out of trouble."

"That used to be my line," he says, shaking his head ruefully. "But point taken."

They hug once more and then Scarlett blows me a kiss and heads out.

Not long after, Jen shows up to collect Piper. Rory introduces her to Oscar briefly, and she and I chat for a quick minute while Rory goes around the house making sure Piper got all of her toys and everything.

He showers her in kisses as usual and grins as the two of them leave. He's gone to visit them at the safe house a few times, but this is the first time they've come over to our place, and I know he misses seeing them as often as he used to.

Soon. Hopefully, it will all be better soon.

Once it's just us and Dad in the house, the atmosphere seems to change a little. The happy warmth isn't gone, exactly, but it's charged with something else now.

Sloan has a determined look on his face, and he sets down his glass of water with a dull thud. He brought my dad back for a reason, and it's time to get down to it, clearly.

Rory and Levi settle on their stools, and Dad and I round out the little war council of sorts, ready to figure out how we're going to do this. Gavin put Sloan in charge, which he's already explained to Dad, and he's taking that responsibility seriously. We all are. None of us will be safe until the Jackals are out of the picture, and we all want it to be over sooner rather than later.

"I have an idea that I've been thinking about for a few

days," Sloan says. "And I think it'll work if we're smart about it."

Usually, this is where Rory would make a joke, but he just keeps watching Sloan, looking to him as a leader and waiting for him to tell us his plan.

"I didn't know it at the time, but Mercy ran into Hugh at that restaurant when we went out together." He glances at me, his steel gray eyes piercing and resolute "You told me later that you thought he was Oscar for a second."

I nod. "Yeah, I did. I mean, I was missing my dad a lot, and the resemblance between them is pretty strong."

"It is." He steeples his fingers, turning to the others. "It was only for a second, but she's seen Oscar almost every day for her whole life, so of course she could tell them apart more easily. But they *do* have a strong resemblance. And on top of that, Oscar is supposed to be dead. Hugh and the Jackals still think he is, at least. So they won't be expecting to see him. We have the codes Hugh uses to communicate with his men, which will help sell it even more."

I rest my hands on the kitchen island, shaking my head in confusion. "Sell what?"

"The lie," he says simply. "The disguise. Our way in."

There's a moment of silence while we all absorb what he just said. Rory and Levi don't look surprised to hear it, so I'm guessing Sloan already broached this idea with them.

It starts to come together in my head what Sloan is suggesting, and my heart skips a beat. I glance at Dad, expecting him to object, but he's got the same determined look on his face as Sloan. Levi and Rory look the same. As crazy and reckless as this idea is, they're all seriously considering it.

They're all seriously insane.

"Are you talking about... trying to pass Dad off as the leader of the Jackals?" I ask, speaking slowly

Sloan nods once, his face set in a stoic mask.

I suck in a sharp breath, ready to object. There's no fucking way this can work. The Jackals aren't stupid, and just because Hugh and Dad look alike doesn't mean anyone will believe this man is the actual leader of the Jackals for more than a minute or so at best. We have the codes, true, but it's just so fucking risky.

But Levi chimes in before I can say anything, holding up a hand as he catches my gaze.

"We're not going to try to insert Oscar into the Jackals permanently or anything," he explains. "It's not a hostile takeover. We just need it to work for long enough to get what we need. Which is access to the Jackal's headquarters. With the codes and his resemblance to Hugh, it should be easy enough for us to get in and out before anyone figures it out. If we can take down most of the Jackal's leadership, then the gang will crumble. We can secure our power in Fairview Heights and take care of any upstarts from the Jackals who try to reform the gang."

Rory pitches in next, breaking it down for me even more, and Sloan interjects with a few key details that he thinks will make this work.

As I listen to them lay it all out, I keep looking for weak points in the plan, reasons to deny it and refuse to let my dad put himself in danger like that. But Sloan has clearly already thought this through, and it shows. He has an answer for every objection I raise, and when he points out that it gives us the chance to end this without risking any more loss of life among the Black Roses, I snap my jaw shut.

I don't know if I'm entirely on board with this yet. It would take a lot of work and a lot of things going right, but it would open up a lot of possibilities that we didn't have before.

"Their headquarters is well protected," Rory adds. "A full on assault on it would only have a small chance of succeeding, and it would risk heavy losses too. Probably mostly on our side, since they'd have home turf advantage and all that."

They're right that this is our best chance to strike a killing blow to the Jackals without them being able to hit us back. It's sort of like a best of both worlds approach to both Sloan's and Gavin's styles. Avoiding an all-out war, but still taking direct action.

My pulse seems to slow down, and I can feel every heavy beat of my heart as I look at the four people gathered around me in the kitchen.

The three men I've fallen in love with and the man who raised me.

If anyone can pull this off, it's them, and I trust them with my life.

But am I willing to risk theirs?

That's not really the right question to ask, though, I guess. Their lives are already at risk, just like mine is, and we'll all be in danger until this is over. Until the war is decisively won.

"Okay," I say, trying to force down the lump in my throat as I nod. "I'm in."

20

Over the next few days, the guys, Dad, and I work on the plan nonstop.

There's so much to coordinate, so much to go over. Sloan has people doing recon on the Jackals' headquarters, making sure we know enough about it to be able to strike it in the best way. He gathers his informants and gets as much information on the higher-ups in the leadership as he can, so that when Dad goes in, he'll go in with enough to make it convincing.

The guys are all busy, consolidating their knowledge with Dad's, and there's barely a spare moment for anything else.

For me, it's strange having my old life and my new life collide under one roof like this. My dad is staying with us, since it's important we keep his presence and the fact that he's still alive under wraps.

One morning, I wake up before the others, feeling weirdly energized. I go downstairs to the kitchen and Dad's already there, making himself a cup of coffee.

If it wasn't for the fact that the guys' kitchen is so much nicer than the one we had back at home, it would be impossible to distinguish this scene from any other morning before all this happened. I always stumbled into the kitchen to find him making that first cup of coffee, humming some song under his breath and taking in the morning sunlight.

For someone who spent so much time doing fights and shit at night, he's been a morning person forever, and he smiles warmly at me when I walk in.

"Coffee?"

"Please." I shoot him a grateful look. "I was thinking about making pancakes."

Dad grins. Pancakes were a staple in our house when I was growing up, and I can tell he likes the idea of reviving the tradition. He pours me a cup of coffee and pulls down a large mixing bowl from the cabinet.

"That's one of the only things your mom ever insisted on making from scratch," he says. "I always told her the box mix would be fine, but she insisted."

"They were the best pancakes," I tell him, going to get the milk and eggs from the refrigerator.

"Yeah. They were." He smiles fondly.

We fall into step with each other the way we used to,

and it feels nice to know that even though we've been apart for so long, none of it has worn off. We pass each other as I go to get measuring cups out of a drawer, moving around together in the large space easily. Having him back makes my heart full, and I fill him in on some of the things that have been going on since he had to go to the safe house outside the city.

The day of his arrival, after our mini war council, I explained to him when I was showing him upstairs to the guest room that I'm married to Sloan now. He already knew about it, since Sloan had told him, sort of asking for his blessing in a way, now that he was able to do that.

It means a lot to me that Sloan actually cared about Dad's blessing, especially since part of why we rushed the marriage was to keep his own father from hurting me or retaliating against me—although in retrospect, I'm not sure that was as big of a danger as we thought.

I know Dad has some idea of how much Sloan means to me in general, which I can imagine he's surprised about, considering how we met and all. But then I consider how he and my mom met, and I realize that maybe he actually understands it better than I would've thought.

I start measuring ingredients out into the mixing bowl, and Dad clears his throat awkwardly, signaling he wants to talk. It's the same way he did it when I was a teenager and he tried to give me "the talk," before we both combusted into awkwardness and I admitted I'd already done the research for myself.

"So..." he begins. "Rory, Levi, and Sloan."

"Yeah?" I respond, glancing at him. "What about them?"

"I feel like I should be asking *you* that. I know you and Sloan are married now, but..." He trails off, making a face.

I have a pretty good idea of where this is going already, even without him finishing his sentence. I've seen Dad studying each of the three men with an assessing gaze ever since he got here. It's not like I'm fucking them all over the house or anything while he's here, but I'm sure he's seen us together. Seen the way we all look at each other.

It hasn't even really occurred to any of us that we might need to hide it or try to be less openly affectionate around him, and that's just a sign of how comfortable we all are with each other now.

But Dad's seen it, and he can clearly tell that there's something going on between me and all three of them, not just me and Sloan.

Part of me wants to try and make him finish his sentence so that maybe I can worm out of this conversation if he doesn't, but another part of me knows I can't hide it from him forever. The guys are a big part of my life, and so is Dad. Besides I'm not ashamed of my feelings for them.

I chew my lip as I crack eggs into the bowl, gazing down at them before answering him honestly.

"I'm with all of them," I say. "On paper, I'm Sloan's wife, but I love all three of them, and instead of having to choose, I get to be with all of them."

Dad's brows rise as I speak, but he doesn't seem disapproving, just surprised. He's been there for me when I got my heart broken by some idiot boy or other in high school, so I know what he looks like when he's ready to defend me, and this isn't it. Which is a relief.

"I had to put my trust in Sloan when Hugh started getting suspicious of me while I was trying to infiltrate the Jackals," he says. "Sloan saved my life, and he had no real reason to. Strategically, it probably would have made more sense for the Black Roses to let the Jackals kill me. But Sloan protected me. I always wondered why it was worth all the trouble, but now I think I understand exactly why he did it. It wasn't about me at all. It was because of you."

I can feel Dad's gaze on me as he finishes speaking, and I glance up at him to find that his expression is strained. I know he's probably thinking about everything I've been through since the night Gavin offered him the chance to pay off his debt to the Black Roses.

"I never should have let Hugh blackmail me into not throwing that fight," he murmurs. "I was trying to protect you from the truth, but I put you in the path of things far more dangerous than that. I don't know if I can ever forgive myself for it."

I open my mouth to tell him that I'm fine, that it's not

his fault. The last thing I want is for him to be eaten by guilt for this. Hugh is the one to blame, not Dad.

But he cuts me off, continuing on. "I've been so damn worried about you, Mercy. I hated that you got caught up in this, and I wished like hell that I could protect you better. But I'm glad that there are three men out there who would raze the world to keep you safe. I don't care if your relationship is unconventional." He gestures around us to encompass the whole house. "Everything about this is unconventional. If it makes you happy, then I'm happy for you. And I'm glad they have your back, come what may."

It's so much more than I could have hoped for, and I dust my floury hands on my pants and then throw my arms around him in a hug, heart swelling.

Ever since this thing between me and the guys became official, I've told myself it doesn't matter what anyone else thinks. And it doesn't. If Dad was pissed at me or ashamed of me, I wouldn't let it change how I feel about my men.

But his acceptance means a lot to me. Maybe he doesn't totally get it, but he clearly supports me no matter what, and that's enough for me.

I never knew it until now, but his relationship with Mom was born of violence and pain. *I* was born of pain. But the house I grew up in was happy and bright. So maybe dad knows more than I thought he did about finding joy in the darkest spaces, and about not questioning the good things we manage to find in this life, no matter how unconventional they are.

We break apart just as Rory comes in, lifting his nose in the air. "What's cooking in here?" he asks, grinning.

"Pancakes, in a second," I tell him. "I'm finishing up the batter now."

"From scratch, too?" He whistles. "Damn, we must have done something right."

"I can't imagine what it would have been," I shoot back with a smirk, finishing up the batter and going to turn the burner on to start heating up the griddle.

Rory pouts and then moves toward the coffee maker where the pot is still half full. "You're so mean, Hurricane. I give and I give and I give."

"Yeah, you give me a headache," I banter back with him, rolling my eyes.

Dad just laughs softly under his breath, stepping out of the way to pull down plates.

Levi and Sloan show up a little bit later, both of them greeting me and Dad with smiles and good mornings. It's so strange to have them all gathered here in the kitchen like this. I've cooked for them before, but the pancake thing has always been something traditional in my family. Sharing it with them makes this little family unit we're building between us feel even more real, and I like it.

I *love* it, a hell of a fucking lot.

Sloan and the others pour juice and get knives and

forks and syrup, and we all sit around the island with our plates, tucking in.

"Oh shit, these are good," Rory groans, demolishing half a pancake in one bite. "I think I'm addicted already."

"Uh oh, Mercy." Levi winks at me. "You've created a monster. He's gonna want these all the time now."

"Not *all* the time," Rory corrects him. "Just on special occasions. Weekends. You know."

Sloan rolls his eyes and pours syrup over his plate. "She's not your personal chef, Rory. You can make pancakes too, if you want them so bad."

"Of course I can make them." Rory's eyes light up, and he turns to me, waggling his eyebrows. "Will you teach me the secret recipe, Hurricane? I promise I'll bring you breakfast in bed."

I laugh, dragging a bit of pancake through the syrup on my plate. "I could be talked into sharing the traditional family recipe. What's mine is yours now, after all."

"Fuck, yeah."

He leans over and gives me a kiss, which is sweeter than usual since he's still got the taste of maple syrup on his lips.

We get through most of the pancakes before the conversation moves to war planning, as it always does. The guys talk strategy, running over the plan for the fiftieth time so they can check it for anything that might pop up and make something go wrong.

I watch Dad scan the guys with his gaze as they talk through it, and I can see that he likes them.

It makes my heart swell, and I bite back a smile, glancing away so I don't break the moment.

We all had a fucking terrible beginning, but things are so different now.

Sometimes out of the ashes of the past, something amazing can grow.

21

EVERY DAY that passes brings us closer and closer to go time.

We can't afford to delay too long, so at some point, the plan has to be good enough. It's set, and we need to put it into action soon. A few days after we all have breakfast together, Sloan decides that it's as good as it's going to get, and tomorrow is the day.

That puts an atmosphere of determination and tension over the whole house, making the air so thick that it's hard to breathe.

We have to prepare. We have to be ready.

I go down to the basement, needing to burn off some excess energy and push out the last bit of adrenaline and fear that course through me. So many things could go wrong here, but we can't focus on that. We can't let ourselves get bogged down in the *what ifs* before we've even started.

Rory comes down with me, and we work out hard together. He holds the bag for a while, steadying it while I punch it hard and fast. My arms burn, and Rory's green eyes bore into me. It's possibly the most serious I've ever seen him look, and he doesn't let up.

"Harder," he says, and there's no sex joke waiting in the wings. "Faster," he urges me, and I do what I can. I give it my all, picturing a Jackal with a gun in the place of the bag and punching the shit out of my imaginary opponent.

We take a break to drink water, and I wipe the sweat from my face. I expect Rory to go for the bag again, but instead, he comes to stand in the middle of the room. He rolls his shoulders and neck, limbering up, and I eye him curiously.

"We should spar," he says with a smile. "It's been a while."

He's right. I don't think we've gone at it since that first time when I was still new here and so angry at all of them. He teased me then, trying to get me worked up enough to lash out and really show him what I could do.

Now I don't need that motivation. I don't have any plans of holding back. Not because I want to impress him and get him to take me seriously, but because I need us both to know that I'm ready for this.

My arms are still burning from hitting the bag, but I ignore that. When it comes to a real fight, I might already be tired and worn down, but that doesn't mean I'll get to stop. I have to be ready for anything, so I finish my drink of water and come to the middle of the room with Rory, facing off against him.

He's still the only one of the guys who has fighting experience like my dad does. Knock down, all out in the ring fighting. The way I learned it. His body easily settles into the stance that will give him the most freedom of movement, and I drop into my own.

Rory's arm is healed up enough that he's barely favoring it at all anymore, and he doesn't seem bothered by using it. Still, I won't go for any cheap shots there at all.

"You going to show me what you've got, Hurricane?" he asks, and then lunges before I have time to respond.

He's fast, but he's also bigger than I am, so I have time to respond, even though it was a surprise move. I twist out of the way and get behind him, hooking my ankle around his to try and bring him down.

He manages to keep his balance, but only just, and when he whips around to face me, there's a smile in his eyes. "Good," he says.

He doesn't go easy on me at all. Every move is a test, and a good one. Rory might not fight like this often, but it's clear that he hasn't forgotten any of the fundamentals. He's clever and quick, and matching and evading his moves forces me to think on my feet and draw on my instincts.

He catches me in a hold at one point, drawing my arm behind me and twisting it up painfully. I bite my lip on the noise of pain and throw my head back, catching him in the chest and throat hard enough that he grunts and lets go.

We go back and forth, trading light, superficial blows and trying to get one over on each other. Rory has determination in his eyes, but I don't think it's about him trying to beat me. I think we both just need this release.

We're giving it everything we've got, and I keep up with him easily enough, even when he starts pushing harder, trying to trip me up or make me make a mistake. I don't fall for it, and I'm impressed with how much I've learned and how much better my reflexes are, compared to when I first got here.

I was so full of anger and righteous indignation back then, but now I'm driven by wanting to keep everyone safe. Maybe that makes it easier, or maybe I've just gotten better. It's hard to say.

Either way, I feel better about whatever is to come because I think I can handle it.

Rory catches me in a grapple, and I let him. We go down to the floor, and he pins me with a gloating smile. I let him hold it for about three seconds and then wrap my legs around his waist. Heat flares in his eyes, and I use that to my advantage, throwing my weight to one side so we end up rolling.

I land on top of him, hands on his shoulders, lightly pinning him to the floor.

"Getting sloppy," I tease. "I didn't think you'd fall for that."

"You knew I'd fall for that," he shoots back. And he's not wrong.

The heat is still there in his eyes, and it flares between us as well. Being on top of him like this takes me back again to that first time, where even though I was so mad at him and so ready to kick his ass, we ended up rolling around on the floor down here, making out, unable to deny the attraction.

My chest heaves as I pant for breath, staring down at him and the hungry look on his face.

"If your dad wasn't in the house, I'd fuck your brains out right now," Rory says, and I can hear how much he means it in the low rasp of his voice.

I grin and lick my lips. "Dad is going over strategy with Sloan right now," I point out. "And I locked the door."

His eyes go even darker, the black pushing out almost all the green at this point. In a move too fast for me to track, he flips me over onto my back, and his hands go to the waistband of my workout leggings, dragging them down my legs.

I swallow hard, arching my hips to help him get them off, heart beating fast from the exertion of our sparring and also from the anticipation of this. I can feel my body already responding, nipples going hard in my sports bra and my pussy getting wet with interest in where this seems to be going.

Rory's hands are big and rough, and he puts one of them on my stomach, pushing me back down until I'm flat on the floor. The other goes between my legs, cupping the heat of my pussy for a second, like he's just feeling it.

Or trying to work me up even more.

I whine softly in the back of my throat, trying to grind against that hand and get some friction or touch or something. Rory just keeps me in place with that hand for a bit longer, smacking my pussy lightly in a way that makes my eyes fly open wide.

He smirks and then moves his hand so he can thumb at my clit. That only lasts for about a second or two. Something shifts in his face, going from playful and amused, to serious and wanting in the blink of an eye.

His fingers slide into me, and he thrusts them hard and deep, working me open until I'm gasping and leaking all over his hand. He watches me, still keeping me held down while I writhe and squirm all over the floor.

"Rory," I moan. "God. Fuck. I need more. Please."

Those seem to be the magic words. He rips his fingers

away and shoves his own pants down. My wetness glistens on his fingers, and he strokes them over his cock, like he's going to use it as lube.

Not that I need it. I'm already soaking wet for him, desperate for more and not caring how apparent it is. The same hunger I feel for him is there on his face for me, and he lines himself up and pushes into me in one go, sliding in with ease.

"Fuck," I groan, tipping my head back and arching against him. "Goddamn."

Usually this is another place where Rory would say something teasing to work me up, but his focus is singular. There's something unrestrained about him. Something desperate. Like he can't wait to be inside me.

I can feel the same thing in myself, the fear of what might happen when we go to the Jackals tomorrow making me cling to him even tighter.

I don't want to lose him. I don't want to lose any of them.

That same sentiment is echoed in every movement Rory makes. He draws himself back and out of me until just the tip of his cock is still inside me. And then he slams back in, bottoming out and hitting that spot I love at the same time.

I cry out his name and then bite down on my lip. Just because everyone else is upstairs doesn't mean I should be too loud. But it's hard to keep quiet when he's fucking me like this. When his cock slams into me hard and deep, taking my breath away and making it impossible to care about anything else.

It's like he wants to make sure there's no way I can forget this. Like he wants me to be able to feel it tomorrow when we launch the plan, a reminder that he's with me and he loves me.

I like the thought of that, and it makes me cling to him, hands at his shoulders, nails biting into the skin through the fabric of his shirt.

I can hear the wet sounds of his cock moving in me, and I wrap my legs around his waist again, forcing him in even deeper.

Rory groans at that, a sound that vibrates through both of us. His eyes were closed before, but they pop open now, and he stares down at me.

We're practically breathing together, both of us panting at the same time, sweat beading on our brows. We're lost in each other, with nothing else in the way, nothing else but this.

Somehow, even though it's hard and rough and dirty, it's also tender. I feel the love for him burning through me right along with all the pleasure. It feels so damned good, and I can't help but gasp his name as it starts to build and build, spreading out from my center to the rest of my body.

I can feel myself going tighter around him, my pussy spasming as the sensation takes over.

Rory seems to love it, the tell-tale signs of my impending orgasm making him move to fuck me even harder.

"You're so fucking good, Mercy," he pants, eyes locked on mine. "You feel so goddamn good. So goddamn perfect."

I open my mouth to respond, but no words come out. Just the desperate moans I can't hold back.

Rory chuckles breathlessly and drives in even harder, slamming right into that spot. I just about manage to bite down on my lip hard enough to hold back the scream that wants to break free, turning it into something muffled and muted.

"Good girl," he teases. "Wouldn't want anyone to know you're down here getting a very different kind of workout."

I wouldn't want my dad to know for sure, but the others? Yeah, I'd be fine with them knowing. I don't have the breath to say that, so I can only hope that Rory gets the message from looking into my eyes and listening to the little noises I'm still making.

"Come on, Hurricane," he urges me, using the same voice he used before when we were sparring. "Come for me. I wanna feel you come all over my cock. And then I wanna come so deep inside you, you won't be able to forget it."

So my hunch before was right. Rory's definitely going to get what he wants because I don't think I could hold back the tide of pleasure roaring through me if I wanted to. And I definitely don't want to.

Each time he batters his cock into me, it just pushes me even closer to my breaking point, and I feel like I'm burning alive, but in the best way.

"Come on," he urges me, and I can tell from how tight his voice is that's he's right on the edge of coming himself.

That thought is enough, and I get pitched headlong right into my orgasm. Again, I have to bite down on the scream so it doesn't burst out and echo everywhere, but it's a close thing. My body shakes and bucks under him, and I gasp for breath.

My pussy clenches around him, and he gives me what I want, following me over the edge with his own orgasm. I can feel him coming in hot spurts, and in the aftershocks of my pleasure, I settle into a bone deep satisfaction.

"Fuck," I manage, still trying to get my breathing back.

I'm sweaty and sated, and Rory looks the same. The grin comes back to his face, and he leans down to kiss me, sweet and soft, which is a contrast to everything else that's happened here today. I still love it, though.

"You're the best, did you know that?" Rory says, drawing back enough that he can see my face. "I love fighting with you like that, and I think you already know I love fucking you. I love how fucking tough you are."

I laugh softly and he kisses me again.

"I mean it," he says. "I'm glad Piper is going to grow up with two strong women as her role models. She'll have two amazing moms."

My heart flips a little to hear that. It seems like a fucking huge responsibility to be a part of the little family unit that cares for Piper, but I love that kid, and I love Rory.

And when I lean up to kiss him again, I make sure he knows it.

LATER THAT NIGHT, after dinner and a nice long shower, I crawl into bed. I'm trying to keep the little bit of calm that I've built up in myself so I don't spiral out of control back into the fear and worry for what might happen tomorrow. Worrying about it won't change anything, and while I don't really believe in fate or anything like that, it can't hurt to try and think positively about it all.

I slide between the sheets and lay there, trying to sleep. I close my eyes and take deep breaths, letting them out slowly. I try to clear my mind of anything but sleepy, tired thoughts. My body is worn out from going at it with Rory in every sense of the word, but my brain refuses to get the message.

I know I need the rest, but I can't make myself fall asleep.

A few moments later, my door cracks open, and in the darkness I see Levi step in.

"I think I could use some company tonight," he murmurs softly.

I smile at him and pat the other side of the bed. "Company, I've got."

He gets in and curls up next to me, pulling me into his embrace.

"I couldn't sleep," I admit, relaxing even more in his hold.

"I figured. That's another reason why I came."

My heart warms, and I settle closer to him.

Levi wraps his arms tighter around me, nuzzling against my neck a little. "You know," he murmurs. "Sometimes I kick myself for not pursuing you harder after our hook up a year ago. I knew even then that you were someone special, and I wanted more."

I smile at that. "Even then, huh?"

"Mmhmm. But then I think that no matter how fucked up parts of it were, maybe everything happened just the way it was supposed to. Because every little step brought us to this moment, right now. And the way things are now is perfect. I couldn't ask for anything else."

I turn to face him in the bed, smiling softly in the darkness of the room. "You're right," I whisper back. "It is perfect. Even after everything that happened."

He smiles back and kisses me softly. It's not a kiss that plans to get carried away, just one that we're sharing between us. A physical expression of the words we already said.

It grows a bit, into us making out, touching each other gently. He rolls me onto my back, his hands roaming over my body, squeezing and massaging my breasts before delving lower and dipping beneath the waistband of my shorts and panties.

A moan escapes my lips when he drags a finger through my folds, but even though I can feel his cock pressing against my hip, he doesn't rush at all. Instead, he works me up slowly and gently, pushing me to the brink with methodical strokes of his fingers and deep, toe-curling kisses.

I reach down and grip his forearm when I come, arching my hips off the bed so that his fingers slip inside my clenching pussy, and he groans into my mouth.

He leans back enough for me to peel my tank top off, shucking his own shirt with one hand. We kick off the rest of our clothes, tossing them to the floor, and when he settles between my legs, the head of his cock brushes my clit, making me shiver.

"Fuck, Mercy. You're so wet. So fucking tight for me."

His words are a whisper against my lips, and as he

speaks, he slides inside me, letting me feel every inch of him. I can still feel the echoes of Rory's touches from earlier today, and of Sloan's from when I climbed in bed with him last night, and as Levi bottoms out inside me, it's like he's completing some kind of circuit, making me whole in a way that nothing else could.

We fuck just like we kissed earlier—like we're not in any hurry, not racing to the finish line. Like we have all the time in the world.

I hope like hell we do.

That thought makes me cling to him a little tighter, burying my hands in his hair as he dips his head to bite and suck at my nipples. He tugs on them with his teeth, sending that burst of pleasure and pain through me that he knows I love so much, and I fall apart around him, locking my legs around his waist as my pussy milks his cock.

"God... oh fuck... fuck!"

He empties himself after a few more strokes, his methodical self-control finally collapsing as he slams into me hard and deep. Then he drops his head to my chest again, bracing part of his bodyweight on his arms as he covers every inch of me that he can reach with soft, warm kisses. He's still inside me, and I arch my back a little to give him better access, loving that even in the aftermath, neither of us wants to stop touching.

He pulls out after a long while, padding to the bathroom for a towel to help me clean up. Then he lies back down beside me and pulls the blankets up over us both.

When he gathers me into his arms, curling his body around mine, I finally feel myself relaxing. My brain catches up to my body, finally realizing that it's late, and it's time to sleep. Leave it to Levi to come in and settle me so completely with his down-to-earth, easy-going way.

I love him, and it's so much easier to drift off to sleep in his arms than it would have been alone.

22

THE NEXT DAY, it's go time.

No more waiting.

No more planning.

We'll either win today... or we'll probably die.

An eerie sort of calm fills me even as I have that thought. I've always been better with *doing*, with having a plan and carrying it out, than with sitting back or biding my time. I don't like waiting, so it's almost a relief to finally be putting things into action.

I can tell the guys are in the same headspace I am, and we go through the day with grim determination. We have to wait until evening to move out, and it's a struggle to do things like make lunch and handle the dishes while we know what's waiting ahead for us, but we manage to do it.

Once it's late enough, we get ready to head out, taking

care of the last few details and double-checking our supplies.

Scarlett comes over before we leave. She knows what we're doing, and she definitely knows how dangerous it will be. I can see the worry in her eyes when she hugs me tightly.

"Be careful," she says, voice low and insistent. "Please."

"I'm always careful," I tell her, and it's more true now than it ever has been, really. I *am* careful, or as careful as I can be. It's just that life has gotten more dangerous around me.

She swallows hard and nods, stepping back.

The guys are in the living room, and they look at me while we stand there. I know there's so much we all want to say to each other. Promises that we'll get each other through this, that we won't let anything stop us. That the plan will work and we'll all come out of it in one piece.

No one really seems to know how to start.

Sloan, who has always been better with actions than words, pulls me into a hug. He holds me for a bit, his face pressed to the top of my head, like he doesn't want to let me go. I cling to him just as hard, my fingers digging into his muscled back through the fabric of his shirt.

When he finally draws back enough to look at me, his eyes are serious. "You remember what I promised you?" he murmurs.

I cock an eyebrow at him, grinning a little as I try to lighten the mood. "Which thing? You make a lot of promises."

"That I'll keep you safe. I'm not going to let anything happen to you."

Each word sounds like a firm oath, and I know he means it completely. My smile slips away as I gaze into his steel gray eyes.

"I know," I tell him, delving my fingers into the hair at the nape of his neck. "I know."

He nods and then draws me into a kiss, clearly not caring that Scarlett and my dad are right there watching us. I don't care either. They both know about me and the guys anyway. This man is my husband, and I'm not willing to die without making sure he knows exactly how I feel about him first.

Our kiss is soft and way too short, but definitely not lacking in feeling and meaning, and when Sloan finally draws away, Rory steps in to take his place.

Just like yesterday, his eyes are serious. There's a smile on his face, but it's not the one he usually wears. He's in *go* mode, ready to get this done, but I can tell that he's just as full of love for me as Sloan is.

"You're strong, Hurricane," he reminds me. "There's a reason I call you that, you know. It's because you're a fucking force of nature. We'll all get through this."

I nod at him, and he pulls me into a crushing hug. We

share a kiss, just as short and intense as the one I shared with Sloan, and then he lets Levi step in.

He smiles at me, tucking a few strands of my dark hair away from my face. The strong line of his jaw looks even more pronounced from the tension I know he's carrying there, but his eyes are warm as he gazes down at me.

"I don't think there's anything I can say that they haven't already," he tells me softly. "We'll protect you, but I also know that you don't need us to look out for you all the time. You can handle yourself. You're strong and smart. We've been over this plan so many times we all know it backward and forward. Everything will work out. Promise."

That's not a promise I'll be able to hold him to if things go wrong and none of us live to see tomorrow. But the words help anyway. His positivity and optimism help, keeping me from getting lost in a torrent of horrible *what ifs*.

"I love you," I murmur. "All of you. So fucking much."

I feel stronger, having them with me, knowing that we're all pulling for the same thing. I feel like with them at my side, there's nothing we can't do.

They go back to making sure everything is ready, loading up the supplies into the car. Scarlett takes her leave, and that leaves me and Dad alone in the living room for a moment.

It's weird to look at him now, as he is. Little things have

been done to make him look more like Hugh. Scarlett, with her skill at makeup, used some shading and highlights to change aspects of his features to match Hugh's more closely.

His nose looks thinner, and his eyes are sharper, and I have to look at him closely to see past all that. He looks like my dad, like the man I've known my whole life, but also... not.

It's disconcerting, but that's good. It means we might actually pull this ruse off.

"This is so damn strange," Dad says. He's finally stopped looking into the mirror, taking in the changes in his reflection. "I don't think I like it."

I laugh and pat his shoulder. "Don't worry. Anyone who knows you knows you aren't like him. You're nothing like him."

He smiles gratefully at me, taking my hand from his shoulder and gripping it tightly. Then he glances in the direction the men went, gazing after them before turning back to me.

"They all really love you, huh?" he asks. "Your men. They'll do whatever it takes to make sure you come out of this in one piece."

"They do." I can see the worry in his eyes, and I wish I could make it go away, but I know that's not possible. "And I feel the same way about them. We're *all* coming out of this alive."

"Yes." Dad nods grimly. "We are."

His voice goes hoarse on the last words, and he reaches out and pulls me into a hug. I hug him right back, clinging to him as I breathe in his familiar scent.

"I love you, Mercy," he whispers. "More than anything. We're going to finish this, and then we can get back to our lives."

"I love you too."

The door opens, and Sloan comes back in, his face serious.

"I got the call," he says. "Hugh has left the Jackals' headquarters. We have to go now."

Dad and I both nod, and we get in the car to head out.

From the information the guys have been collecting over the last few days, they know exactly where the Jackals' headquarters is located. It's a building they were already aware of and knew was an important Jackal location, but now we're reasonably sure that it's where they operate from. Where most of the higher-level players in the gang will be at any given time.

It's the heart of their organization.

And tonight, we're going to make that heart stop beating.

We have no way of knowing how long Hugh will be gone or how much time we have, so we have to act fast. Him coming back in the middle of our operation would be a fucking disaster.

We all pile into the car, which is a bit of a tight fit, but we make it work. Sloan drives quickly, turning the head-lights off as we enter Jackal territory. Everyone in the car is quiet, all of us lost in our own heads, getting ready for what's going to happen next.

We pull up to the curb a few blocks away from the building, around a corner and out of sight, then climb out of the car.

Unlike the last time we rolled up to a Jackal building, none of us are wearing bulletproof vests or anything. We have to look like we're not planning anything, after all, but I hate that it's necessary for our ruse. It means that if this goes wrong, we're that much more likely to die.

Sloan pops the trunk and pulls out the ropes that we brought with us. I give him my wrists, amused in a way I didn't think I would be when he comes over to tie them together. It's such a different set of circumstances than the last time we were like this, when he was so fucking angry with me, yanking me around while he tied my wrists so I couldn't run from him.

So much has changed since then. Back then, we were still trying to hate each other, and we didn't trust each other for shit. Now, there's no one I'd rather have by my side than him, Rory, and Levi.

The ropes are still scratchy, but there's a comfort that Sloan is the one who's doing this. He's gentle, his fingers brushing my wrists in a way that's soothing and grounding.

He's careful not to hurt me, and he ties the binds in a way that I can easily get out of when I need to.

"That good?" he asks when he's done.

I test the ropes, then nod. "Yeah. Thanks."

Sloan gives me a little smile that makes warmth bloom in my chest, and then he leans in to kiss me. That helps settle me, even though I'm still not as nervous as I thought I would be, facing this sort of thing.

Once my binds are in place, the guys all turn to face Dad, ready to play their parts in this. It's hard to watch as he draws back and punches each one of them in the face, bloodying them up a bit. They all take it with no complaints, bearing the pain well, but I still wince at the sight of it. I hate that it's necessary, even though I know it is.

It has to look like there was a fight. Everyone knows the guys wouldn't come willingly with Hugh without putting up some resistance.

They rough their clothes up, tearing holes here and there, and smearing some of the blood around to make the effect work.

"Ready?" Dad asks us all once the job has been done well enough.

Everyone nods, and we all start to move out, heading around the corner and down the quiet, dark street.

They keep me behind them for the most part, until we get near enough to the building. Then I take my position closer to Dad, giving him a tense smile to show I'm ready for this.

Dad pulls out a gun and fires it once into the air before pressing the barrel against my temple.

It doesn't take more than a matter of seconds before the sound draws attention, and backup in the form of a group of Jackals come running out of the building toward the source of the sound and us.

Dad takes a deep breath and snarls at Sloan, Levi, and Rory, his entire demeanor changing in an instant.

"I'll shoot her right here and now," he growls. "You think I won't? You stole her from me last time, but that ends tonight."

He laughs, and it's a chilling sound that I've never heard him make before.

The Jackals come tearing around the corner, and my stomach clenches into a tight knot. If they react too quickly, the men I love could die. Hugh's soldiers could just open fire right here and now and take them out, and all of this will be for nothing.

But just as we were counting on, they don't fire right away, even though they have their guns out and aimed.

My three men step back, holding their hands up, looking angry and pissed while they play their roles. I know it's all an act, all faked for the benefit of the Jackals, but my body can barely tell the difference. Adrenaline is surging through my veins, and I can feel my heart thudding hard in my chest.

"That's right," Dad says. "You wouldn't want anything to happen to her, would you? Your little wife. Your little *whore*."

He says it mockingly, and my stomach twists. It's all a lie, but the words still sting.

Levi's eyes flash with what looks like real anger, and Rory looks pissed as fuck too. No matter who says it, their instinct to protect me is strong enough that hearing anyone call me a whore probably makes them want to fight. Sloan spits in Dad's direction, the way he would if this were a real threat, probably.

"Take them alive," Dad snaps to the gathered Jackals. "We can use them. As long as we have her, they'll do what I say." He presses the gun more firmly to my temple. "And there's plenty we can get out of them before we decide what to do with them. Bring them inside."

That's the key to all of this.

We *have* to get inside under the ruse that Dad is Hugh.

The guys and I are bait, the lure that will hopefully sell this whole lie.

Now we just have to hope it works, or we'll die before we even get inside the Jackals' den.

23

THERE's a heart-stopping moment where the Jackals all just stare at Dad, and I'm sure they've already seen through his disguise.

But then one of them nods, and they all move forward, closing in on my men and grabbing them roughly. We're badly outnumbered right now, but as long as the Jackals think they're under orders not to kill them, it should be fine.

The enemy gang members start dragging the guys into the building, and Dad follows, still keeping a tight hold on me. My nerves are on edge, making my breath come in shuddery gasps, but I don't try to hide my fear. There's no reason to, when it helps us sell the pretense that I'm Dad's captive, afraid for my life and those of my men.

It's dark on the street, since a lot of the streetlamps out here have burned out or been shot out. Once we get into the light inside the building, it'll be easier to see the differences between Hugh and Dad, so the guys start to struggle more as we pass through the doorway, trying to jerk away from the men holding them so the attention stays on them and not Dad.

"Get your fucking hands off me," Rory snaps, jerking away from the big bruiser who has a hold on him. "You son of a bitch."

"You're lucky we're not supposed to kill you," the bruiser growls back, tightening his grip.

"Because your leader is a fucking coward who takes hostages instead of fighting like a man," Levi chimes in bitterly.

"Don't worry," one of the Jackals says with a harsh laugh. "I'm sure we'll all be *real* nice to your girlfriend."

Sloan's head snaps around, a murderous look overtaking his features. He looks like he's going to launch himself at the asshole for even opening his mouth, and the smaller, wiry guy holding on to Sloan digs his gun deeper into Sloan's back.

"None of that now. Keep walking."

"You sure we can't just get rid of them now?" one of them turns to ask Dad. "They're gonna be trouble."

Dad just shakes his head, keeping his face hard and neutral. "We can use them, and I want to get every piece of information I can out of them before we kill them. We may even be able to use them as hostages to force the Black

Roses to negotiate with us. If they decide to be trouble, there are ways to deal with that."

It sounds ominous, and I have no doubt that he's drawing on his knowledge of his brother to come up with something Hugh would actually say and do. Until recently, they hadn't seen each other in years, but they grew up together, so I'm sure he knows his brother well. And the time he spent trying to infiltrate the Jackals earlier probably helped him learn more about who is brother is now. Hopefully, he picked up enough of his speech patterns and mannerisms to sell this.

The other Jackals don't say anything as they keep shoving us farther into the building. We pass a lot of the men that Sloan's spies have identified as the higher-ups in the Jackals' order. They see us with who they assume is Hugh, and I can only imagine word is going to spread through the building pretty quickly that he has some high-value hostages right now.

We're dragged into a room that looks like it must be used for interrogations and those kinds of things.

The Jackals who aren't holding my men at gunpoint fan out along the walls and covering the exits, looking like they're just waiting for one of us to make a wrong move so they can retaliate. All the bad blood between the two gangs is very apparent, and I force myself to stay calm.

We have a plan.

It'll all be fine.

Dad pushes me down into a chair in the middle of the room and ties me to it, jerking his head at the Jackals behind him. "Tie them up too. I want to have a little chat with them all."

The gang members don't hesitate to follow his command, shoving all three of my men roughly into chairs and yanking their hands behind their backs as ropes are produced to tie them up. I know that, unlike my binds, theirs are real, and it sends a tremor of fear through me to think about how vulnerable we've made ourselves to sell this part of our deception.

If any of the Jackals figure out that my father isn't Hugh now, they could execute each of the men I love before any of us could even move to fight back.

That won't happen. Dad knows his brother. He's doing well.

"You're making a big mistake," Sloan grunts, straining against his bonds as he glares at Dad. "If you think my father will let this go without retaliation, you're wrong. He'll—"

My dad strides over and backhands him across the face, making his head whip to the side. The gathered Jackals all react with glee, some of them making noises of approval while others grin. I can see the muscles straining in Sloan's neck, and I know how much effort it must be taking to restrain his natural impulse to fight back. He looks back at my father with his lips curled back in a snarl, then spits a bloody gob of saliva at his feet.

"Fuck you."

Dad chuckles. "Big words. But I'm not worried about you *or* Gavin. The Black Roses are weak, and no one is weaker than your father."

Sloan's jaw clenches, his nostrils flaring as his chest heaves. He glares in furious silence at my father, who glances at the assembled Jackals who escorted us into the room.

"Leave us," Dad commands. "All of you."

There's a moment of silence, and a few of the Jackals look around at each other in surprise. Fuck. This is obviously out of character for the role Dad is supposed to be playing, and I can practically feel the atmosphere in the room shift as everyone tries to figure out what's going on.

My heart thuds so heavily that it rattles my ribs, and I do my best to keep my thoughts from showing on my face.

Come on. Just go, you fuckers. Leave.

Dad turns to the men who stand at the perimeter of the room—lower-level guards, I'm guessing.

"Go!" he barks in a tone I've never heard him use before. The guards jerk to attention and then quickly file out of the room, obviously afraid of provoking their leader's wrath.

A few other men linger though, and I lick my lips as it becomes nearly impossible to breathe. One of them, a man with dark hair that hangs down to his shoulders, steps forward and glances at my men before looking at Dad.

"Are you sure, sir?"

Instead of nearly shouting the command like he did before, Dad let's his features relax a little. He steps forward, murmuring something to the shaggy-haired man. I know what he's saying, even though I can't hear the words. He's using the codes I taught him—the one that strange girl who tracked me down at the boutique made me memorize.

My pulse spikes again as a whole new kind of worry overtakes me. That woman could've been fucking with me. She could've been trying to set us up, intentionally feeding us bad intel. She could've been wrong about the codes, and even if she was right, it's possible that Hugh could've changed them by now.

Glancing sideways, I catch Levi's gaze. His brown eyes are steady and reassuring, and keep looking at him as I drag in a slow breath and release it. If I'm about to die, I wouldn't mind if his eyes are the last thing I see.

But then the man Dad is speaking to makes a soft noise in his throat.

I wrench my focus back to him in time to see him nod and step back, then turn toward the door, jerking his head toward the others to indicate they should follow. Dad speaks to one other Jackal member, and whatever code he gives, it seems to fool that man too. In the space of less than a minute, the room has cleared out entirely.

The air leaves my lungs in a sharp rush, and I look up at Dad with wide eyes.

"You did it," I breathe, keeping my voice low.

He nods, looking relieved, terrified, and determined all at once. He waits for a few moments that seem to last forever, then gives me another sharp nod before turning and striding over to the chairs where the men are tied.

I quickly undo the binds on my wrists and the ones strapping me to the chair beneath me, then hurry over and help Dad untie the guys. It takes longer than I'd like, especially since every second counts right now, but after a minute or two, all three of them are free.

"You know what to do," Dad says shortly.

And we do. We spent hours talking over this, so there's no hesitation as all five of us begin to pull out the C-4 that's been strapped to our bodies, hidden beneath our clothes where the Jackals wouldn't see it. The bulk of it is being carried by me and Dad, since it was less likely that the Jackals would try to search either of us, but the guys have some strapped to their legs and hidden in their shoes.

It doesn't take long for us to pull it all out, and then we move quickly to place the clay-like substance at strategic points around the room, making sure each lump is armed with a charge. My racing pulse slows a little as we work, despite the nerves that still rampage through my body. I'm better at doing than sitting, and having a task to focus on helps channel my nervous energy.

When I've placed the last of the C-4 I was in charge of, I glance around at the guys and Dad. Rory is just finishing up, setting a lump of the explosives in place on the far side of the room, and he dusts off his hands as he straightens.

"Good to go," he says quietly, his green eyes burning the same kind of determination I can feel in myself. "Let's get the fuck out of here."

This will be the hardest part. We were able to get in under the ruse of Dad being Hugh, but now we need to get out without any of the Jackals coming into this room. Dad can't exactly call them all back and have them escort us out, and we need to be well away from the building before I press the button that will detonate the explosives.

So we need to keep playing our roles, but also go for stealth as much as possible. It's a tricky balancing act, and I can feel sweat trickling down my back as Dad quickly binds each of our wrists again, using the same slip knots that Sloan used when he tied me up outside. Then he pulls his gun from the waistband of his pants and wraps one arm around my torso, pinning my back to his front as he presses the gun to my temple.

Standing like this, I can feel his heart beating as hard as mine is, and it grounds me a little, reminding me that I'm not the only one who's terrified. He's scared too, but my dad is one of the best fighters I know. He knows how to push through fear and adrenaline and fight smart, and he taught me to do the same.

We can make it out of here.

We've come this far.

"Ready?" he murmurs.

"Yeah."

He cracks the door and peers out, then nods and gestures to my three men. They go first, walking a few steps ahead of us, and Dad follows with the gun still pressed to my temple. If we pass any Jackals, it'll look like Dad is escorting the men using the threat of killing me as leverage to make them comply. It's odd for him to be doing it alone, just like it was a little out of character for him to want to be left alone in the room with all of us, but I have to believe he can sell it.

We start making our way toward the building's exit. This time, instead of struggling or drawing attention, my men are walking with their heads down, looking beaten and cowed and doing everything they can not to draw attention. We take a slightly different route than the one we took when we entered, avoiding passing through the most heavily populated part of the building, but we can't avoid other people entirely.

When we pass by a couple of Jackals standing together in a hallway, my skin prickles with tension. They glance our way, immediately standing at attention when they see Dad, but he jerks his head in a way that's obviously meant to dismiss them, shoving me forward and making me walk a bit faster.

My shoulders bunch with tension as we leave the three men behind, but before I can even allow myself a breath of relief, a voice calls out from behind us.

"Hugh!"

I feel my father suck in a breath behind me.

"Keep walking," he hisses, and we pick up our pace even more.

"Hugh! Wait." The deep voice is vaguely familiar, and as the man draws up beside us, I realize why.

It's one of the men who was in the room after Hugh abducted me, the day Niko tried to rape me.

My stomach flip-flops, and I keep my gaze focused straight ahead as Dad glances over at him.

"Not now," Dad grunts. "Whatever you need, it can wait. I'm dealing with our prisoners."

"Yeah, that's the problem." The man's gaze flicks to me, his eyes narrowing. "After Niko died, you said this one was going to be mine instead. That once we recaptured her, I could punish her for what she and her men did to him."

"There's been a change of plans," Dad says gruffly, his grip on me tightening. "She's needed for another purpose."

The Jackal's jaw clenches. He shoots a glance at the three men walking ahead of us, then leans in to talk to Dad in a low, urgent tone. "You said I *deserved* this. For being loyal to you. Others doubted you when you took over, and for the way things have been going since then, but I never did. I stood by you. I did whatever you wanted. And you promised I'd be rewarded for that."

"And so you will," Dad grits out. "But this is a personal matter. Mercy is my daughter. My *blood*. You need to understand that."

He puts steel in his tone, warning the guy to back off, but the man doesn't seem to care. He just keeps following us as we make our way through the building, and then he steps in front of me and Dad entirely, cutting off our path.

"I'm just saying that's bad for business." His fingers tap against his thigh. "You can't go around making promises and not keeping them. That's not how you operate, is it?"

"I do what's necessary."

The Jackal makes a noise in his throat. "Yeah, I believe that. But you remember what you told me, don't you? After Niko took a bullet between his eyes, and I asked you whether this little bitch is really worth all this trouble?"

"Of course I remember, and I'm telling you that you will have what you want, once I'm done."

The big man cocks his head, taking a small step closer to us. "No. What did you say to me, Hugh? What did you promise me exactly?"

Oh, fuck.

The question is too pointed, and there's no way for Dad to know the answer to that. I hold my breath, my entire body so on edge that my skin aches.

Fuck, fuck, fuck.

Dad falters for a second, and that seems to be all the burly man needs to prove himself right. His eyes flash with anger and shock, and in a smooth motion, he draws his gun.

"That's what I thought. You're not Hugh. He doesn't go back on his word, and if he does, he doesn't put up with being questioned about it for so long."

Realizing the ruse is up, Dad shoves me away from him, out of the line of fire. The Jackal's gun goes off just as Levi barrels into him with his shoulder, and his shot goes wide, missing Dad. Without giving the man a chance to recover or aim again, Dad puts a bullet between his eyes, just like Niko got.

But now our cover is well and truly blown.

Shouts sound from deeper inside the building, and the men we passed in the hall earlier all come tearing after us. Rory scoops up the dead Jackal's gun and shoots at them. Dad does the same, firing off two rounds and clipping one of the men before turning to me.

"Run!"

I don't need him to tell me twice. With Sloan and Levi on either side of me, I bolt down the hallway. Rory and Dad are right behind us, still firing at our pursuers to hold them off.

I can hear more shouts in the distance, but we're so close to the exit now.

We're so fucking close.

My chest heaves as I keep my head down and sprint, digging into my pocket for the device that will detonate the explosives.

We burst through the door and out into the night, and just as I'm about to put on an extra burst of speed, Levi, who's a step in front of me, skids to a stop.

I crash into his back, my heart thundering.

What the hell?

I look up to see what happened, and my breath catches in my throat.

It's Hugh. The *real* Hugh.

He's back, and he's standing there looking furious. When he sees me, he points his gun right at my chest, his eyes narrowed.

"What the fuck is going on here?" he demands, cold fury in his voice. When he sees Dad behind me, he looks even more pissed off. "Oscar. You're supposed to be dead."

My heart pounds in my chest, adrenaline and fear mingling together into a heady cocktail that makes my hands shake a little. Behind us, I can hear several of the Jackals who were pursuing us exiting the building, boxing us in between themselves and Hugh.

"Oh, Mercy." Hugh gives me a cruel, condescending look. "I wanted to give you a chance. But I should've killed you weeks ago."

"Do it," Sloan murmurs from behind me, and it takes

me a second to realize he's not talking to the man in front of us.

He's talking to me.

Oh. Fuck.

There are a million reasons why this is a bad idea. We're not far enough away from the building, and we left enough C-4 inside to level the place.

But we're out of options.

I glance sideways, catching Rory's gaze, and he gives me the tiniest nod. Tears sting my eyes, and I wish I could kiss him or hug him or tell him how fucking much he means to me. How much they've all changed my life.

But there's no time for any of that.

With trembling fingers, I press the button on the detonator in my hand, setting off the explosion we've rigged up.

There's a split second where nothing happens, and my heart drops all the way down to my stomach. Time seems to slow down for an instant, and then the explosion rips through the building, deafening and powerful.

The sound rings out, splitting the night and obliterating every other noise, and the force of it hits me in the back like a fucking truck.

24

THE AFTERMATH of the explosion is all dust clouds and the ringing of my ears.

Smoke and debris float through the darkness. The night air is dimly lit, and the building has been torn apart.

I drag myself up off the ground with a groan that I feel more than hear. Fuck, it feels like I *actually* got run over by a goddamn truck. I've got shrapnel wounds and bruises, my cheeks and arms stinging with rocks and bits of brick and wood and glass and whatever the hell else is embedded in my skin.

My head feels fuzzy, and the ringing in my ears is shrill and piercing. When I reach up to push my hair out of my face, my hand comes away wet with blood.

Everything seems muffled and slow moving, and it takes me a second to focus enough to get my bearings.

The first thing I notice is that I don't see the guys or

Dad. I don't know where they are, and a frantic look around doesn't make them appear. Fear rises inside me like a tidal wave, because even if we did manage to destroy the Jackals, it won't matter if we don't all come through this together.

I stagger on my feet a bit, swallowing hard. My throat is dry from the shock and the dust, and my tongue feels like sandpaper. I blink, peering through the billowing dust as my heart pounds out a staccato beat in my chest.

In the distance a little way away, there are shapes moving in the smoky darkness, and my heart lurches as I try to make them out. I take a step toward them, and then another, hoping they're friendly and not Jackals who might have managed to make it out of the building before it blew.

Once I'm close enough, the shapes come into focus, and my skin turns to ice.

It's Dad.

And Hugh.

They must've been thrown by the blast just like I was, and I can tell they're both still shaking off the effects of the explosion. But that hasn't stopped them from going after each other with fists and knees and elbows.

Dad's holding his own, all of his fight skills serving him well now, but there's a raw fury in Hugh that terrifies me. He's not going to give this up without a fight. His legacy has been destroyed, all of his most loyal soldiers taken down. He's got nothing left to lose, and I already know how vindictive and vicious he is.

He'll kill Oscar, brother or not. It makes no difference to him.

"Dad!" I call out, the sound of my own voice cutting through the muffled feeling in my ears.

Both men glance over at me, and that fills me with fury. Only one of them is my father, and it's not the one who'd pass a paternity test. For him to respond to that word is like a slap in the fucking face.

Dad's features go slack with relief for an instant as he realizes I'm alive. He turns back to the fight, but he's a second too slow. Hugh takes advantage of his brother's momentary distraction, rearing back and headbutting my dad in the throat, making him choke and stagger back.

The fucker pushes his advantage, slamming his shoulder into Dad's stomach and knocking him to the ground.

Hugh stands over him, breathing hard. There's an ugly, gloating look on his face, and a sort of grim satisfaction that he can't hide. He draws a gun from his waistband and aims it right for Dad, preparing to take him out.

Panic floods me, and I look around for something, *anything* I can use as a weapon. There's a rock or a chunk of blasted brick on the ground by my foot, and I don't hesitate long enough to figure out which one of those things it is. I just pick it up and throw it, aiming right for Hugh's fucking head.

It stuns him just in time, and when he fires, it goes wide, the bullet hitting the asphalt instead of Dad's face.

Hugh snarls in anger and whips around, aiming a shot for me before I can react.

The bullet grazes my arm, clipping me, and I yelp in shock and pain. Hugh keeps the gun raised, aimed right at my heart. His face is dirty from the explosion, and he looks like a cornered animal, eyes wide and teeth bared.

"You should have joined me when you had the chance," he says. "You *owed* me that. Then none of this would have had to happen."

"I'd rather die than join you," I spit. "You think raping my mother gives you any right to call yourself my *family*? If you really believe that, you're insane."

He scowls, his eyes dark with anger, glinting in the flames of the blasted out building. "And if you think I won't kill you because you're my daughter—"

"I am not your fucking daughter!" I cut him off, giving in to the rage that burns in my stomach as my shout echoes in the air around us.

He laughs, and it's a bitter, hollow sound. The gun stays steady in his hand as he steps closer to me. "Keep telling yourself that. Although I have to admit, I expected more from you. I always thought you were like me, but you're like your mother after all. Weak. Breakable. Pathetic."

Cold, animalistic fury rushes through me.

I don't even think. I just move so fast I surprise even myself, and maybe that's why I manage to catch Hugh off-guard too.

He pulls the trigger a second too late, but I'm already too close, shoving his arm aside as I hurl myself at him. The gun goes off right next to my head, making my ears ring, but I ignore it.

I aim an elbow at his face, catching him on the chin, and then grapple for the gun, trying to wrest it from his grip. We struggle for control of it, but when I manage to break his hold, I can't get my hand around the grip. The gun flies out of his hand and skitters over the ground several yards away.

Hugh grunts a curse, punching me in the stomach before he tries to get his hands around my neck.

No. Fuck, no.

Remembering the horror of having Niko's beefy hands choking the breath out of me, I don't give Hugh a chance to tighten his grip, slamming my forearms against his to break his hold.

He's not going to get the upper hand here. He's not going to win this.

I rear back and punch him across the face, sending him staggering away from me a few steps. When he looks back up at me, there's blood in the corner of his mouth and his eyes are cold.

"This is for Mom," I grit out. And then I hit him again with everything I have in me.

Hugh goes down to one knee from the force of my punch, blood and spit flying from his mouth. He lists to one side, and I pray that he'll go down, but when I step in for another punch, he recovers enough to sweep my legs out from under me.

He grins in triumph, one hand going to my throat again and the other fisting my hair. He yanks my head up by the hair, trying to slam it back into the pavement, but I twist in his hold, clawing at his wrist hard enough to leave bloody lines from my nails.

He hisses at the pain but doesn't let up.

Both hands go around my neck, and he starts squeezing with a force that makes me certain he's trying to kill me. He wants me out of the picture for good, and he's not afraid to do it himself.

My lungs burn, and I look around wildly as I struggle beneath him.

Just out of reach, I see another chunk of stone, and I stretch my arm out, trying to grab it. My fingers brush the jagged edges, and I try again, managing to shift the large chunk close enough to me to get my hand on it.

I choke down a half breath of air, and it hurts, but it

gives me enough to be able to start bashing the rock into Hugh's arm, making him let me go.

Before tonight, I would have said the fight with Hugh's big bruiser for my freedom from him was the hardest I've ever fought in my life. But this is something different.

We're both angry, both desperate, and neither one of us will stop short of killing the other.

It's knockdown, drag-out, dirty, and vicious.

We grapple with each other, rolling around on the concrete, each trying to get and keep the upper hand. My chest is heaving, my throat is sore from being choked, and my body aches from everything that's already happened tonight.

And Hugh uses my exhaustion to his advantage.

When one of my punches goes wide, he leans down, pinning me to the ground with a heavy forearm across my neck. His other hand reaches out sideways, and I think for a moment that he's winding up to hit me. But then a triumphant smile spreads across his face, and he straightens, releasing the pressure on my neck and gripping the gun he just picked up in both hands.

Fuck.

My breath catches in my throat. I lost track of where the gun landed, but our fighting brought us close enough to it for Hugh to reclaim his weapon, and he slides his finger over the trigger as he pants for breath.

"Say hi to your mom for me, will you?" he mutters.

But he never pulls the trigger.

A figure hurls itself out of the smoky darkness around us, and before I can even register that it's Sloan, he's knocked Hugh off of me. They land on the dusty pavement next to me, and Sloan's fist collides with Hugh's face. He straddles the older man, pinning him down just like Hugh pinned me, and before Hugh can raise the gun or react at all, another blow rains down on him.

And another.

And another.

And another.

It's a flurry of fists, each punch so vicious and hard that it sounds like wood snapping.

Sloan doesn't speak or even yell. He just keeps hitting and hitting until Hugh's body goes limp beneath him. And even then, he doesn't stop. There's nothing recognizable left of Hugh's face by the time Sloan lands his last punch, and as his fist falls for the final time, he lets out a feral, hoarse yell.

Staggering to his feet, Sloan snatches the gun from Hugh's limp hand and stands over the man's prone body.

Then he points it at Hugh's chest and empties every last bullet left in the clip.

25

My body feels numb, and my ears are still ringing, making everything around me feel like it's miles away. The ground is rough beneath my palms as I press up to sitting, staring at Sloan where he stands a few feet away from me.

He drops the gun and spits on Hugh's body, then turns toward me.

Even through the haze of smoke and the flickering light of the flames that light up the darkness, I can see every line of Sloan's face as our gazes meet.

He looks like an avenging angel, dirty and bloody as he towers over the body of his enemy.

And I scramble to my feet and run toward him.

Because he's *my* angel, dammit.

My beautiful, brutal angel.

He wraps his arms around me tightly as our bodies

collide, and I wheeze a little when he presses against my sore ribs, but I hug him back just as tight.

"You're okay?" he rasps, pulling back so he can look me over.

I nod. "Yeah, I'm in one piece. Are you?"

"Yes."

"Where are Levi and Rory?" I ask, licking my dry lips.

His face hardens. "I don't know. I got trapped under a chunk of concrete, and I couldn't find them when I woke up. You're the first person I saw. You and Hugh."

My stomach drops, making me feel dizzy and lightheaded.

Fuck, no. Please.

We can't have gotten through all of this just to lose them. I can't face the thought of going through life without two pieces of my heart.

"Rory! Levi!" I scream the words, spinning away from Sloan to scan the destruction around us.

Sloan grabs my hand, holding me steady and keeping me on my feet as we stagger toward the wreckage of the building, scanning the ground around it as he calls for his friends too.

"Mercy!"

I whip my head around to see Rory and Levi running toward us. They're both grimy and blood splattered, but they're on their feet. They're alive.

Tears blur my vision as a rush of relief so powerful it's

almost painful surges through me. I let out a choked sob and race to meet them, slipping on the chunks of rock and cement.

I reach Levi first, wrapping my arms around him and clinging to his back, and Rory envelops me in his arms too a second later.

"Thank fuck." Rory buries his face in my hair, breathing me in even though I have to smell like dust and blood and smoke more than anything good. "A couple of the Jackals made it out of the building before it blew. They got hit by the blast but recovered enough to try to take us down."

"Where are they now?" Sloan asks, his voice tight.

"Dead," Levi says shortly. "Where's Hugh?"

"Dead."

"Good," Rory grits out, finally stepping back from our tight embrace. "Where's your dad?"

"He fell." My mouth goes dry as a new wave of worry rushes through me. "But he's alive. Or at least, I think he is. Hugh fucking sucker punched him. Headbutted him and tried to kill him."

"Let's go."

Sloan jerks his head, and I cast around to get my bearings, then lead the men toward where I saw my dad go down.

He's still on the ground, passed out where he fell during his fight with Hugh, but when I kneel down and set my fingers to his neck, there's a pulse, and I can see the gentle rise and fall of his chest.

He's alive. Thank fuck.

The last vestiges of dread fade from my chest, and I sit back on my heels, taking deep breaths as I try to steady myself. It's been a long fucking night.

"Let's get the fuck out of here," Levi says, glancing around.

"Good goddamn idea." Rory chuckles, although he doesn't really sound amused.

There are enough dirty cops in this town that they'll look the other way about a lot of shit, but for something like this, there's no way they'll just cover it up or ignore it. Already, I can hear sirens in the distance.

Sloan and Rory grab dad and carry Dad to the car, sliding him into the back seat, and we all pile in. Then Sloan cranks the ignition and peels out, leaving the burning wreckage of the building and the bodies behind.

It's a quiet drive, all of us dirty and hurt and exhausted, so when Dad starts to stir with a little groan, I notice immediately.

I hug him when he opens his eyes, as best I can in the car, anyway, and he hugs me back, smoothing a hand over my hair.

"What happened?" he asks, glancing around. "Is everybody alright? Did everybody get out?"

"Yeah. We're all present and accounted for," I tell him.

I hesitate, remembering the sound of Sloan's fist hitting Hugh's face over and over, and of the bullets striking his body. I don't know which thing killed him, but I don't really care. "Hugh is dead."

I watch my dad's face as I speak, expecting to maybe see some flicker of pain in it. Hugh was his brother, after all, and sometimes family is more than a little complicated. Even with all the hate between them, it's possible there was love at some point too.

But all I see in my dad's features is relief. The same relief I felt when Sloan put the last bullet in Hugh's body.

"Then it's over," he says, letting out a breath. "Good."

As he drives, Sloan pulls out his phone to call Gavin and update him on what's going on. It's quiet enough in the car that I can pick up snatches of the conversation from both sides.

Gavin asks questions about the damage and how many of the Jackals were taken out in the blast, and Sloan answers him as thoroughly as he can, giving the details that we know. There's a lot we don't know, and a lot we'll have to sort through and figure out later—finding out exactly which members of the Jackals were eliminated by our strike tonight, and if there are any left who might try to rise up and become threats. But the job we set out to do was accomplished, and that's enough for now.

"Any casualties on our side?" I hear Gavin ask.

"None," Sloan says. "We're all out and alive. Some injuries, but nothing life threatening. It was a success."

There's a moment of silence while Gavin processes that. I know he was imagining a huge casualty list. Losing people he's in charge of, people he's responsible for.

But with Sloan's plan, it didn't have to come to that, and I imagine his father is relieved as hell about that.

He better be proud too. I know I am.

"Good job," he says finally. There's something in his tone that lets me know he feels the same pride that burns in my chest, and I let a smile pull at my lips. What Sloan accomplished is huge, and hopefully it will save us all a lot of danger and stress in the long run.

I hope this will mark the beginning of Gavin ceding more control to Sloan over time. It seems like things have improved between them a little, at least. Sloan has definitely proved himself to his dad, not by following him in everything, but by standing up to him.

By the time they finish their conversation, Sloan looks satisfied. His hands are bloody and bruised, and I make a mental note to have them checked out by the Black Roses medical technician. With the way he was waling on Hugh's face, I wouldn't be surprised if he broke something in his hand.

I'm sure he would say it was worth it though, and I can't really disagree.

My biological father's death was brutal and savage, but so was the man himself. He got what he fucking deserved.

We finally make it home, and I find that Gavin was already one step ahead of me. He sent someone from the Black Roses who specializes as a medic to meet us there and have a look at our injuries.

Dad's hurt the worst, but once the medic looks him over, he says he's going to be okay. He's got a mild concussion, but nothing broken, no life threatening injuries at all.

The rest of us have assorted bruises and cuts and scrapes that will need to be cleaned, and some of them need to be wrapped. The medic takes a look at my shoulder where Hugh shot at me and makes me sit at the kitchen island so he can stitch it up.

He has me breathe in and out deeply and makes the call that my sides are just sore and none of my ribs are cracked from tussling with Hugh, though he does say if it doesn't feel better in a couple of days, going to a real doctor is probably a good idea.

I promise that I will, then drag Sloan into the room to get his hands checked out. Nothing is broken, thank fuck. Just a lot of split knuckles and bruises.

We get dad situated in bed according to the medic's orders, and then we go upstairs and part ways to clean up.

I feel grimy and sooty and banged up, and I peel myself out of my filthy clothes, noting with a wry smile that there's another pile I'd probably rather burn than try to deal with.

Anxious to clean the dust and blood off my body, I hustle into the shower, running it hot like I always do and hissing when it pours over my cuts and scrapes. The soap doesn't help, making them sting and burn slightly, but it's so nice to watch the dried blood and grime swirl away down the drain as I wash up.

I stay in the shower longer than is strictly needed to get clean, letting the heat of the water soak into my tired muscles.

Eventually, my fingers start to prune and the water starts to lose some of its heat, so I step out and dry myself off, grabbing the bathrobe Rory bought me a while ago from the back of the door so I can wrap myself up in it.

Usually, I'd just go for a simple towel, but I feel the need for the extra fluffy comfort tonight. I'm still alive, and earlier tonight, I really didn't know if I'd live to see tomorrow. So, fuck it. I'm spoiling myself a little.

I grin at that thought, stepping out of the bathroom and into my bedroom. Then I stop short, my eyebrows shooting up.

All three of my guys are in here already, freshly showered themselves and already re-dressed in sweats and t-shirts.

They all have looks on their faces that I can't quite decipher, so I cock one eyebrow and glance at them all.

"Um... what's up?"

It doesn't seem like anything bad, so I'm not too worried. Just curious.

Sloan leans against the doorframe, arms folded with a tired but pleased grin on his face.

Rory gets up from the bed where he was sitting, and Levi comes closer as well. They stand in front of me for a second and then, just as I'm about to ask them again what the hell is going on, both of them drop to one knee in front of me.

My eyes fly open wide with surprise, and my jaw drops, but nothing comes out. I'm not sure what I could say anyway, and they don't seem to need me to respond before they start talking themselves.

"Mercy," Levi says, going first. "You are the strongest, bravest, kindest woman I have ever met. You never quit when you know something is right, and you have so much heart that I'm awed every day to stand next to you. And grateful that you want me there."

He glances at Rory, who grins. "Levi forgot hottest, so I'll add that in here. But he's right. You're amazing. Every day that we get to spend with you is a good day, and we've decided that we want every day to be like that. We want you with us for the rest of our lives."

"We know we can't make it official on paper," Levi adds. "But that's not a big deal to us if it isn't to you. We just want you to be ours. We want to marry you too."

My heart squeezes, and I press a hand to my mouth as a rush of emotions flow through me. Even though I already planned for the two of them to be included in the whole *being married to Sloan* thing, the fact that they're here, proposing to me after everything, just makes it all a million times better.

"Yes," I say, my voice a little muffled. I lift my hand away from my mouth and repeat it again, just so they'll have no doubt at all about my answer. "Yes, of course."

"Thank fuck." Rory blows out a breath, his eyes gleaming with amusement and happiness.

They both grin and get to their feet, taking their turns to kiss me.

Sloan comes over and steals a kiss for himself as well, and sandwiched between the three of them, I feel like I could take on the entire fucking world.

Because I've got three dark, avenging angels who love me.

26

THREE MONTHS LATER

"You ᴋɴᴏᴡ," Scarlett says, eyeing me up and down in the mirror. "There are a lot of perks to being with three guys, but I gotta say, having more chances to wear hot wedding dresses is definitely up there."

Jen and I both laugh. She's not wrong.

It's been a few months since the whole thing with Hugh and the Jackals, and finally Scarlett is getting her wish for me to be able to have a real honeymoon.

But first, I'm having another wedding. Because why the hell not?

Scarlett, Jen, Piper, and I are all in a hotel room in downtown Fairview Heights, preparing for my second wedding ceremony, and Scarlett is practically giddy, even if she's not the one getting married.

My dress this time is different from the one I wore for the courthouse wedding. That time was more barebones, and the dress was something more like the one concession to the idea of an actual wedding. This time, it's a real party, and the dress I have was chosen to match that.

It's strapless and sleeveless, leaving my shoulders and arms bare to show off my tattoos. The push up strapless bra I have on under the dress gives my tits a nice lift, filling out the front in a way designed to draw the eye. The bodice is tight-fitting and covered with lace, and it flares out into a full skirt that swishes around my feet as I walk. It's not so much material that I feel like a cupcake, but when I turn to ask Piper how I look, she smiles up at me with wide eyes.

"Like a princess," she breathes.

I'll take that.

"Thanks, squirt," I tell her with a broad grin. "You look good yourself."

She beams and does a little twirl in her flower girl dress, spinning around a few extra times for good measure as we all laugh and applaud.

Scarlett is my maid of honor again, and she and Jen help me get ready, fixing my hair and touching up my makeup.

"I never thought I'd see anyone get Rory down the aisle," Jen says, using a curling iron to give my hair soft waves. "He never seemed like the type. I knew he wasn't going to marry me, and I thought he'd be doomed for the bachelor life forever."

"He just needed someone who can put up with him,"

Scarlett chimes in. "And his many dad jokes."

"The key is letting him know when he's not funny," I tell them. "It doesn't make him stop, but I like to think it keeps him humble."

We laugh at that, and Jen moves around to curl the other side of my hair. I'm so happy that Jen and Scarlett get along so well. I knew they would, since they're both badass women, and with less to worry about after the fall of the Jackals, we've all had more time to hang out together.

A lot of things have changed since our attack on the Jackals' headquarters. The gang itself has mostly fallen apart.

They still exist, technically. Plenty of their members weren't caught in the blast that ripped the building apart, but they're smaller and weaker since they lost all of their top members for the most part.

Their financial and business infrastructure crumbled, and without money coming in, they haven't been able to make up the ground they lost after the explosion.

Besides, in the clean-up from the explosion, some things were salvaged that allowed law enforcement to pin several of the remaining Jackals with crimes they'd committed, so that took out even more of their numbers.

Things have been a bit chaotic in the months since, but in a good way. There's been a lot to do to secure the Black Roses' power in Fairview Heights, and I've been right at my men's sides as they do it.

There's even been talk of expanding our territory now that the Jackals have lost most of theirs—and now that Sloan and Gavin are working better together as a team. So they could each sort of take point on one part of the territory and run it the way they saw fit.

Aside from being busy with all the changes, Sloan has been much less stressed lately, since things are so much better with his dad. It makes me glad as hell to see it. I think they've finally hashed out all the bad blood that existed between them since Sloan's mom died, and their relationship has grown beyond just a father and son dynamic to two partners who butt heads occasionally but still respect each other.

Jen and Piper are back in a house of their own after everything, and I know Jen is beyond relieved to be out of the small safe house where they were hidden away under the constant watch of the Black Roses. It's better protected than the one they lived in before, and closer to our place, so there's not as far to go if something goes wrong.

Rory was serious about keeping her close, although he's not especially thrilled that one of the Black Roses seems to be getting extra friendly with her these days.

I told him that's what happens when you're around a handsome man who keeps you safe all the time and would do anything to protect you.

Rory just grumbled at that, muttering something about how it was different with us and that doesn't count. I know he's not jealous, or even really mad about it, just being protective of his friend and the mother of his daughter. But he'll come around, I'm sure.

Scarlett and Jen step back together and I look at my reflection once more. I look like myself, but happier and hotter than usual. There's a flower tucked behind my ear, bright yellow and orange blooming out from the white center, and it really brings everything together.

"Are you ready?" Scarlett asks.

"Yeah," I say, grinning at her. "More than ready."

She's already getting emotional, and she fans her face with her hand, trying to dry the tears welling in her eyes without smudging her makeup.

I pull her into a hug, grabbing Jen too for good measure.

"Thanks for helping me get ready," I murmur, and then laugh when I feel Piper's little arms come around my calves from behind.

We take the elevator up to the top of the building, all of us piling inside as Jen holds Piper in her arms. The ceremony is being held on the landscaped rooftop, with a view overlooking the city, and even though this wedding won't be legally binding, I don't care.

It's perfect.

A makeshift aisle has been set up between the two sections of seats, leading to the spot where Sloan, Rory, and Levi are waiting. The few people we wanted to have with us are lined up along that aisle, and my dad waits outside the rooftop door, a smile on his face.

When I step outside, his smile grows impossibly wider, and he looks me over, pride shining in his eyes.

"I wish your mom was here to see this," he murmurs roughly, shaking his head. "She'd be so proud of you—of who you've become."

"You don't think she'd find the three husbands thing kind of weird?" I ask him, grinning back.

He shakes his head. "Nah. She was a rebel. And she'd just be happy that you're happy. That's all she ever wanted for you. That's all I want for you now."

He pulls me into a hug, careful of my dress and hair, and I hear him clear his throat as he tries to get his emotions in check. I smile into his shoulder and hug him back, so fucking grateful that he's here for this and able to walk me down the aisle. Not just that he's alive to do it, but that he's *willing* to do it. That he's accepted my unconventional relationship and has even gotten close with all three of the men I love.

Piper goes down first as the flower girl, scattering handfuls of soft petals to line my way. Once she reaches the end of the aisle, Rory scoops her up and peppers her face with kisses, making her giggle. Then he hands her off to Jen, who's standing next to Scarlett as my second maid of honor.

The music changes to something soft and light, and I

start my walk with Dad, my arm threaded through his. He has one hand on mine, beaming with pride as we head for where the guys are all standing, dressed up and so fucking handsome, waiting for me.

They light up as they watch me walk toward them, their gazes devouring every inch of me—my dress, my hair, my face. I love the way their expressions are both hungry and tender, and I can already feel my face starting to ache from the smiling I'm doing. It'll only be worse by the end of the night, I'm sure, and it'll be a damn miracle if I can get through this without tearing up.

I've never been much of a crier, but I'd rather cry happy tears than sad ones, and today, they'll be the happiest of my life.

We reach them as the song slowly comes to an end, and Dad hugs me once more before stepping back and out of the way.

Leaving just me and my guys.

The way it all began.

Our officiant, Malek, isn't anyone with any legal power to marry us, just one of the Black Roses who's known all three of my guys for years. Everyone in the gang is aware that I'm with all of them by now, and if anybody has a problem with it, they know better than to say it out loud.

Malek says a few short words welcoming everyone, and although there's nothing flowery or polished about his speech, he speaks with confidence. Then he gestures to us for our vows.

Levi steps up first, an almost shy smile on his face. His dark brown eyes shine with happiness, and he reaches for my hand before he starts.

"Mercy, I told you before that this is exactly what I wanted for my future. The only thing that mattered. All of us together, happy and healthy and alive. I never knew what my perfect life would look like until you came into it, but here you are, and this is all I need. It's that simple, but it's everything."

I grin back at him, remembering the day he told me those same words, when he showed me the picture he'd drawn of the four of us. I press one hand over my heart as he lets my hand go and steps back so Rory can take his turn.

Rory's already grinning, and instead of taking my hand like Levi did, he starts unbuttoning his shirt instead. I look on in surprise, which turns to stunned shock when he reveals a new tattoo over his heart.

The letter M, for my name, in elegant script.

It's the most basic of all of his tattoos, but I think it just became my new favorite

"My love for you is simple," he says. "It doesn't need an explanation or a reason for being. It just *is*." He cocks a brow, flashing me a wicked grin. "And I told you, way back when, that you'd better be prepared for the tat, didn't I? So I'm following through on that."

I burst out laughing, but I'm crying too, overwhelmed with so much emotion. My eyes are wet as he buttons his shirt and takes my hand.

"I promise you that you'll never be lonely. If you're sad, I'll do what I can to fix it. I've been told I'm very funny," he adds with a wink. "You're a part of my family, and you already know that I'll always do whatever it takes to keep my family safe. I can't wait to grow old with you, Hurricane."

By the time he finishes, I'm very glad Scarlett insisted on the waterproof mascara, because I can feel the tears streaking down my cheeks.

When Rory lets go, Sloan moves in. We've already done this once, and when he looks at me, there's a serene happiness in his face that is still such a surprise to see from him. He used to be so angry all the time, and little by little, I've seen that bleed away as we've settled into the new normal of our lives. Not that he can't still get worked up sometimes, but I have to admit, I kind of like fighting with him from time to time... and making up with him.

"I meant every word I said in the courthouse," he says. "And I mean it even more now. Every day, I will love you more. Every day, I will want you more. Every day, I will make sure you know how precious you are. My love for you will never stop growing."

It's all I can do to nod through my tears, and when Malek turns to me expectantly, I draw in a deep breath.

My throat is tight, and I clear it quickly as I turn to Levi.

"I think I knew it, all the way back then. That first night we ever met, I think some part of me knew you could change my life if I let you. If I gave in to that spark I felt between us. It scared me then, but it doesn't scare me now. Now that spark is a fire, a blaze that will never go out. It can warm me up and burn me down, and I want it to do both. I love you, Levi. Thank you for envisioning our future when the rest of us couldn't quite see it yet."

He nods, holding my gaze as his eyes glisten, and I lick my lips before turning to face Rory. I've never been great at expressing my feelings, but the words come easily when I look at these men—they pour out of me without thought or effort, straight from my heart to my lips.

"Rory, you taught me what family is and what it can be," I say softly. "Watching you be a dad was one of the things that made me fall in love with you. The first time I saw you with Piper, I was a goner. Your light shines so bright, and anybody who gets to stand in that light is so damn lucky. You make me laugh every day, and..." I grimace, hiding the smile that tugs at my lips. "I probably shouldn't admit this, but I even like your bad jokes."

"Ha. Knew it." He smirks, but even though amusement twinkles in his eyes, there's something else burning in them too. Something fierce and so full of love that it makes my heart flutter.

Finally, I turn to Sloan, reaching up to wipe the tears from my eyes so I can see him without my vision going blurry. He smiles at me, and in a flash, I feel like I can see our whole relationship play out in my mind's eye—everything leading up to this moment.

The ups and downs. The hatred and resentment. The passion and overwhelming need.

"I'll love you forever," I say simply, my voice dropping a little as my heart beats faster. "I'll fight with you forever. I'll fight *by* you forever. Because you're mine."

Scarlett lets out a muffled laugh that she hides behind her hand, and I'm sure she's probably remembering the conversation we had where I told her the guys weren't mine.

Fuck it, I was wrong.

Because they definitely are.

They're mine, and I'm theirs.

Malek lifts his eyebrows approvingly as I finish my vows, then raises his hands and gestures to the four of us. "Then I now pronounce you bound to each other. You may kiss your husbands."

I don't need the urging, and I finally kiss all three of them, trying to pour my love and gratitude and promises into each kiss while the small group of our loved ones look on and cheer.

AFTER THE WEDDING comes the reception, and just like last time, we plan to party hard—it's just a bigger party this time.

We booked a hall in the hotel, and there are food and drinks and music. The atmosphere is raucous and festive as all of the people I love most in the world celebrate my second wedding, and I move between our guests, accepting well wishes and compliments and praise.

I have a drink in my hand and a smile on my face as the celebration plays out around me, talking to Black Rose members who came to the wedding and teasing Jen about the one who keeps gazing at her with intense, hungry eyes.

And then, on the edges of the crowd, I see someone I recognize. Someone I definitely didn't invite.

It's the woman from the dress shop—the one who gave

me the codes that ended up being key to our ability to take the Jackals down.

Curiosity and wariness pass through me, the two emotions vying for dominance, but I step away from the crowd and approach her where she's standing in the large open doorway, leaning against the doorframe.

Her blue eyes scan the room, and she looks over everything with a detached air, like she's here but not *really* here.

Like some part of her is a million miles away.

"It looks like everything worked out for you," she says when I reach her.

"Yeah, it did." I hesitate for a moment, then add, "Thank you for your help. Your info on the Jackals was really useful."

She nods. Her silver hair falls around her shoulders, and she's wearing a t-shirt today that reveals more of the ink I thought I saw hints of when she found me in the boutique dressing room.

"Hugh died?" she asks, something hungry sparking in her eyes.

"Yeah."

"How?"

"Um..." I pause. I'm tempted to clean it up or just give her the abbreviated version, but something about the way she's looking at me makes me decide against it. She looks like she needs to hear this, even though I don't quite understand why.

"He was beaten to death," I say. "He tried to kill me, but before he could, Sloan tackled him and put his fist through his face. Over and over. Then he shot him. Emptied half a clip into his chest."

For the first time, a small flicker of emotion shows on her face. Her lips curve up just slightly—not quite a smile, but almost one. "He died in pain?"

"Yeah, I would say so."

That strange, feral sort of hunger shines in her dark blue eyes again, and she nods. "Good."

I stare at her, intrigued and somehow a little unnerved by this mysterious woman. She can't be much older than I am, but there's something about her that makes her seem almost timeless. Like what she's seen in her lifetime is more than a normal person should ever witness.

"What's your name?" I ask.

"It doesn't matter." Her face shuts down into a mask again, the smile disappearing from her lips. "You can just call me Ghost."

She pushes away from the doorframe where she's been leaning, and before I can say anything else, she slips away.

I stare after her, curious and a little unsettled. I don't think she has any beef with the Black Roses—she did help us, after all. But she's clearly got shit going on.

The sound of Piper's delighted giggle brings me back to the party and the fact that this is a time to celebrate, not worry about things that may or may not have anything to do with me. Whatever "Ghost's" story is, it's not mine to uncover.

I turn around and see Piper standing on Rory's feet, her little hands in his as they dance together on the dance floor in the middle of the reception hall. It's adorable, and I can't help the grin that spreads across my face as I watch them.

Piper catches sight of me, and her eyes light up.

"Mercy!" she calls in her sweet, high voice, taking one hand out of Rory's to wave at me. "Dance with us!"

"Sure, squirt. I'd be honored," I tell her, coming over to take Rory's free hand.

The music is lively, and the three of us dance and laugh while Rory takes turns twirling us.

I come out of a twirl to see him looking across the dance floor to where Jen is dancing with Andy, the Black Rose member who's been staring at her longingly all night. I remember him from when he watched out for me and Scarlett when we went dress shopping, and how chill and nice he was.

He's looking at Jen like she's the most beautiful thing he's ever seen before, and I smile while Rory scowls in their direction.

"Behave," I tell him, hitting him in the arm lightly. "It'll be okay. Andy's a good guy. He's on *our* side, remember? He's not the enemy."

Rory makes a face. "We'll see about that."

I laugh. "He really isn't. I promise. Remember what you taught me about family, and how we make our own? Well, your family might be getting ready to expand again, so you'd better get used to it. Who knows? Andy could become a permanent part of your life."

"I wasn't consulted on this," he says, his lips turning down in a pout, but I can see amusement hiding behind the scowl.

When I lean up to kiss him, he palms the back of my head and deepens it for a second. Then he goes back to making Piper laugh by twirling her so her pink flower girl dress flares out around her.

A cleared throat catches our attention, and I look up to see Gavin standing there.

"May I cut in?" he asks in his deep, commanding voice.

Rory tenses just a little. Things have been way better between me and Gavin since the takedown of the Jackals, but there's still a tiny edge of protectiveness in the guys when it comes to Sloan's father.

At least it's clear he never actually tried to get me killed—well, except for the time he told Sloan to "take care of me." But he was never in league with Hugh, and he never offered me up to the Jackals. Hugh came up with the plan to abduct me all on his own.

Anyway, this day is supposed to be about happiness and moving forward, not holding on to old grudges, so I agree with a small smile. "Of course."

Gavin moves in to put one hand on my waist, and the music changes to something slower and easier to talk over.

"I know we didn't necessarily get off on the right foot," he says as we begin to dance, and I laugh softly.

"Yeah. That's one way to put it."

Gavin nods, as if acknowledging how loaded that sentence is.

"I did what I had to do as leader of the Black Roses," he tells me. "None of it was personal." He pauses, then adds, "But it *is* personal now. You're married to my son and his two captains. That makes you family. Things haven't always been easy between us, but I'd like it if we could start fresh. Wipe the slate clean."

I lift my eyebrows, a little surprised to hear him say that. But I don't argue. "Yeah. I'd like that too."

He smiles softly. "You're very good for Sloan. You've pushed him into becoming a better man than I am, just by being in his life. You're good for all of them, really, and by extension, good for the Black Roses. The reason my organization has thrived for so long is because of a strong sense of family. And you've made three of the most powerful members a family. You've bound them all together, and they will be a nearly unstoppable force now."

I almost roll my eyes at Gavin's "father of the groom"

talk, because it's so typical of him and not what a regular father of the groom would say at a time like this. Still, his words mean something to me. I'm not sure either of us will ever forget what happened in the past, but I do think we can move on from it.

"I hope you're right about that," I tell him. "I want to see the Black Roses flourish."

There was definitely a time in my life when I would have held everything Gavin has ever done and said against him, and used it as a reason to hold a grudge and not trust him. But I've grown and changed since then, so as the dance winds to a close, I step back and hold out one hand.

"A clean slate," I agree, and he smiles and shakes my hand.

Sloan, who was probably watching our whole exchange from the edge of the dance floor, swoops in and steals me away from his dad as soon as the dance finishes. Gavin claps his son on the shoulder, and Sloan pulls me into his arms.

The music playing is perfect for a slow dance, and I smile up at him, so full of love that my heart feels like it might burst.

My arms are around his neck, and his large hands feel perfect at my waist. We dance to the song, but to be honest, I barely hear it. It's like we're in our own little world, caught up in the spark and the feelings passing between us.

His gray eyes are full of emotion, and I can read every one of them perfectly. It's such a change from when he shut me out at every opportunity, and I fucking love it. He spent so long trying to hide from me, but now he lets me see everything.

He lets me *know* him.

And the more I know, the more I want to learn. I don't think I'll ever stop wanting to crawl inside Sloan's soul.

"You look so beautiful," he murmurs, dipping his head so that his words are just for me.

"You're not so bad yourself."

He makes a noise low in his throat, and I feel his gaze sliding over my exposed shoulders and arms, like he can't wait to follow that path with his hands and mouth later.

When the song ends, he kisses me again, and I lean into him, taking comfort in how strong and solid he always is and always will be.

Levi is waiting when we break apart, and I smile warmly at him as he comes to whisk me into one more dance. We sway together on the dance floor, and I rest my head on his chest, listening to his heart beat.

"Did you have a good day?" I ask.

He chuckles. "Best day of my life. You?"

"Same."

"I was thinking about Logan earlier," he says quietly, a touch of sadness creeping into his voice as he talks about his brother. "How much I wish he could've been here. It's the only thing that would've made this day even more perfect."

I squeeze him a little tighter, reminding him that I'm right here. "I get that. I felt that way the day we all went to the courthouse, missing my dad. I'm so glad he got to be here today, but I wish my mom could've been here too."

"I think they'd be happy for us." He tips my chin up with his fingers, dropping a kiss to my lips. "If they could see us now. I think they'd be proud."

"Yeah, I do too," I murmur.

"I guess one thing that losing him so young taught me is that nothing is guaranteed in life." He runs his hand up and down my back, his fingertips dragging over the fabric of my dress. "Tragedies happen. Loss happens. But that's why I want to make the most of everything I have. I'm so glad you said yes when we asked you to marry us, Mercy. Because I want to spend as many days of my life married to you as possible."

Fuck. When he says shit like that, I can't help but kiss him.

I wrap my arms around him and press my chest against his, and we spend the rest of the dance with our lips locked together.

As the song starts to wrap up, Levi spins me so my back is to his front and he can wrap his arms around me from behind as we sway together.

"Look around," he murmurs into my ear, and I do.

On the other side of the room, Dad is talking to Scarlett and a couple other Black Rose members. Jen and Piper and Andy are standing off to one side, and Jen blushes at something Andy says as Piper tries to mash a cupcake into her face without getting frosting all over her dress. Gavin is holding court with Malek and a few others, and Sloan and Rory are watching me and Levi with hungry looks on their faces.

"All these people are here because of you," Levi says, his breath ghosting over my ear as he pulls me closer. "Because of us and our love. This is our family."

EPILOGUE
ONE YEAR LATER

I LET myself into the house after a coffee date with Scarlett, waving at her before she pulls out of the drive way to head back to her own place.

We have so much more time to see each other now that I'm back in school and we have similar schedules, so coffee dates after class have become a regular thing again, just like they were back before any of this started.

For all the things that have changed, that's one thing that hasn't, and I'm glad.

With things more or less back to normal, I'm at a better school than before, with my degree funded by Black Rose money. I'm also actively involved in Black Rose business, mostly with Sloan and the others, handling things when they're necessary and attending the meetings and all of that.

Clearly, I've proved myself after the whole mess with

Alex because no one gives me shit anymore. But that might also be because I'm essentially married to three of the most powerful men in the gang, and the daughter-in-law of their leader.

Either way, the Black Roses have been flourishing, holding on to the power we grabbed after the fall of the Jackals.

The Jackals themselves are basically defunct now. There are some upstart gangs trying to come together, sometimes led by former members who want to try to make it big again or exact revenge on us, but the Black Roses are powerful enough to keep them down.

For all intents and purposes, we control the city right now—and I intend to help it stay that way. The stability is good for everyone, including the people I care about who aren't a part of the gang, so it's not just because I like power or anything like that.

I've seen first-hand that the city is better off with the Black Roses on top than the Jackals, or with the two gangs fighting.

The house is quiet as I make my way deeper inside, and I head to the kitchen to rummage in the fridge, mind on dinner.

Sloan comes in while I've got my head stuck in the fridge barefoot and dressed down in sweats and a worn t-shirt, and I glance over my shoulder at him. I swear I could feel his eyes on me even before I heard his footsteps—it's something that always seems to happen, a hyperawareness of my men that connects us almost like a physical thing.

"You're home late," he murmurs as I shut the fridge and turn around.

"Coffee date with Scarlett," I tell him. "What are you feeling for dinner?"

He doesn't even answer my question. At least, not in words.

Instead, he stalks toward me and wraps one arm around my waist, practically dipping me backward as he kisses me ravenously. It's like he hasn't seen me in weeks, even though I just kissed him goodbye this morning. Not that I'm complaining.

When we break apart, I'm breathless and a little dazed.

"Well, that answers that question," I tell him, licking my lips as I chuckle. "Clearly you're hungry for me."

"I am." He nods, and it's not even a joke back.

He drops his head for another kiss, and I make a soft, needy noise against his lips, clinging to him as I kiss him back.

Rory and Levi come walking in just in time to see this display, and I can feel their eyes on the pair of us, watching it all happen.

The atmosphere in the kitchen shifts from comfortable and homey to hot and steamy in a second, and I pull away from Sloan to catch my breath, laughing.

"I don't know about you guys, but I'm *starving*."

I love when we all converge like this. I have a relationship with each of the men separately, but all together is my favorite. It feels so fucking right. Like we're all supposed to exist together, as a unit.

Sloan picks me up and sets me on the kitchen island as Rory and Levi approach. There's no question of what's about to happen here, and Sloan starts undressing me, tugging my pants down but leaving my panties in place.

He drops to his knees between my spread legs, and I suck a breath of anticipation, always eager for him to go down on me.

He clearly wasn't kidding about wanting to have me for dinner, although maybe this counts more as starting with dessert. His mouth is hot, and he licks me through the soft cotton of my panties first, teasing me until I'm panting and rolling my hips where I sit on the counter.

Levi moves in and takes my hand, kissing his way up my arm to my shoulder in a trail that leads to the sensitive skin of my neck. He applies his mouth there, with just an edge of teeth that makes me buck in surprise and moan out loud.

Rory applies himself to my chest, moving to the other side of Sloan to hitch my shirt up over my breasts and drag my bra down, exposing my tits to the air and his gaze.

He looks at them with hunger in his eyes, and wastes no time getting his hands involved too, palming and cupping my tits roughly.

I can feel how wet I'm getting, how I'm soaking into my panties for Sloan to lick up. He slips the panties to the side so he can work his tongue into me, and I'm a breathless mess while they work me up.

Rory and Levi coax me to lay back on the island, their hands pulling at my shirt and my bra until I'm naked from the waist up for them.

They descend on me, their mouths on my neck, my chest, my stomach, kissing and licking and sucking dark hickies in places no one else will be able to find them.

Levi bites down on one of my nipples and I cry out, bucking against Sloan's face as he feasts on me. The only thing I can focus on is them and the way the heat and pleasure are rising in my body, every single touch getting a reaction.

When the orgasm barrels into me, it's fierce and overwhelming. My toes curl as I practically hump Sloan's face, smearing my wetness everywhere while he keeps licking into me.

It seems to go on for longer than usual, and I tremble my way through it, letting Levi and Rory plant their kisses on my cheeks and my lips until I can breathe again.

They all move back a bit, letting me sit back up. I slide off of the counter, my legs a little wobbly and my underwear soaked through.

It's time to take them off for good, so I shimmy out of

them and leave them on the kitchen floor, not caring even a little bit about the mess.

"I'll be upstairs if anyone needs me," I say, looking at each of the men in turn with a teasing expression on my face. Then I turn and walk out of the kitchen, butt naked.

I make it halfway up the stairs before the first pair of arms wraps around my waist, scooping me up.

"You're such a tease," Levi says, whispering it in my ear with that deep voice I love so much.

He turns me around so I'm bent over the railing, looking down into the living room. My legs are spread wide, giving them all a good view of how wet my pussy still is, and I hear all three of them groan behind me.

There's shuffling as they shift positions, and one of them goes down to their knees behind me.

I can tell it's Rory from the way he eats me out, bold and teasing, the swirls and loops of his tongue giving him away. He holds my hips tightly, not giving me anywhere to go, and makes me take it as he works his tongue with wild abandon.

"Fuck! Rory..." I moan, bucking my hips back. My fingers curl tight around the railing, holding on for dear life while my legs shake from the sheer pleasure of it all.

A hand comes down hard on my ass, spanking me hard enough that there has to be a mark left behind. I cry out from the pained pleasure that shoots through me, and I can feel my clit throbbing with each pass of Rory's tongue, even though he hasn't gotten around to licking there yet.

But Sloan picks up the slack, winding his arm between me and the railing and finding that slippery, sensitive bud with his rough fingers.

He rubs at it in time with Rory eating me out, and my moans and whimpers get louder and higher pitched as they work me up toward another orgasm.

From the stairs above me, Levi bends down to kiss at my neck, providing a gentle contrast to the explosive sensations Sloan and Rory are giving me.

I feel caught between the three of them, unable to stop myself as I career toward the edge and then fly right off of it, pitching headfirst into another orgasm that has me screaming in pleasure.

After that, I'm not feeling quite so sassy anymore. My knees feel like jello, and my head spins with how good it all is.

"One of you is gonna have to carry me up the stairs," I pant, because I sure as fuck am not going to be able to make it on my own at this rate.

As always, it's Rory to the rescue for these kinds of things, and he sweeps me up and over his shoulder, slapping my ass a couple times for good measure.

It just makes me even wetter, which feels like it shouldn't be possible, but here we are. He takes me to the bedroom and dumps me on the bed, where I sit up enough to watch all of them get naked too.

It's a sight that never gets old, and I lick my lips, anticipating what's to come.

Sloan steps back a bit, letting the other two move toward the bed. It's like him to get off on the control of it, telling his friends what to do.

"Levi," he says, voice rough. "How wet is she?"

Levi grins and works three fingers into my pussy with ease. I'm open and wet from being eaten out and coming twice already, and his fingers are thick and long, making me squirm and try to grind on them.

"She's soaking," he murmurs. "I think she's having a good time."

"Why don't you fuck her and find out?" Sloan asks.

Levi doesn't need to be asked twice. He grabs my ankles and drags me down the bed until my ass is right at the edge of the mattress. Then he lines his cock up with my pussy and shoves in hard, seating himself in one go.

I make a wailing sort of noise that's pure pleasure, and when he grabs my hips to hold me still, I feel his fingers dig into my skin.

It feels so fucking good, especially when I'm already sensitive from coming twice in such a short time.

Before I can start getting too close to another orgasm though, Sloan directs Levi to let Rory have a turn.

Rory fills me up, taking away the empty feeling left

behind by Levi pulling out. His fingers find that same spot on my hips, and he batters into me hard, making me take every stroke of his thick cock.

By this point I'm just babbling, trying to remember how to breathe and begging for more all at the same time. I urge Rory to take me harder and faster, and he does for a bit. But then Sloan moves in, taking his own turn with me.

He gives me everything I was begging Rory for, fucking me with almost punishing thrusts, like he can't get enough. I know I'm going to have bruises left behind from how tightly they're holding on to me, and I will definitely be feeling this hard fuck in the morning, but that's a good thing in my book.

I try to gasp Sloan's name, but it just comes out as another moan, another desperate plea for more.

They share me between the three of them, making me come over and over again until they've all come inside me too.

My heart races, and my chest burns as I gulp down grateful breaths of air, trying to remember how to function while the aftershocks of my orgasms wash through me. The guys collapse on the bed with me, sweaty and sated, and even the *idea* of having to move feels like way too much effort.

Levi echoes my thoughts when he laughs a second later. "I guess we're doing pizza for dinner tonight. I couldn't cook if someone paid me right now."

"Your cooking isn't good enough to pay for anyway, so that's fine," Rory shoots back, his voice a little hoarse from exertion.

Sloan laughs under his breath, and I smile to hear them joking around with each other like this. It's goofy and fierce and perfect and *ours*, this thing we've created between us.

I kiss the tattoo on Rory's chest, and he lifts a hand to run his fingers through my hair.

Warm and comfortable and sated beyond my wildest dreams, I can't help but think about how lucky I am. I know a kind of love that very few people ever experience. And I didn't just find it once. I found it three times.

I remember what Levi said about how they all never wanted the same woman before me, and how the flip side of that is true too. I never wanted three men at the same time before. I never would have even thought it was possible to want that, much less make it work.

But each of these three men fits perfectly to a part of my soul.

And all four of us?

We make a perfect whole.

Mad Love

**Sinners of Hawthorne University
(dark new adult romance)**
When Sinners Play
How Sinners Fight
What Sinners Love

**Black Rose Kisses
(dark new adult romance)**
Fight Dirty
Play Rough
Wreak Havoc
TBA

(contemporary romance standalone)
Say Yes

**Magic Blessed Academy
(paranormal academy series)**
Gift of the Gods
Secret of the Gods
Wrath of the Gods

Printed in Great Britain
by Amazon

84651798R00202